The Mapkeeper
& the Rise of the Wardens

KATIE CASH

Book one of The Mapkeeper series. First edition.

Cover design by Diana Buidoso

ISBN: 0692568506

ISBN-13: 978-0692568507

ACKNOWLEDGEMENTS

I would be remiss if I did not extend my deepest thanks to my husband, who has supported my dream of publishing a novel from conception to publication. To my developmental editor H. Fryer, without whose incredible and unwavering constructive criticism I would not have produced my best possible work, I thank you immensely. The ongoing love and support of my family brought life and fresh meaning to the sometimes painstaking process of writing, editing, and repeating. Thank you, and I hope to have your continued patience and understanding as I forge on with my writing career! To Diana Buidoso, who rapidly and skillfully modified draft designs to craft a stunning final cover image—you exceeded my expectations and I am so grateful. Finally, I want to thank my readers! I look forward to interacting with you and receiving your feedback as I continue to write The Mapkeeper series.

Visit the author's website at

www.katiecashwriting.com

Email the author at

thekatiecash@katiecashwriting.com

CHAPTER 1

Morning came too soon. *Beep. Beep. Beep.* Lucy's alarm increased in volume the longer she ignored it. She was not a morning person. Squinting, she rolled over and silenced it with a slap.

School day, she thought, flopping back into the shallow rut in the mattress that her body had formed over the years. *Get up and get dressed.* She rolled out of bed, her brain foggy and her body on auto-pilot. Stumbling into the bathroom, she brushed her teeth, combed her hair, and washed her face. That always woke her up a bit. Today was Monday—the start of a new week.

Her brothers were stirring as Lucy threw on jeans and a t-shirt behind her L-shaped curtain. After tugging on a pair of wool socks, she picked her way through piles of Mack's and Luke's clothing and ambled toward the kitchen. She started the coffee pot for Mack and put the kettle on for herself. She was a tea-drinker. She shuffled to the cupboard and poured a bowl of her favorite sugar-laminated cereal. Like a sleepwalker on auto-pilot, she gazed absently out the kitchen window as she ate. Snow. The base layer had increased two-fold overnight. *It must be twenty inches,* she thought.

The Barnes family lived a short distance from Frostbite High, where Mack was a senior, Lucy a junior, and Luke a freshman. Lucy and her brothers walked the ten minutes to school together each morning, sometimes tossing snowballs and other times walking in silence, absorbed in a sleep-induced morning lethargy. Their father left before sunrise each morning to prepare fishing boats for the morning catch at his marine mechanic shop, so they were on their own in the mornings.

Luke trudged into the kitchen, eyes half open, not bothering to say good morning. They shared an understanding that none of them were expected to act like civilized humans in the morning. He pulled a couple of pieces of bread out of their bag and stuffed them into the toaster, setting the timer for "extra light." Luke preferred his toast just warmed. Dad called it "Luke's hot bread."

Lucy poured boiling water over a tea bag as Mack lumbered into the room. He grabbed a box of cereal and poured so much into a bowl that it spilled over onto the counter and floor.

"Oops." He bent to sweep peanut-butter flavored pebbles into his cupped hands and tossed them into the sink.

"Way to go," she smirked. Her older brother ignored her.

Bing! Luke's tepid toast popped out of the toaster and he smeared a thick layer of peanut butter on each slice. Lucy savored her last bite of cereal, rinsed the dish, and went to the closet to retrieve her purple puffer jacket.

"I just finished *Tentacle Mythology* last night," she called over her shoulder to Luke and grinning to herself at the memory of the book. "It was so good I couldn't put it down! You should read it before I return it to the library."

"Mmk," she heard Luke burble through a mouthful of food. She and her younger brother devoured books so quickly that they'd almost read through all the books Frostbite High Library had to offer. She knew he would enjoy *Tentacle Mythology* as much as she had.

⁎

The walk to school was gorgeous and still. The gentlest snowfall drifted from the gray sky, dusting last night's snowfall with a fresh layer of fluff. The padding of snow muffled the cozy sounds of the small town coming to life.

To Lucy's surprise, there was a large crowd of townspeople gathered around Frostbite High. They spilled into the parking lot, crammed shoulder-to-shoulder against one another, trying to get a glimpse of something at the center of the school's outdoor courtyard. Lucy's curiosity was piqued—nothing interesting ever happened at Frostbite!

"What's going on?" Luke asked.

"I don't know... I don't remember any of the teachers saying there would be an event on Monday," Mack replied.

The Barnes siblings quickened their pace. *Crunch crunch crunch.* Their rubber boots bit into the fresh packed snow. The low murmur of excited voices emanated from the crowd and people pointed toward the center of the courtyard, standing on tip-toes to get a better view. An inexplicable apprehension formed somewhere deep within Lucy's stomach, but she shook off the unwelcome chill that slithered its way up her spine.

The siblings weaved through several parked snow mobiles and reached the edge of the crowd in the parking lot, where they shouldered their way in until they had a clear view of the courtyard. A small group of people were seated in high-backed chairs on stage, but Lucy couldn't make out their faces.

"Who are they?" Mack asked a man who was squeezed up against him.

"It's Mr. Quincy and his staff," the gray-bearded man muttered. "He's supposed to make some special announcement, just for us here in Algid." The man's eyes darkened with mistrust.

Fearing the worst, Lucy's heart constricted. Mack shot an anxious glance at his sister and began to shift his weight from one foot to the other, clenching and unclenching his fists. The fact that the Representative of the People, the highest authority in the entire country of Apocrypham, was visiting their little town of Algid had to mean that something was amiss.

An unsettled hush fell over the crowd as Mr. Quincy stood with majestic grace from his chair at center-stage. He was shorter than Lucy expected—a thin, petite man—and wore his typical attire: a dark suit and white collared shirt with a tie, the same type of clothing he always wore when he was interviewed on Commune TV. His dark skin and thick-brimmed glasses made it impossible to discern his expression from a distance.

"Good people of Algid, Frostbite High, and Principal Mungsworth: thank you for your kind reception. I must admit, I was not expecting such warmth from the chilly town of Algid," he joked, though he did not smile.

A smattering of forced laughter rippled through the crowd. Mr. Quincy's microphone squeaked in protest, filling the silence following his brief pause. "It is wonderful to be back in the north, as I have a particular fondness for this region. It is so beautiful, especially following a fresh snowfall." He held his hands out, catching sporadic snowflakes in his spindly brown hands.

"I want to take this opportunity to thank you all in person for the wonderful work you do day in and day out in support of Apocrypham. You are all truly indispensable. I must apologize for arriving unannounced, but this was an unexpected trip. Still, I see word does indeed fly in a small town." He flashed his sparkling set of too-white teeth. Lucy shot Mack a discreet, incredulous look— Mr. Quincy had *no idea* what life was like in a small town. Mack rolled his eyes in agreement.

"My friends, I have wonderful news to share with you. As

you know, Commune representatives are always on the hunt for outstanding citizens who would excel working with us in the Capital. Well, my friends, one of your very own has been hand-selected to join us as a member of my personal staff in a position that has recently become available!" Mr. Quincy paused and smiled at one of the enormous black-suited body guards flanking him. The guard chuckled, his massive round belly bobbing up and down.

Get on with it, Lucy thought with a flash of irritation.

"Now that it's past seven o'clock, am I correct to assume that all the high schoolers should be present, Principal?" Principal Mungsworth jumped out of her seat and nodded in frantic agreement. She was a petite woman with bizarrely plump arms. Mr. Quincy seemed pleased with her reaction. "Good. In that case, will Miss Lucy Barnes please come forward?"

Lucy's stomach dropped. She couldn't believe her ears. *Did he just say my name?* she wondered as the reverberating silence enveloped her, seeming to press in on her. Her palms immediately began to sweat.

"Is Ms. Barnes here?" Mr. Quincy and his entourage scanned the crowd of students and onlookers. The people surrounding Lucy gawked at her, open-mouthed. She glanced at her brothers, but they appeared to be as dumbstruck as she was. Most of the people around Lucy knew who she was—after all, it was a small town. They began to edge away from her, forming a pathway leading to the courtyard stage.

This is not happening, she told herself as her ears began to ring. She felt as though she were watching the scene unfold from somewhere outside of her body. *What could the Commune possibly want with me?* She glanced at her brothers, pleading with her eyes for one of them to tell her it wasn't real. Mack shrugged and gestured toward the stage, encouraging her to move. She hated being the center of attention, and yet here she was being summoned on stage in front of the entire town!

"All right Lucy!"

Her classmates and the townspeople began to cheer her on as she felt her feet begin to move. But she saw the hollowness in their eyes as they clapped, for they shared her mistrust of the Commune. Her stomach performed several acrobatic flips deep inside her abdomen as she realized that everyone was looking at her.

"Way to go, Lucy!"

People fist-pumped the air and clapped as the throng parted, making way for their champion. Nausea twisted her stomach, threatening to rise in her throat. She couldn't process what was happening, though her feet were moving of their own accord. The crowd was a blur of clapping people, but Mr. Quincy was crystal-clear on the stage, smiling with crossed arms as he watched her draw nearer. His large, pointy nose poked out between the lenses of his black glasses as if reaching toward her.

"Ah, there she is. Come on up, Ms. Barnes," he boomed into his microphone.

Why is he talking so loudly? Lucy's feet somehow carried her through the crowd all the way to the stage. The clapping of the crowd died and people began to quiet, anticipating Mr. Quincy's next move.

Lucy's autonomous legs climbed the steps to the stage and one of Mr. Quincy's bodyguards offered her a ham-like arm. She took it with one hand, allowing him to lead her to center stage, where Mr. Quincy stood with one hand outstretched for a handshake. She shook it and watched him grin as he assessed her. A chill shot down her spine and she tore her gaze away. She did not trust this man.

"Ladies and gentlemen, today is a proud day indeed for Algid! After careful consideration of many individuals across the country, Ms. Barnes has been hand-selected by Commune officials to serve in the Capital on my personal staff. Let this day be remembered always, and may each of you bear in mind that you too can accomplish great things! Be your best at all times, for you never know who is watching!" He winked and grinned, but the people of Algid did not return his smile.

Lucy gazed out at the crowd, numb with shock. She found her brothers among the throng. They both wore deep frowns, their apprehension written on their faces. The sight of the crowd made her knees go weak—she feared they might buckle at any moment. *Don't pass out,* she willed herself.

Mr. Quincy eyed Lucy over the tops of his glasses. "Well, Ms. Barnes, we have much to discuss. I don't think Principal

Mungsworth will mind if I borrow you for the morning to sort matters out." He winked at Principal Mungsworth, who sprang to her feet once again, wringing her hands at the mention of her name.

Mr. Quincy gave a shallow bow and gestured toward the door that stood open at one end of the stage. Lucy gulped, realizing she had no choice but to go with him.

His four beefy body guards flanked her and together, the small group exited the stage to a smattering of clapping from the townspeople. Lucy's stomach sank as she looked over her shoulder and found her brothers' faces once again.

Behind her, Mr. Quincy faced the crowd and raised his hands, proclaiming, "Thank you for tolerating my visit, good people of Algid! Fear not, we will return Ms. Barnes to you very soon!" He shot a stony glance at Mack and Luke before following Lucy and his guards through the door and snapping it closed.

CHAPTER 2

"Follow me," commanded one of Mr. Quincy's oversized goons from behind his dark reflective sunglasses, which he still wore despite being indoors. He led Lucy to a conference room at the end of the hallway and gestured for her to enter ahead of him. Her stomach hadn't stopped churning since the moment she'd heard her name announced.

Lucy swallowed hard. He was more than twice her size, and there were three replicas of him hot on her tail. Sucking in a deep breath in an effort to calm her out-of-control heartbeat, she obeyed, though the thought of going into a room with these brutes from the Commune terrified her. The other three body guards and Mr. Quincy followed them inside the room, which was quite dark.

"Please have a seat, Ms. Barnes." Mr. Quincy instructed her as her eyes adjusted to the dim lighting. One of the guards flipped a switch on the wall and the swath of ceiling lighting sizzled to life with a soft hum.

The conference room was furnished with only a single long wooden table and about a dozen chairs. Lucy pulled one of the stiff wooden chairs back from the center of the table and sat, clasping her shaking hands in her lap beneath the lip of the table. Mr. Quincy rounded the table and selected the chair opposite her. Two guards sank heavily into the seats on either side of him and the other two took position beside the door through which they'd come.

Her mind whirred with possible reasons why this was happening to her as her stomach fluttered. She rubbed her palms against her jeans. Despite the cold, they were damp.

"Ms. Barnes, do you really believe you have been hand-selected to serve as a member of my personal staff?" Mr. Quincy leaned in, a smirk playing at the corners of his lips. His guards chimed in with a chorus of deep, throaty chuckles.

"Uh, no..." she managed, crossing her arms and looking away. She swallowed to moisten her dry throat.

"Well, you're right," he replied, leaning back in his chair. "You do not have any special skills, you are of ordinary intelligence and bravery, and you do not set yourself apart from other citizens in any way whatsoever."

He stared her in the eyes. Her nostrils flared, but she held his gaze. She was furious, but refused to show it. *He's just trying to provoke me*, she told herself. "No, Lucy, I brought you here not because I wanted to, but because I *had* to." He smacked the table, making her flinch.

"You are not special, but for reasons I promise that I will never comprehend, it seems the most undeserving people are chosen for the greatest honors in this world." He looked left and right at his guards for affirmation. On cue, they nodded in grave agreement.

Mr. Quincy reached into the breast pocket of his jacket and extracted a yellowed piece of folded parchment and laid it on the table between himself and Lucy. "Do you know what this is?"

Lucy felt an inexplicable tug within her, as if some force was pulling her toward the strange parchment. She was suddenly energized by a warmth that spread from her core out to her limbs and replaced the nervous jitters in her stomach.

"No." She stared at the piece of paper. She had never seen it before, yet her intuition told her it was of incredible importance to her.

"This is the map. Lucy, I am about to tell you things that very, very few people have knowledge of." He leaned back and sighed, rubbing his temples with a thumb and forefinger. "Again, not because I want to, but because I must. To give you some idea of the significance of this information, the only people who share it are me, my four personal body guards, the Minister of Defense, and the National Historian. It is a blood secret that *must* be well-guarded. This is of dire importance. Do you understand?"

He leaned forward, staring into her eyes through his square-framed glasses. Despite her innate dislike for Mr. Quincy, Lucy felt the power of his solemnity from across the table.

"...Yes, I do, Mr. Quincy." He paused for a moment, holding her eye contact for emphasis.

"Very well, then. It is time. Karl. Gregor. Unfurl the map." The guards on either side of him stood and grasped the parchment at both ends, unfolding it in unison. As it unfurled before them, it began to glow! They released the map as soon as it was opened, leaping back and shielding their eyes against the brightness emanating from the map. A strange surge of energy welled up inside her and her heart began to pound.

The glow flickered out almost as soon as it began, and all that was left was an aged, ordinary-looking map on the table before them. Her heart rate calmed with the dissipating of the light. The map was larger than an ordinary piece of paper, but still small enough for a single person to hold.

"Interesting, no?" Mr. Quincy leaned forward, making a point not to touch the map.

"Yes, very interesting." Lucy had to agree. She felt nearer to normal now, though the unfamiliar pull toward the map persisted. Her mind was clouded with confusing, conflicting emotions.

"This is no ordinary map. It contains a certain power, the full extent of which is still unknown to mankind. You see, only one person is capable of manipulating this map. It is a portal between our world and a parallel universe called Praxis." He paused to assess her reaction, but she steeled herself, keeping her face blank as she listened. "Map control passes from one person to the next at the discretion of the map, or whenever the previous Mapkeeper passes away."

Mr. Quincy stared into her eyes. "Lucy, the Mapkeeper passed away two days ago, and the map named you as its next keeper. See?" He pointed to the bottom right corner of the map, careful not to touch it. Sure enough, her name was scrawled across the corner in elaborate penmanship.

Lucy Barnes, Mapkeeper.

She was stunned, unable to believe her eyes. Suddenly, she became aware that she craved the map. She wanted to hold it. Hesitating at first, she reached for it, pausing to glance up at Mr. Quincy.

"Go ahead." He gestured to the map with a resigned sigh, as if disgusted with the notion of Lucy touching the map.

But it drew her in! She slowly reached toward the parchment with both hands and to her shock, it began to glow as her hands neared it. The strange warmth inside her returned, flowing from her core throughout her body. As she grasped each side of the map, a gentle, tingling buzz flowed from her hands through her arms and into her body. She was exhilarated! Holding the map felt right, as if somehow it completed her.

She held it up at eye level, lost in its simple beauty. Through the gentle pulsing glow, black inked lines depicted the world Mr. Quincy had called "Praxis." Captivated, she examined features labeled Glacial Lake, Doldrums Forest, Dark Sea, and Dour Mountains. Her heart climbed into her throat with excitement. Was it possible such a place existed?

As if slapped with a wave of realization, she decided that this could not be true. Mistrust of Mr. Quincy once again dominated her mind.

"It's marvelous, isn't it?" Mr. Quincy asked. Lucy nodded her agreement, determined not to speak until she had a better handle on what was going on; why these strange, unfamiliar feelings were coming over her. "The map seems to take well to you. That's a good sign. I guess it really has chosen you as the next Mapkeeper." He seemed disappointed.

"You see, the last Mapkeeper's passing was unexpected. The moment we learned of his passing, we traveled to his location and obtained the map, for it must be safeguarded at all times. If we were ever to lose the map..." Mr. Quincy trailed off, glancing at Karl and Gregor. "Let's just say it would be beyond disastrous, Lucy. The map is our only known portal to Praxis. Our laboratories in the Capital have conducted extensive analysis of the map, and are still unable to identify the source of the map's power or determine how it works. All we know is that the Mapkeeper is able to manipulate it to a limited extent."

Lucy still held the map, the glowing warmth pulsing gently through her body. She listened to Mr. Quincy's story as she gazed at the treasure in her hands. She didn't know what to believe, but every instinct within her writhed at the thought of cooperating with the Representative of the People.

"The last Mapkeeper retained possession of the map for

over fifteen years before his passing two days ago," Mr. Quincy continued. "The Mapkeeper is called upon to travel back and forth between Apocrypham and Praxis as necessary to assist the people and creatures of Praxis. The Mapkeeper is known throughout Praxis as a powerful individual with the ability to assist them in ways no one else can."

Lucy tore her gaze from the map and looked up at him. *Why me? What can I offer that no one else can? This must be some sort of trick*, she decided. Despite her internal struggle, she refused to show self-doubt in front of Mr. Quincy. She kept her lips sealed shut and showed no emotion.

"We must never allow this precious connection between our worlds to fade," he continued, pushing his glasses higher on the bridge of his oversized nose. "One day, I hope to discover a means to allow for greater passage between our worlds. As the new Mapkeeper, you must learn to harness the power of the map through your unique connection to the map. It will not respond to anyone else, but it will take time for you to learn to manipulate the map. You must be patient. You will undergo this process alone, and only time and practice will make you a proficient Mapkeeper. Just keep in mind that the skills you learn will be of vital importance in Praxis. I cannot elaborate further. You must travel to Praxis for yourself to discover if and how you are needed at this time."

Lucy's stomach began to churn again. The warmth and confidence the map seemed to bring disappeared and dread slithered to the forefront of her mind. *He must be lying. What does he really want with a soft-spoken, nobody of a bookworm like me?*

"Do not make the mistake of underestimating the power of the map, Lucy. This is not a game. This is our only portal to another world. You must be very careful using the map, and you must also keep the map's existence a secret from everyone, including your family. Can you do that, Lucy?" His bottomless, dark brown eyes met hers once more.

She eyed Karl and Gregor. Enthralled as she was by the map, her mistrust of these men overpowered the incredible sense of wonder she'd experienced a moment before.

"Yes," she replied, eager to end the meeting and go home.

"I announced your addition to my staff to serve as your cover story. You will need a valid reason to explain your sudden disappearances to teachers, friends and family. I have meticulous notes for you describing what to tell them about working in the Capital. Of course, you must tell them much of what you do is top-secret and cannot be divulged. But you will still need some basic details to abate suspicion.

"Oh, and one more thing: you will be... *supervised* while in possession of the map. As I am unable to select the Mapkeeper myself, I hold myself accountable for the actions of the Mapkeepers chosen by the map. Do you understand?"

Lucy's stomach dropped, her heart constricting with fear. *Supervised?* She remembered to move her head up and down in a nod, though her mind reeled at his terms. She relished the dying glow of the map in her hands, clinging to the final trace of warmth it supplied her hands before returning to its inert state.

"But I don't—I don't want to leave Algid. It's my home," she stammered, her heart thundering. She couldn't imagine life without her brothers and her father. *I will run away before I let Mr. Quincy dictate my life*, she decided. Her blood chilled at the thought of the Commune tracking her movements.

"It's not up for debate." He slapped the table again. "You have been chosen, and now you have no choice but to comply." His dark eyes glittered behind his glasses. "And be aware that at any given time, I will know whether you are in Praxis or Apocrypham."

Her eyes widened as she felt every hair on her body stand on its end all at once.

"You will return to Algid and tell your family that your staff assignment in the Capital will begin in a few days. Then monitor the map. It will notify you when there is need for you in Praxis. That is all the advice I can give you. Now we must go. Now we must go," he snapped, glancing at the expensive leather-banded watch on his wrist. "I have two more meetings this evening and it's a long train ride back to the Capital," he muttered with annoyance."

Mr. Quincy stood, Karl and Gregor rising with him. Lucy gazed down at the map again, conflicted by an innate mistrust and an unexpected, soul-deep longing. Unsure of what else to do, she folded it along the creases and tucked it into her jeans pocket. It was a perfect fit.

Her heart continued to pound in her chest as she followed the four body guards out of the room and down the hallway toward an exit at the back of the building. Her head spun, unable to discern whether this was all real.

A light drifting snowfall met them when they stepped outside, flouring Lucy's hair with soft, fuzzy flakes. Her mind was an utterly muddled mess.

CHAPTER 3

"Where did they take you?" Luke asked, wide-eyed.

"What did they say?" Mack prodded, unable to contain his concerned curiosity as the three siblings walked home after school. It was their first opportunity to be alone together since Lucy had returned.

All day since being dropped off back at Frostbite High, she had endured relentless questioning about what her job at the Capital would entail and what Mr. Quincy was like. She'd gone from a quiet girl her classmates labelled "antisocial" to a celebrity in a few short hours.

With each question she delivered the generic, canned story Mr. Quincy had provided: "In a few weeks I will begin working on Mr. Quincy's personal staff, but my exact job description wasn't revealed yet. I'll work part-time at the Capital, spending the rest of my time at home here in Algid," she recited again and again

"What was Mr. Quincy like?" everyone wanted to know.

"He seemed nice enough," she had choked out several dozen times behind an exhausting false smile. She recoiled inside each time she forced it out. Her long-held dislike of Mr. Quincy had not decreased since meeting him face-to-face. Rather, it was stronger than ever.

All day she'd felt like she was in a haze, going through the motions of being alive since the encounter. Not having had time to process everything that had taken place, she still wasn't convinced that it was all real, and the constant attention was starting to give her a headache.

"I still can't believe this is happening," Lucy admitted to her brothers, grateful to be alone with them at last as they walked home from school. She glanced over her shoulder, then around at the little log cabins and brick homes of Algid. She didn't dare reveal anything out in the open. "But I'll have to tell you guys the details later."

A vision flashed across her mind: Mr. Quincy and a staff of white-garbed, antiseptic, soulless Commune employees tracking her position from somewhere in the Capital. A thin bespectacled woman with a too-tight bun rattled off reports to Mr. Quincy, who sat behind his team of professional stalkers, sipping a beverage and barking orders as one of his goons rubbed his shoulders. She shuddered, willing the unpleasant image to vanish from her mind.

They walked for several minutes in silence. Lucy stuffed her gloved hand into the pocket of her jeans and touched the map.

She was excited to discover that it grew warm beneath her fingertips! She admitted to herself that the mystery of the map was intriguing, but her suspicion edged out her curiosity. If Mr. Quincy supported something, she would remain guarded against it.

"Do you think Dad knows about my new assignment?"

"There's no way he couldn't. The whole town knows by now!" Mack grinned. He was right—there had been an immense turnout that morning at the high school. They took their usual route home through town, but today, clusters of finger-pointing people lined the sidewalk ahead.

"Let's go this way." Lucy grabbed Luke's coat sleeve and tugged him off the sidewalk into the snow-dusted woods. Mack followed.

The quiet hum of small-town life diminished as they trod along a narrow deer trail into the solitude of the deep woods. They walked in silence for several minutes, listening for signs of life among the trees. They knew this part of the woods well, and a few minutes later, Lucy came upon a familiar, thick fallen tree trunk and plopped down on it.

She scanned the surroundings, straining her ears through the silence. Her brothers fell to their seats on the log beside her. When she was sure all was quiet, she spoke in a whisper.

"It was insane! They gave me this map that has supposed magical powers and is a portal to another universe." She scrunched up her face in disbelief. She knew her level-headed brothers would have a hard time believing it, too.

"Umm..." Mack and Luke looked at one another, incredulous. Lucy pulled the map out of her pocket. It began to glow as she unfolded it on her lap. Her brothers' eyes bulged.

"See? It kind of glows and warms up when I touch it. It's sort of like... like it responds to me. When I come near it, I feel it pulling me in..." She trailed off, losing herself in the incredible detail of the map. The inked black lines were thicker where less precision was necessary, but fine as spider silk in areas of minute detail, like the A-frame wood-trimmed houses of the village. The thought of exploring the map's power both enticed and frightened her.

"So... why you?" Luke's question jerked her back into the moment.

"I have no idea! Apparently the map chooses its keeper. See?" She pointed to her name at the bottom right corner of the map. Her brothers seemed suspicious, but impressed. "They said the previous Mapkeeper held the position for over fifteen years! But I can't figure out what I did to be chosen..." She trailed off. She felt as though the past day were nothing but a dream, unable to wrap her head around the possibility that this was real. She rubbed her forehead—the dull ache in her head was beginning to develop into a pounding headache.

"So what does the Mapkeeper do, anyway?" Mack leaned in to get a closer look.

"They said I'm supposed to try to figure out how to read signs the map puts out. How to make the map work for me. If the people of the other world, called Praxis, need help, I guess somehow the map lets me know. And then I'm supposed to be able to use the map as a portal and do whatever they need me to. I don't know—it's as confusing to me as it is to you. I don't even know if I believe it's real. It's crazy, right? It can't be real."

"I don't like that Mr. Quincy is involved." Luke voiced what they were all thinking. "We should tell Dad. This is all way too weird."

"Please, don't tell anyone else!" Lucy interjected, a chill of fear creeping up her spine. "I'm not supposed to tell anyone at all, so I'm trusting you both not to tell anyone. Mr. Quincy said if I lose his trust he'll move me to the Capital!" A knot formed in her stomach at the thought.

"Don't worry Lucy, I won't tell a soul." Luke met her gaze.

"Me either," Mack promised, wide-eyed. They knew better than to test the Commune. "I still can't believe that Mr. Quincy himself came to talk to you. It *must* be a big deal in one way or another," Mack mused, rubbing his chin in thought.

Overwhelmed, Lucy re-folded the map and slipped it back into her pocket as she stood. She glanced over her shoulder, half expecting to see Commune agents creeping out from behind tree trunks and coming for her. She shuddered. She still couldn't believe the map was magical. This had to be some sort of Commune ploy. A terrible trick.

"We should keep moving. Who knows if we're being watched," she muttered. Her brothers must have been thinking the same thing, as they were already scanning the surrounding woods too.

"Don't worry Luce, I've gotten pretty good at fighting since Drew and I started wrestling after school," Mack offered. His mention of his best friend Drew was a momentary distraction.

"Is he coming over today?" Lucy asked.

"Yeah, he's coming by after soccer practice to watch the Form of the Nation address. I told my coach I wouldn't make it to practice today because of what happened to you—he understood."

"Oh, that's right, the Form of the Nation is tonight! I completely forgot. Can't believe it's that time of year already," Luke said. They made their way along the deer path through the woods toward their side of town.

"Maybe I should just bury the map in the woods," Lucy blurted out. "If I ditch it, I won't have to worry about it, right? I don't want this thing anyway."

"Uh... yeah, I guess..." Luke agreed with hesitation.

"I don't know, that might be a bad idea," Mack retorted. "What if Mr. Quincy retaliates somehow?"

Lucy deliberated for a moment, considering on one hand potential punishments the Commune might dole out if she ditched the map... but held back by the mysterious connection she felt to it. Shaking her head to free herself from the inundation of unsettling thoughts, on impulse she yanked the map out of her pocket and ran several dozen paces off the deer trail, stooping to dig a hole in the snow. She pressed the map deep into the drift and covered it, skimming her glove along the top of the flaky mound to even out the surface.

"There," she announced, breathless and rosy-cheeked as she rejoined her brothers on the trail, brushing snow off her gloves. "I don't want it. I'm leaving it here."

They exchanged a look of uncertainty, but shrugged and fell into step beside their sister. The Barnes siblings emerged from the woods at a point where they would only have to pass a few houses to get home. By taking the trail through the woods, they had avoided the heart of town, which was sure to be overrun with nosy neighbors. Lucy set a brisk pace, head down and hands balled up in the pockets of her puffer jacket. The boys kept up.

"Hey there, Lucy! Heard you're the newest celebrity in town!" Mr. e called from across the street. He was standing on his front porch beside his wife, waving frantically.

"Yes, Mr. Moscowe, I guess so!" She waved back and smiled without stopping.

Crunch crunch crunch. Their rubber boots smashed footprints into the fresh pad of sidewalk snow. In a few minutes they would be home.

"Hey, Lucy!" Mrs. Beadleback appeared out of nowhere in

front of them, layered up for the cold. Lucy jumped, startled. It was rare to see Mrs. Beadleback venture outside. *She must have been waiting to ambush us*, Lucy thought with irritation. "I saw you this morning at Frostbite! Where did Mr. Quincy take you? Is it true you're going to the Capital for good?" The plump, middle-aged woman fell into step beside Mack. The Barnes siblings did not slow down.

"No Mrs. Beadleback, I will travel back and forth to the Capital, where I will work as a member of Mr. Quincy's staff."

Mrs. Beadleback was not discouraged. The short, squat woman scurried along beside the siblings, awkward beneath too many layers of outerwear. "How exciting! Why were you chosen? Did they tell you?" She scampered around behind them and popped her head in between Lucy and Luke, trying to insert herself into the group.

Lucy turned away from Mrs. Beadleback and rolled her eyes in Mack's direction. They had almost reached the end of the block—just a left turn and a half-block until they were home. "I'm not sure why they chose me—they didn't say. I'm sorry Mrs. Beadleback, but we have to get home. Nice seeing you!" She waved, putting the other arm around Luke and making a sharp turn at the corner of their street. Mrs. Beadleback had no choice but to accept the blatant dismissal. The woman shuffled home, no doubt with the intention of planning her next ambush.

"I'm nobody for seventeen years, and now all of a sudden everyone wants to be my best friend," she complained under her breath to her brothers.

They could see their house now, and the little log cabin had never seemed so inviting! Several more faces peered out windows as they passed, and Lucy scanned the neighborhood, her senses heightened.

They set the fastest pace possible without breaking into a run. As they approached, she saw their father Peter step out onto the porch. He stood with his arms crossed, his posture straight as a match stick. Worry lines creased his face, though his expression was devoid of emotion.

"Hi, Dad!" Lucy called. They ran the final steps across their snow-covered yard, past the big evergreen tree and up the front steps. Lucy gave her dad a hug, relief washing over her. He returned the embrace, squeezing her against his chest.

"I heard you had a busy day today, Luce! Hi, boys. Let's go inside and you can tell me all about it." Peter peered up and down the quiet street before ushering his children inside, closing and locking the front door. A light snowfall began to coat the town of Algid.

Lucy and her brothers removed their jackets and boots and hurried to the living room to settle in and discuss the day's happenings as Peter plopped into his favorite armchair. He wore one of his standard plaid work shirts and jeans with thick woolen socks. He blew on a steaming mug of coffee as his children dove onto the couch, enfolding themselves in blankets and sinking into the doughy cushions.

"Let's choose our words with care, kids. You know what I mean by that," he said in a low voice, giving them a 'don't say anything stupid' look. "I was hard at work troubleshooting the outboard motor on a six-meter when my assistant Sam came running in and informed me not only that the Representative of the People was at Frostbite High, but that he'd selected my daughter for some prestigious honor. I dropped everything and Sam and I got to Frostbite as fast as we could, but by the time I arrived you'd already been whisked away. Some neighbors filled me in on everything that happened. I was about as shocked as I'm sure you were, Luce. At first." His eyes were suddenly sad, focused on some far-off thought.

"It's okay, Dad. They just needed to take me somewhere private to talk about my future job working part-time on Mr. Quincy's staff in the Capital." She looked down at her hands in her lap, desperate to tell her father what really happened that afternoon, but she knew it would have to wait until they were alone together. Her dad was right—they could be under close surveillance. The thought was both terrifying and infuriating.

It was clear that Peter understood, because he began to ask all the questions that would be expected of him.

"When will you start? Did Mr. Quincy say what your role will be? How will you travel between home and the Capital?" She provided the canned answers Mr. Quincy had instructed her to give. Peter's act reached its climax when he announced, "Well, I am honored that my daughter was selected for this rare and prestigious opportunity!" Mack chuckled aloud. Lucy never thought they would hear their father praise the Commune, but she smacked Mack's leg and he quieted. This was serious business.

"I'm honored too, Dad. I can't wait to start. I'll let you know when I receive word to report to the Capital. I'll travel by the Intercontinental Railway."

"Why does it have to be you?" he asked. Her heart ached for him, but she continued with the act, terrified of what the Commune might do if they overheard her telling him the truth.

"I really don't know, Dad." She shrugged, unable to meet his gaze for fear of bursting into tears. She knew her father was dying to know the truth, and Lucy sensed a deep strain of sadness beneath the surface of their false conversation. It wrenched her heart.

"Well kids, I can't say I'm happy that my daughter will be spending time away from the family, but after all the Commune has done for us—providing security and protection, teachers for our schools, and transporting goods across Apocrypham, I guess our time has come to give back." He forced the words, but his eyes were shadowed with deep unhappiness.

Lucy couldn't meet her father's eyes. She longed more than anything to tell him everything and to ask his advice. But she also knew that the truth was nothing short of disturbing. He would be opposed to her involvement with the map, but since she might not have a choice, maybe it was best that he not know about it. Guilt gnawed at her. *I'll think of a way to tell him*, she promised herself.

There was a knock at the front door, and then a key turned the lock and it opened. *Click.* Lucy's heart leapt into her throat and her body tensed.

Her father jumped out of his seat. "Oh, Drew, it's just you." He walked over to shake Drew's hand, relieved. "How are you? It's been a few weeks." Lucy let her breath out and relaxed, sinking back into the plush couch cushions beneath her.

"I'm doing great, Mr. Barnes! I've still got an edge on Mack for number of goals scored this season. I'm at 22 and he's at 21." Drew flashed his straight, white smile. Lucy took a deep breath and tucked a stray lock of hair behind her ear. "Hey, man, speak of the devil!" Drew tugged his boots off his feet and flopped onto the couch next to Mack. "You plan on catching up to me with a goal or two at our game on Friday?"

Drew shook his head, tousling his long dark hair as he settled into the couch. Lucy loved his hair. It had the perfect amount of wave, falling around his head in an arbitrary, athletic way. He was tall and tan, with more muscle than most boys his age. He was the kind of guy who seemed to have a natural talent for just about everything he tried.

"Hey Drew," Lucy said with a smile.

"Hey Lucy! I heard about what happened today. Are you okay?" His dark brown eyes were soft with concern. She sensed that he would do everything in his power to help her if she ever needed it.

"Yeah, I'm fine. I guess they chose me to work in the Capital. It'll be a part-time gig though. Just whenever they need me." She looked down, wishing she could tell him everything.

"That's cool, I guess. Are you okay with the idea of it?"

"Yeah... It is what it is, you know?" She tried to smile, but she felt awful. She couldn't stop envisioning the map buried in the forest, glowing beneath a pile of snow.

Mack flipped on the television. "It's seven o'clock," he announced. "The Form of the Nation is starting."

CHAPTER 4

Mr. Quincy bared his wide, bleached grin for the camera. His plain green tie was tacked with perfection to a starched collar, dangling down to folded hands atop a mahogany desk. His dark, gelled comb-over and thick-brimmed black glasses added an aura of professionalism to his lean, dark, youthful face. His gaze was locked on his audience.

"Good morning, Apocrypham. As your Representative of the People, I am pleased to come before you once again in my annual Form of the Nation address. My friends, times have never been better for us. Here in the Capital we see the economic results of your everyday efforts. Once again our citizens have worked hard all year, producing record yield across the board! I look forward to introducing you to a few of your fellow citizens from across the country.

"I had the honor of meeting some of you in person over the past year during my annual visitations. My friends, you are thriving in every corner of this nation! We must never forget how we got where we are today and that the freedoms we enjoy are a luxury inaccessible to the rest of civilization. Exalt Apocrypham."

Lucy sneaked a look at her father as the camera cut to the first portion of the program, which this year happened to feature their hometown of Algid in the northernmost reaches of Apocrypham. Peter's stony worry-lines deepened. He was nearly as well-weathered as the fatigued fishing boats he serviced at his marine mechanic shop. His tanned, leathery skin blanketed a frame composed of small but firm muscles and strong bones. He was always cold.

Lucy's attention snapped back to the television. A representative from the Capital was interviewing one of the Commune-appointed teachers from her high school. It was Ms. Goker, Lucy's least favorite teacher. She was a mean, pudgy, middle-aged English teacher with a distaste for teenagers.

"Oh yes, Frostbite High is one of the best high schools in the entire nation," she bragged. "Our English department is second-to-none, as evidenced by our superior annual nationwide aptitude test scores. We pride ourselves in putting education first. Not sports, not recreation, and most of all, not the counterproductive social quests of juveniles!" Ms. Goker frowned into the camera with her bulging dark eyes, shaking a sausage finger at the viewers. Lucy shuddered. She shared a smile with her two brothers, Mack and Luke, who sat on the couch beside her. The whole school knew what a tyrant Ms. Goker was.

The camera panned to a full-screen shot of the high school. It was a large, five-story building paneled with dark blue one-way glass windows. Heavy white double doors dominated the front of the building, with "Frostbite High" inscribed on a large granite slab above the doors. The parking lot was equipped with spots for a variety of vehicles. Many students rode miles to school on snowmobiles, some drove cars, and others took the bus.

The scene cut to Main Street, which led from the center of Algid to the waterfront. Algid bordered the Northern Sea, the coldest ocean in the world. A Commune reporter guided the cameraman down Main Street, identifying the various shops that lined the broad, lamp-lit boulevard.

"On my right you'll see Mrs. Coventry's Bakery, where I'm told you'll find the best baked goods this side of the equator!"

Mrs. Coventry, like her fellow shopkeepers, stood dutifully outside her store. She was plump, with a shock of wrinkled skin and a wiry mop of salt-and-pepper hair. She waved at the camera, baring a gap-toothed grin and ruffling her lace-trimmed apron in delight. "And next door is the local woodworker. He begins with high-quality northern lumber and whittles it into unique, intricate furniture pieces!" Mr. Wealder grinned and waved, his petite body swaying with the momentum of his moving arm.

"Finally, this year we'll be going up close and personal with the local marine mechanic." The reporter guided the cameraman across the street to the waterfront. They'd reached the northernmost end of Main Street, where Peter's shop was located.

"Good afternoon, Mr. Barnes. Would you be so kind as to show us around your shop and tell us a little bit about what you do?"

Her father gripped the armrests of his chair as he watched himself on screen. Lucy and her brothers glanced at one another, exchanging a silent agreement to keep quiet as they watched their father's moment on national television. They knew how much he mistrusted the Commune, and that he had been selected to be interviewed against his will. Of course, he hadn't made his dissention known. Peter had made one thing very clear to his three children as they grew up—the Commune was not to be trusted, but dissention could *not* be voiced.

Center-screen on their television, Peter glanced at the camera before turning his back to show the reporter inside his shop. He guided the man around, explaining the docking and lift systems he used to secure boats while he worked.

"Here is my tool bench. Times are good here in Algid, but they could always be better. I lack many of the tools I need to perform all the services necessary to repair and maintain these fishing boats. A simple oil change is never a problem, but—"

"Thank you for your time, Mr. Barnes!" The reporter cut Lucy's father off. "Your shop is very quaint! We from the Commune are so grateful for the work you do to ensure these important vessels are able to continue their work and provide fish for your town and the rest of Apocrypham!" The reporter ushered his cameraman out of the shop. "Next, we'll be showing you a beautiful panoramic view of the Northern Sea. This stunning sea is the backdrop your counterparts from the north are privileged to enjoy every day!" The camera swept across the glittering sea as the helicopter hoisting the camera crew took to the sky.

Lucy stole another glance at her father. His knuckles were white. "Kids," he licked his lips and began, "As I'm sure you can tell, this interview wasn't my finest moment in the eyes of the Commune. There are certain standards they expect to be upheld. They expect citizens to portray happiness and prosperity for the camera regardless of the truth. I failed to meet that expectation, and it's possible I may be punished for it."

"Dad! What are you saying?" Luke cried.

"I'm not saying anything bad is going to happen, son, but I'm being realistic. The Commune is a corrupt organization that will do anything to save face. They want to portray a prosperous nation that is grateful toward the government. Those who are subversive hinder the Commune from achieving its goals—and that is intolerable in the eyes of the Commune."

"So are you saying they could punish you for saying you needed more tools?" Mack's mouth hung open.

Peter seemed tired. "I don't know, Mack. You never know with the Commune. All I know is my feature was cut short—and it didn't end on a good note. The only way I imagine they'd allow me a free pass is because of you kids. They already—" he cut himself off. His eyes were far away. Despite Lucy, Mack, Luke, and Drew's undivided attention, Peter appeared to lose himself in a flurry of memories within his mind.

"Dad? Are you okay?" Lucy prompted. She hated to see her father this way. She'd seen it a few times before when he spoke of the times when their mother was still around. He didn't speak of their mother often. She and her brothers knew very little about their mother, though Peter had told them she was courageous, outspoken, intelligent, and beautiful. What happened to her, the children did not know.

"Yes, yes I'm fine. Sorry—I was just remembering something. I need to go out to the garage to collect a few items to bring to work tomorrow." He stood and left the children alone in the living room as a dazzling shot of the Northern Sea panned across the screen.

Lucy met her brothers' eyes, sharing in their alarm. She didn't dare speak her fears aloud for fear of substantiating them: would the Commune take their father away?

CHAPTER 5

The Commune camera crew transitioned to the next segment of their annual production with a breathtaking shot of a vast, plateau-peppered desert. The arid land of south-western Apocrypham boasted expanses of colorful sands due to upwelling of various minerals, the reporter explained. Patches of teal, neon green, and electric red minerals bejeweled the bright orange sand.

The helicopter passed over several massive quarries abuzz with construction equipment and people, where the reporter noted that workers were mining rock, precious metals, and minerals.

"Do you guys think Dad is okay?" Luke asked his older siblings. The three Barnes children had always been very close. With their mother gone, they felt a compelling need to stick together. Aside from their father, they were all each other had.

"He'll be fine, Luke. He's a little rattled by the interview but I think it'll be okay..." Mack trailed off, glancing at his sister. Drew shifted, uncomfortable despite his closeness to the Barnes family. He'd spent so much time with them that he was practically part of the family.

"It's going to be fine," Lucy agreed, as much in an effort to convince herself as her younger brother. "Dad has taught us since we were kids not to trust the Commune. We can put on a good front if someone from the Commune ever shows up to question us. Dad just got frustrated in his interview... he's never been good at masking his emotion." Her heart constricted with pain as they discussed their father's interview. It brought back the hurt of their absent mother, making Lucy wince. She pushed the feelings away, unable to bear the sadness.

Luke crossed his arms, unconvinced. The Barnes children had witnessed the brutality the Commune was capable of. Dissenters disappeared. Ordinary, law-abiding citizens were fitted with Commune tracking devices at random. It was said that the ankle strap tracking devices reported citizens' everyday movements and were monitored somewhere in the Capital. Over the years, Lucy had seen temporary tracking devices fitted to her father, a few neighbors, and several of her friends at school.

Public trials of traitors and spies were broadcast on Commune TV, and the sentence for the guilty was always execution. Images of wailing defendants being dragged away were caged in the Barnes children's minds.

"Turn that garbage off," their father would scold, but often Commune TV was the only channel they picked up. At best, they'd receive three or four channels at a time, but most days there were alleged technical difficulties due to snowstorms or equipment failure. Somehow, Commune TV never experienced outages.

"And now, we bring you to Scaldsburg, the hub of life in the desert here in southwestern Apocrypham! Scaldsburg specializes in medicine, services for the transcontinental railroad, spices, mining, drilling oil, and natural gas. That's right—without Scaldsburg, you wouldn't be able to drive an automobile, build houses, or even have medicine when you are sick!"

The reporter's eyes bulged atop his goofy grin. Mack and Drew rolled their eyes at his over-exuberance.

The reporter led the cameraman down a wide, packed dirt road lined with shops. Everything seemed to be built right up from the dirt—there was no pavement. The reporter approached a tall middle-aged woman standing outside a jewelry shop. "Hello, there! You must be Mrs. Leftwick, the local jeweler. Can you tell us a little bit about your business, ma'am?"

"Certainly!" Mrs. Leftwick beamed at the camera, her thin glasses reflecting the sun's sharp rays. She unveiled a long, thin-lipped smile, managing to show just a sliver of teeth. "Please, step inside and see my collection of precious metal jewelry." She gestured to a long glass display cabinet. "The metals are all mined here in the desert and hand crafted into the fine shapes you see. I adorn my handmade jewelry with local semi-precious stones, and export my products nationwide for other Apocryphites to enjoy." She smiled at the reporter, entwining her bony fingers in front of her body.

"Just lovely, Mrs. Leftwick! You are a true master craftswoman. Dave—get a close-up of this turquoise stone set in sterling silver!" He summoned the cameraman closer, holding up a large pendant necklace. Lucy was taken aback by the beauty of the piece. She would never reveal it in front of her brothers, but she wished their father had the money to buy her something like that. She relished the thought of being able to dress up, though in Algid, impractical clothing was scarce and frowned upon. Her day-to-day attire consisted of jeans and a t-shirt indoors, or jeans, boots, and her purple puffer jacket outside.

The reporter smothered Mrs. Leftwick with chirpy partings as he backed out of her shop. Mrs. Leftwick beamed and waved at the camera as the Commune crew moved off down the road.

"Next, we will pay a visit to the main medicinal factory," the reporter declared. Shopkeepers and residents lined the road, intrigued by the spectacle as the crew approached a towering, rectangular white building. Several small glass windows freckled the face of the massive structure.

A serious-faced man in a white lab coat and thick black-framed glasses stood at the access gate awaiting the crew. He shook the reporter's hand and swiped a plastic access card. The massive iron gates guarding the grounds slid open. The building was encircled by hundreds of assorted cacti planted in a sea of red rocks.

"Here, I'm told Scaldsburg produces hundreds of

medicines which are distributed throughout the country. Over 5,000 people are employed at this facility alone!" The reporter spread his arms in a grand gesture as a hoard of sweat beads matured on his forehead.

The man in the white coat led the camera crew to the large glass double doors. He paused to swipe another plastic access card, then approached an eye-level sensor, removed his glasses, and allowed an orange laser beam to scan his eyeball. The sensor rewarded him with a shrill beep and the thick glass doors released with a hiss of pressure, bulging ajar.

The program rattled on, but Lucy couldn't concentrate on it. Her mind wandered as she stared at the screen, the scenes blurring together and failing to register. She couldn't stop thinking about the map and Mr. Quincy's strange orders. Confusion and anxiety were waging a war inside her head, though she kept a straight face and pretended to be absorbed in the show.

Does this have something to do with Mom's disappearance? Is it some sort of trick? Are my family and I in danger? A terrible vision of Mr. Quincy laughing at her flashed across her mind's eye, but sudden pain and the metallic tang of blood on her tongue jerked her back to reality. She'd chewed one of her fingernails to the nub.

"Excellent—it's 1:58! We've made it just in time. Our viewers are in for a real treat!" The reporter sprang into action on screen. "Dave, get in position for the shot!" Lucy's attention was recaptured by the reporter's enthusiasm. The camera crew was at a train station in a town somewhere near the middle of the country called Ryesville.

She watched as the cameraman secured the camera to its tripod facing west, where the train tracks disappeared into a field of swaying golden grain. Gusts of wind left pulsating impressions among the stems. Lucy marveled at how the stalks heaved and caved like wave tops on the ocean as the wind pressed and released their tips. A black speck appeared on the horizon and a distant whistle was just audible over the swishing of grain. The speck grew as the seconds passed, until Lucy could make out a dark smoke cloud rising from a stack atop the train.

"There she is!" The reporter jumped into the scene to narrate the train's arrival. "Ladies and gentlemen, the two o'clock is just moments away. The Intercontinental is vital to our nation's success. It enables us to transport goods across the country and to the Capital, sharing our resources, making it a true symbol of this great nation's unity! As you know, following the Third Great War of 2127, our nation was thrown into turmoil when the world economy collapsed. But while other nations warred and ravaged and starved, our isolationism saved us. We strengthened our already-superior military and beefed up our defenses, including the Great Fence that keeps the rest of the world out. We *survived*.

"No one else lives like you do, Apocrypham! You see the terrible images of extreme poverty from the rest of the world on Commune TV. We *must* remain ever-grateful to the Commune for providing ongoing military protection to sustain us! There is no better representation of everything we stand for—independence, working together, and industriousness—than the Intercontinental Railway!" He threw his hands high in triumph and was engulfed in a great rush of air as the huge black train sped past him, just an arm's length from where he stood.

Troubling as his speech was, chills still ran up Lucy's arms. He managed to create quite a climactic moment with the train's arrival. She rolled her eyes, chastising herself for succumbing to the reporter's obvious attempt to inspire nationalism.

The camera panned away from the reporter to follow the train as it squealed to a stop at Ryesville Station. Several men in cornflower collared shirts hopped down from the train and sprang into action, filling out paperwork, opening side-car doors, setting up ramps, and unlocking train car hatches.

Ryesville Station workers opened sheds storing local goods awaiting export. The blue-shirted Intercontinental workers busied themselves unloading heavy pallets and stacking them in neat piles next to the sheds. Once the offload was complete, the workers loaded the cars to maximum capacity with boxes of produce, clothing, and livestock. Chickens clucked, roosters squawked, men gestured and shouted, and dust clouded the air. Lucy was captivated by the blur of organized commotion.

"As you can see, unloading and loading the Intercontinental is a busy process!" The reporter injected himself into the scene, stepping in front of the camera. A cheeky Ryesville station worker leaned into the edge of the scene. He smiled at the camera, baring an alarming set of gappy teeth, gray at the gums.

Lucy cringed, grateful that they had a dentist in Algid.

The station workers finished loading the train, sealed and locked the hasps, and stepped away from the tracks. With a prolonged toot of its whistle, the train discharged a cloud of steam and began to chug away from Ryesville station.

Lucy sensed the mistrust of the gathering of locals who loitered around the station. Mothers clung to their squirming children amid a crowd of rigid, somber faces. *It seems that attitudes toward the Commune are no different in Ryesville than they in Algid*, Lucy thought with an involuntary shudder. She pulled a woolen blanket around her shoulders and tried to shake off the sudden, eerie feeling that someone was watching her

The reporter was engulfed in steam as he made his final remarks. "Well folks, this concludes this year's on-scene coverage for the Form of the Nation address. Thank you for joining us. It has been our pleasure to provide you with a glimpse into life in various cities that comprise our great nation! We now hand it back over to the Representative of the People, the honorable Mr. Quincy."

The screen flickered as the program cut to Mr. Quincy, who sat behind a heavy wooden desk with flawless posture.

"Welcome back, people of Apocrypham. I hope you enjoyed this year's peek into life across Apocrypham. Our country is the best and strongest nation on this earth today! As you know, when the world economy collapsed during the nuclear attacks of the Third Great War, the nations of the world went to war. Everyone suffered. Countries were wiped out. Those who survived were left without central government, alone and unprotected. But we were smarter than that. And with the protection of our military, we remain safe from infiltration to this day. The horrors and suffering of the outside world will remain outside our borders.

"Here in Apocrypham, we know peace and prosperity. Under the Commune, you are protected from those who would destroy us. They want what you have. They want everything you work hard to produce. But together, we will continue to live our peaceful lives. Together, we will keep foreigners out and maintain order!" He pounded the desk with a fist. His dark black eyes flashed. Not a single hair fell out of his glassy comb over. "My friends, together we are the future, not just of Apocrypham, but of the world." He spoke slower now, emphasizing each word. Lucy's upper lip curled.

The national anthem began to play as the camera zoomed out, signaling the end of the Form of the Nation address. Mr. Quincy shuffled some papers on his desk in a staged effort to appear occupied. Mack sighed and switched off the television.

"Did you guys notice how the people were standing off at a distance when the Commune crew was leaving?" Luke asked. "They must feel the same way people around here do," he muttered.

Mack nodded. "I noticed it too."

Goosebumps formed on Lucy's arms despite her blanket cocoon. "Stop!" she insisted in a low voice. "You both know you can't talk like that, even here. Especially after what happened with Dad! You never know if we're being watched—"

"Or listened to." Peter finished her sentence in a hushed voice. He had returned from the garage without making a sound. "Boys, Lucy is right to be cautious. The things I've told you all your lives about the Commune and how we must behave are now more important than ever. There will be a time to finish this discussion, but it is not now." Peter's tone dictated the end of the conversation. Sighing, he sank into his favorite chair.

The children regarded their father with the deepest respect. They were old enough to have pieced together the fragments they knew of his past and to begin theorizing as to what may have happened to their mother. Lucy sensed that it was part of what made him such a grave, closed-off man.

"Well, another year, another Form of the Nation. Nothing new there. Let's get ready for bed, everyone," Peter said with a forced smile that did not reach his eyes. Lucy and her brothers complied.

"Well, I'll see you tomorrow," Drew said, waving to the Barnes family as he stretched and sauntered to the front door. Lucy hoped that he was right.

The siblings shared one bedroom. It was all their father could afford for the family, but Lucy didn't mind. She had her own corner curtained-off, and Luke and Mack each had a bed on the opposite side of the room. It was all they knew, and they were content with what they had.

Lucy made it to the bathroom first, brushed her teeth, and hopped into bed. As she lay on her back with her eyes closed, she couldn't stop visions of the map from flashing across her mind's eye. She tossed and turned, unable to find a comfortable position despite her weariness. She threw the blanket off her body, but later ended up pulling it back over her legs, alternating between feeling too hot and too cold.

After an hour she gave up trying to fall asleep, pulled out her *City-Bright Commune Light* flashlight, and peeled the top book off her statuesque "to-read" stack, which towered up from the floor beside her bed. She made it through a hundred pages before sleep overtook her at last.

CHAPTER 6

⁂

Lucy blinked awake to the sound of a robin chirping outside her window. Exhausted, she rubbed her eyes, sat up, and pulled back the bed curtain. Dawn's first rays pierced the frosty panes of the bedroom window. Luke and Mack were both still asleep, balled up in thick messes of quilts and sheets. Mack's mouth hung agape, soft snores escaping with each breath.

The map. Mr. Quincy. *Was yesterday real?*

A glow caught her eye at the edge of her vision. She glanced at her bedside table and her stomach immediately knotted into a tight ball. The map was sitting on the corner of the table, pulsing with soft glows of light.

For a moment she stared at it, inexplicably relieved to see it again. As she reached out and picked it up, the wash of relief was replaced with a cold chill of fear. *How did it return to me?* she thought. Her heart began to race. Her eyes darted around the room, scanning for signs of Commune spies. Her breath quickened and the skin on her arms prickled with apprehension.

She eased out of bed, careful not to wake Mack and Luke. On tiptoes, she peered out the window to make sure no one was watching her. Her head spun. *This can't be happening,* she thought.

She slipped back into bed and slid the curtain shut. Unfolding the map, she ran a quivering hand over its soft, ancient surface. A bright glow followed her hand across the paper and vivid color illuminated the black illustrations atop the pulsing light. Lucy let out a gasp as warmth stirred within her. She couldn't believe her eyes!

Mesmerized, she examined the map's details. In the lower right corner above her name was an intricate compass rose. It had an eight-point star at the center, with long arms budding out in the four cardinal directions and shorter arms in the ordinal directions. At the far right side of the map in the East was Doldrums Forest, a vast, dense thicket of evergreens. To the northwest of Doldrums Forest were rolling green foothills, and beyond those in the far north were steep, craggy mountains capped with snow. They were labeled Dour Mountains.

South of the mountains and foothills was a large body of water labeled Glacial Lake. Though there were numerous evergreen trees scattered throughout the countryside and around the lake, one tree stood out—a giant among its peers. It was a massive canopy tree with sprawling roots and a thick trunk. It grew on the southeastern shore of Glacial Lake and was labeled Tree of Virtue in elegant script. *Does this tree have special powers?* she couldn't help but wonder. It seemed to exude radiance. Lucy was entranced as she explored the various features of the map.

A large castle labeled Tropos Castle dominated the center of the map atop a hill overlooking a quaint village. The winding dirt road leading up the hill from the village to the castle was labeled Royale Byway. The castle was guarded by a large wooden drawbridge and a moat. It was many stories tall and was dotted with tall, thin windows. There were half a dozen spires atop the castle, several of which were embellished with long red flags. The rooftop tiles were bright red as well.

To the west of Tropos Castle and at the base of the hill was a small, ramshackle wooden hut labeled Alchemist's Cottage. It was connected to the village by a thin dirt path. The village occupied the bottom left corner of the map. It was charming—little cottages lined the streets along with trees, flowers, and cobbled roads. It was not a large village. Smaller than Algid, Lucy estimated.

In the northern part of town was Main Market Road, which was lined with small shops, stalls, and stands. In the south, just north of where the Royale Byway met the village was a wide road labeled Central Square Promenade. It was lined with homes and dead-ended at Central Square, a circular plaza encased by narrow buildings with sharp-slanted roofs. The tallest structure was a thin pointed clock tower at the easternmost edge of the circle. Lucy envisioned lots of activity in Central Square at the heart of the village.

North of the town, past the Alchemist's Cottage, the western end of Glacial Lake emerged from behind the castle hill. Beyond that were open grassy fields, and in the far northwest lay the Dark Sea.

It looks like the Northern Sea, Lucy thought. The Dark Sea was drawn on the map with heavy churning swells crashing ashore at a rocky place called Pernicious Landing. She cringed—it looked like a mariner's worst nightmare.

"Hmm..." One of her brothers made a waking noise.

Tearing herself away from the map, she folded it with care and slipped it into her pocket. Grabbing a set of clothes, she slipped out to use the bathroom before her brothers got up. She made sure to transfer the map from the pocket of the jeans she'd fallen asleep in yesterday to the front pocket of today's pair. She washed her face and brushed her teeth, her mind absorbed with images of Praxis. In the living room, she was surprised to find her father hadn't left for work yet.

"Morning, Dad." He lifted his head from the book he was reading. It was a thick diesel engine mechanic's manual.

"Morning, Luce. You get enough sleep?" He cracked a smile. Lucy loved the way his eyes wrinkled up when he smiled, and she was glad to see that he seemed at ease this morning.

She grinned, appreciative of his sarcastic joke. "Yes, I did, thank you very much!" She made her way to the kitchen. "You're late getting to work this morning."

"Yeah, I like to enjoy a bit of quiet at the shop before the day starts. That wouldn't have happened this morning, so I stayed here where I knew I'd get some peace." Peter closed his book, stood, and stretched. "You going to stay out of trouble today?" He frowned at his daughter.

"Of course!" Lucy smiled. "I'm always careful. And I promise I'll keep my guard up."

"I know you will. Come here." He took a few steps toward her, arms open wide. Lucy rushed into her father's arms, longing to tell him about the map. His fresh flannel button-up work shirt felt soft and clean against her cheek. She breathed in his scent, savoring the moment. Bar soap, coffee, and a trace of engine lubricating oil. Hot tears sprang into her eyes, unbidden. She didn't want to be the Mapkeeper, but the map seemed to have other plans. She clung to her father, feeling safe in his arms—even if it was just for a moment.

Peter held her out at arm's length. "Well, I'm off to the shop. Tell the boys to have a great day for me. I love you." He pulled her in for one more quick squeeze, then grabbed his ratty old ball cap and strode out through the garage door.

"I will. I love you too Dad!" she called after him. She watched him leave and waited until she heard his snow mobile start and drone off down the road. It wouldn't be long before the boys were up. She pulled the map out and sank into the couch. Mr.

Quincy had said something about the Mapkeeper being able to manipulate the map.

Color and warmth spread through the map in a sparkling sheen when she rubbed it. She tucked some loose hair behind her ear and flipped the map upside down, puzzled. The back side was plain—no markings whatsoever. She flipped it back to the front side, inspecting each marking. She searched for hidden words or pictures. Finding none, she tried rubbing the map harder.

The map cooled as the colorful ink faded to plain black. Puzzled, she held it up to eye level. She had no idea how to harness the power of the map, but rather than allowing it to frustrate her, she told herself that she didn't mind. It relieved her of having to worry about whatever responsibility came with being the Mapkeeper.

"Hey," Luke grumbled as he shuffled through the living room toward the kitchen. None of the Barnes children were fond of mornings. There was a half-hour grace period where it was understood that no one should be expected to have much energy.

"Hey." Lucy pocketed the map and followed him into the kitchen.

"Mack and I were talking last night," Luke whispered, "and we think maybe we should go back into the forest and dig up the map." He pulled two slices of bread from the bread box and stuffed them in the toaster.

Lucy's eyes darted to the kitchen window. The curtains

were shut.

Mack walked in, his hair a complete mess. "Yeah," he chimed in.

"Too late. Look what showed up on my nightstand this morning." She pulled the tip of the map out of her pocket to show them. They huddled together in the center of the kitchen. "It's so strange. It glows, gets warm, and turns colorful when I rub it sometimes, but that's it."

"You said you felt a connection to the map, right?" Luke asked.

"Yeah. It's weird. I don't really know how to explain it."

"Have you considered that maybe it reacts to more than just your touch? Maybe it responds to your state of mind, too," Luke speculated. Lucy considered the idea. Mack just shrugged.

"I guess that could make sense... But this is all crazy. I'm not planning on using the map anyway."

"Why don't you at least try to see if you can make it do something?" Luke whispered.

She sighed and pulled out the map. Closing her eyes, she took a deep breath, trying to empty her mind and be at peace, but she couldn't force frustrating thoughts of Mr. Quincy and the Commune from her mind. Sudden warmth from the map surprised her. Opening her eyes, she saw the vortex of color form at the center of the map and expand until the whole map was once again alive with color—and now motion!

"Whoa!" Luke exclaimed in a hushed voice.

"That is awesome." Mack agreed, wide-eyed and alert despite having just woken up.

The map was alive. Leaves on trees stirred as if blown by a stiff breeze, the surface of the lake rippled, the castle turret flags whipped in the wind, and large swells exploded with fury against the rocks at Pernicious Landing in the northwest. Lucy's arms and legs tingled with warmth.

"You were right, Luke!" Lucy exclaimed, unable to contain her delight.

Nervousness overcame her. What if the Commune really was listening in? Or worse—watching them? "I should put this away." She folded the map and stuffed it in her pocket, heading to the cupboard for a box of cereal. Her brothers didn't object.

"Lucy, I hope you know that if you go, we're coming," Mack asserted. His blue eyes were grave.

"You guys can't... it's too risky!" she protested. "Besides, Mr. Quincy said no one besides the Mapkeeper has ever gone to Praxis. I don't think it's possible."

"We're coming." Luke stepped toward her, intent. His toast was burning. The three of them stood for a long moment facing one another. Lucy's gaze swept from Luke to Mack and back. It seemed there was no dissuading them.

"I mean, if it's possible, that would be great. But as of now I don't think I'm even going," she replied, shrugging. Remembering his breakfast, Luke whipped around to salvage what was left of his toast. Mack's brow furrowed in concern. Protecting his sister was his main concern.

"I heard you talking to Dad this morning. He still doesn't know about the map, right?" Mack asked.

"Right."

"I'd better leave a note for him just in case," Mack said with a grimace of guilt. "I feel bad...but he'd feel better to at least know we're all together." He pulled a pad of paper and a *Commune Ink, Inc.* pen out of a drawer and scrawled a note.

"That isn't necessary, Mack," Lucy insisted, annoyed. "We aren't going anywhere." She left the kitchen.

In silence, they gathered their belongings, donned boots and jackets, locked up the house, and set off for school. They hurried, trying once again to avoid contact with nosy neighbors. When they reached Mrs. Beadleback's house, Lucy glanced up in time to see the curtains in her front window swish shut. The door popped open and the woman waddled out, overdressed as before.

"Hey kids! Going to school?" she called, toddling after them.

"Yes, Mrs. Beadleback, but we're running a little late so we've got to hurry! Sorry there's no time to chat!" Lucy called over her shoulder as they picked up the pace. Lucy peeked over her shoulder a few seconds later and saw a disappointed Mrs. Beadleback give up, realizing she wouldn't be able to catch them. One of three scarves draped around her shoulders plopped onto the icy sidewalk. She bent at the waist to snatch it up, layers of puffy winter jackets ballooning around her. With a final frown of determination, the woman shuffled up the path toward her house.

"Maybe this afternoon then, Lucy!" she called. Lucy waved over her shoulder as the siblings rounded a corner. They hurried down the street toward a cul-de-sac that backed up to the woods. Trees would provide the cover they needed to get to school. Parting shin-deep snow, they cut between two houses and trekked into the woods without further incident.

"Let's hurry. I don't see anyone following us," Mack urged in a hushed voice. They tramped deeper into the woods through thick drifts of untouched snow. The forest around them grew dense and dark. Glancing back, Lucy could see the white glow from the natural opening in the woods that led into town.

"Let's turn here. I don't want to lose my sense of direction. We need to head west and parallel the edge of the woods," she said. Her brothers nodded in agreement and they shifted course, keeping the faint light of the forest's edge in view.

"You're not going to try ditch the map again, are you?" Luke asked, kicking a stick that was half-buried in a snow drift.

"I want to," Lucy laughed, nervous. "But no, I guess I'll hang onto it and see what happens." The map warmed as they walked, becoming hotter and hotter. "Whoa, this thing feels like it's going to burn a hole in my pocket!" She jerked the map out, holding it away from her body by a corner. It pulsed, emitting blinding light. Her heart rate skyrocketed and the woods began to fade, her vision blurring around the edges.

In a panic, she grabbed each of her brothers by an arm. The woods expanded and contracted, rippling like the surface of the sea. Everything grew darker and a great rush of snow seemed to surround them. Her stomach dropped as if she was in a high-speed elevator, and then everything was black. The only sound was the deafening rush of air.

Thud. She crumpled in a heap. Grass crushed against her left cheek. She still gripped the map in her left hand. One of her brothers was sprawled across her legs, pinning her down. An unidentifiable bony joint belonging to the other brother jabbed into her neck from below. Brightness compressed her pupils to pinpoints as she blinked her eyes open, trying to focus. Tugging her legs free, she pushed herself up to her knees, sitting back on her heels and trying to orient herself. She rubbed the back of her neck—it felt like she'd fallen off a roof! Her brothers sat up too, groaning.

Lucy squinted, allowing her eyes to adjust to the direct sunlight. They were in a field of grass atop a small hill. It was a cloudless, sunny day, and the twittering of birds permeated the air. Taking a deep breath, she took in her surroundings. Nausea clenched her stomach, but she was awestruck at the same time. She stood, turning in a slow circle to take it all in.

"Whoa..." Luke murmured, whipping his brown hair out of his eyes as he stood.

At the base of the grassy hill about a half mile away, Lucy could see a town. Beyond the town, a large castle loomed atop a crowning hill. Beyond that, a wide lake stretched across a broad green valley. To the northeast, Lucy could make out a dark, thick forest. In the backdrop, sharp, snow-capped mountains loomed, shrouded in a fine mist. It was all just as the map depicted!

A jolt of nerves shot through Lucy's veins. "This is unreal," she muttered, scratching her head and glancing down at the map in her hand. Mack was picking a tuft of grass out of the zipper of his jacket. Luke had already shed his. It was far too warm for their winter layers.

"Look!" Luke pointed toward the town.

At the edge of town, a group of people on horseback were riding toward them. The lead rider held a tall pole topped with a billowing red forked pennant. Three riders followed behind him.

Mack and Luke glanced at their sister with a shadow of fear. Lucy swallowed her own alarm, battling back the jitters that rose in her throat and faced the riders in a show of bravery.

CHAPTER 7

The Barnes siblings shed their winter jackets and tossed them into a heap. Lucy stepped toward the riders, hoping to appear peaceful. She clasped her hands in front of her body and planted her feet. Mack and Luke took place on either side of her. The riders galloped closer. Now Lucy could see them with clarity. The leader was a handsome man with light brown hair that blew in the breeze as he rode. He held the red pennant in one hand and held the reins with the other. He squinted at the siblings with guarded curiosity. He had a strong jaw, broad shoulders, and an athletic build. He wore simple clothing—black pants and a loose white linen work shirt.

The others, two men and a woman, flanked him and were all dressed in similar attire—tall leather riding boots and comfortable clothing. They rode healthy-looking horses with fine leather saddles. The woman's hair was tied in a long tail down her back with thin leather rope. All four of them rode with easy confidence. Three saddled horses without riders were being guided behind the riders by leather ropes.

"Good day to you, strangers. My name is Cadmus," the leader addressed them. "We come in the name of King Muttongale, rightful ruler of Praxis. Please state your names and your purpose." The riders slowed and reined in their mounts, coming to a collective halt several paces away from the siblings.

"My name is Lucy Barnes and these are my brothers, Mack and Luke. We—um, we come in peace… from a place called Algid." Lucy tried to project her voice. The riders loomed over her astride their steeds. The horses side-stepped, energetic and eager to trot.

"Lucy Barnes of Algid, what is your purpose in Praxis?" Cadmus challenged.

"I, uh, inherited a map which brought me from my world to this one." She held the map up in one hand. Though her explanation felt feeble, the map pulsed a gentle, pleasant warmth through her body.

The eyes of the riders softened and they exchanged a round of brisk nods with one another as if some shared secret had been verified. Amid a chorus of snorts and huffs, the riders dismounted and the leader walked toward Lucy, leading his horse by its reins.

"Lucy Barnes of Algid, we have been expecting you. Welcome to Praxis." He bowed before her, taking her free hand and kissing it, his striking blue eyes never breaking contact with hers. Lucy instinctively tugged her hand away at the unexpected touch. Flustered, she looked away and fished for the proper way to respond to his startling greeting.

She gazed at the ground and mumbled, "Um..."

Cadmus averted his eyes and stepped back. "We invite you to join us. There is much to discuss. In fact, there will be a great celebration in your honor this evening. We have been waiting for the return of the Mapkeeper for quite some time." She blinked, struggling to process everything he was saying. "Dark forces are stirring in Praxis, Lucy," he went on, looking her in the eye. "Those who wish us harm are growing stronger. The signs foretold by our grandfathers' grandfathers are being realized and your service is very much needed at this time." Her stomach twisted into a knot at the comment about dark forces stirring. *Am I expected to do something about it?* She shifted her weight from one foot to the other and stared at her feet as she toed the ground.

Cadmus mounted his steed and motioned to one of the other men, who nodded and led the three extra stallions toward the siblings.

"Hello, my name is Quinn." The man introduced himself with a kind smile, offering them each a set of reins. Exchanging a look of concern, the Barnes siblings communicated without speaking: none of them knew how to ride.

Lucy's apprehension grew as she watched her horse stamp at the ground with impatience. She'd seen plenty of horses on TV of course, but only now came to the realization that she had never seen a horse up close. It was so... big! Quinn held the reins toward her, waiting for her to accept them.

Mack had taken hold of his with confidence and was stroking his horse on the nose. Lucy already knew he would be a natural, like he was with most everything. Taking a deep breath, she stepped forward and took her reins, though the huge animal unnerved her greatly. Its sudden, jerky movements caught her off guard. She stepped away from the beast, clenching the reins as far from her body as possible.

"Are you unfamiliar with riding?" Cadmus asked.

Heat flushed Lucy's face—everyone was staring at her! In a single gliding motion, Cadmus slid out of his saddle and lodged the red pennant in the grass. In three swift strides, he was at her side. He slipped the leather reins out of her hand and stepped up to her horse.

"Easy, girl." He calmed the horse, stroking its nose and whispering in its ear. The muscular chestnut stallion visibly relaxed at his touch. Cadmus turned to Lucy and held out a hand. Grateful that Luke's horse was now rearing and absorbing the attention of the other bystanders, Lucy accepted Cadmus' offer of assistance. He led her to the stallion and placed her hand on its nose.

"Shh... easy, Nel," he cooed. His presence seemed to calm the beast. "Try to be still," he directed Lucy. "The horse will relax when you do."

She stared into the horse's large black eye. She had no idea what it was feeling. *How did he know?* She continued to pet its nose gingerly. "Okay. Are you ready to mount?" Cadmus took her hand once more and she nodded, though she was fighting back an intense rush of nerves, both about riding for the first time, and being in this bizarre place with these strangers.

He stepped up next to the saddle. "Nel is comfortable with you now. She'll let you on with no problems. Here, put your left foot in the stirrup." He held his other hand at shoulder height, and she found herself taking it. "One, two, three!" She stepped up and he lifted her with ease. Her right leg swung around and she plopped into the saddle. "Now, take the reins. Pull toward you to slow him down, and give a gentle dig with your heels to get him going. Remember—gentle." Cadmus flashed a grin, then turned, unearthed his pennant, and mounted his horse.

"Whoa! Whoa, Brig!" Quinn and the woman were attempting to get Luke's horse under control. It was a wild-looking black and white spotted mare. Safely astride her horse, Lucy couldn't help but giggle nervously at the sight, though her stomach was still doing somersaults. Luke was in the saddle, clinging to the saddle horn for dear life. His horse reared with a sharp whinny. Lucy glanced back at Mack, who was already trotting in circles astride his gray mount as though he'd been riding horses all his life. Her gaze shifted to Cadmus, who was watching her younger brother with a vigilant eye.

At last Luke's assistants managed to get Brig under control, and the group started off together toward the town. Lucy gave Nel the gentlest nudge, but she didn't move. She nudged her again, a bit harder this time.

Nel took off, almost throwing Lucy off her rear end! Tugging on the reins with all her strength, Lucy managed to recover from the shock and whiplash in time to stay on the horse. Her heart thundered and she bounced wildly as Nel caught up with the group.

Despite her nearly incapacitating unease, Lucy forced a smile. *Just try to go with the flow and figure this out as you go,* she told herself as they crossed the soft, grassy field at a rapid gallop. To Lucy's surprise, the muted collective thundering of hooves was soothing. On her right, Luke clung to his reins in a mild panic. She laughed out loud at the sight of his long, boyish hair blowing straight back in the wind while he struggled to stay upright in the saddle, clinging to the horse with his thin legs. She knew he would be all right—Luke was more athletic and physically capable than he gave himself credit for.

Mack rode well, keeping pace in the center of the group, just behind Cadmus. Lucy was proud of him, and his confidence gave her strength. He looked so muscular and grown-up. The unknowns of what lay ahead troubled her deeply, but she felt safer with her older brother by her side.

They reached the town and slowed to a trot. Lucy was grateful to be at the back of the group—that way Nel followed the cues of the rest of the horses and she didn't have to work the reins much. She tried to relax, for she had been squeezing so tightly with her thighs that her muscles were on the verge of cramping.

They were on a wide dirt path now, which led to a cobbled avenue lined with quaint A-frame houses. The houses were colorful, with intricate wood-worked faces. Most had dark shingled roofs and shuttered windows with overflowing flower boxes beneath them. Charming pink, white, and purple buds nestled in the boxes, flourishing in the warm weather. Little round doors with center-mounted knobs popped open as the riders trotted past, and the heads of curious villagers poked out in hopes of catching a glimpse of the strangers.

Children playing with a ball in the street up ahead were shooed to the side by a teenage girl. The girl met her gaze with shocking deep violet eyes, but glanced away as soon as their eyes met. She wore the same hair style as the woman in the riding group—a pony tail secured with thin leather rope. *I wonder what it's like to grow up here*, Lucy thought, still in disbelief that any of this was real. The eyes of the villagers only increased her nervousness.

"We'll take the Royale Byway up to the palace where you will meet the royal family and be shown to your quarters." Cadmus explained, turning in his saddle to face her.

She swallowed hard and her eyes narrowed. She met Mack's gaze as her brother turned to look at her. Thinking through the situation, at the moment she saw no reason not to trust Cadmus and this group of strangers—they hadn't yet done anything to cause her to believe they were a threat... but she would prod him for more information.

"We're... staying in the palace?" she replied. She wasn't sure she had the proper manners to mingle with royalty. Glancing down, she noticed several grass and dirt stains on her jeans.

"Of course!" Cadmus seemed surprised. "You are the Mapkeeper, after all. And besides... it's not safe for you in town right now." He faced forward and increased the pace to a light gallop. She gulped.

The road widened and began to climb up a gentle, sloping hill. Lucy could see the castle in the distance between patches of evergreens. It was tall and majestic, overlooking the town on the crest of the hill. She remembered seeing this hill on the map.

They galloped onward in silence. *What did Cadmus mean when he said, "it's not safe for you in town right now?"* she wondered. She was now in the middle of the pack, surrounded by riders. They'd shifted position without her noticing. She scanned the surroundings, her nerves on edge. Parts of the road were entirely shadowed by dense groves of trees. *Could this all be a trick? Are we in danger?*

Mack rode on her left side. He smiled at her, bringing her a small amount of comfort. Luke was to her right, at last looking a bit more relaxed in the saddle. He was too focused on riding to notice Lucy trying to catch his eye.

The dirt road wound uphill through the trees. Lucy could see Cadmus up ahead, the red pennant whipping and snapping in the wind high overhead. His white shirt billowed behind him like the sail of a ship. The road here was lined with many more red pennants identical to the one Cadmus bore, strung high on shafts of gold.

The group rounded a final curve in the road and Cadmus eased the pace to a trot. The trees thinned around them and they spilled out into a clearing. Across a large field of grass, a wide moat encircled the castle. Lucy shaded her eyes against the sun, tilting her head up to take in the view. She gasped: the castle was massive! Tilting her head up so far that she almost felt dizzy, she could just make out the arched window slits hewn in the stone near the top of the spires. It was just as the map pictured it!

She stuffed a hand into her jeans pocket and felt the comforting crinkle of parchment.

More red pennants flapped in the wind high above, affixed to the tops of spires. A thick wooden drawbridge rested in the raised position across the moat. Two armored sentries wielding crossbows and sheathed swords rode to meet them, their helmets concealing everything but their eyes. A neatly shaved stripe of red plumage adorned the tops of their helmets. Cadmus reined in his steed and turned sideways in a show of submission.

"Good day to you both!" he called as they approached.

"Good day, Cadmus," one of the guards replied. "I see you've brought our guests." He peered beyond the front line of the escort party and eyed the Barnes siblings. Turning toward the castle, the guard signaled a cohort on the other side of the moat, who in turn began to lower the drawbridge. It groaned in protest, straining against its rope constraints as it lowered. *Wham!* Lucy winced as the dense wooden bridge slammed into the grass and the guards motioned for the group to dismount.

Lucy and her brothers followed suit when their escorts hopped down from their mounts. Four young stable hands scurried across the drawbridge and snatched up the reins, trotting with light-footed agility alongside the horses toward the stable across the lawn.

Cadmus held out his arm. "Lucy, may I escort you across the bridge?" She hesitated, unsure whether this was truly a good idea. Glancing at her brothers for reassurance, she tried to ignore the fact that her stomach felt like a gaping hole in her abdomen. Mack and Luke looked uneasy, but did nothing to stop her. Snapping her head away from them and back to Cadmus, she hesitantly accepted his arm. The rest of the riding party were already crossing.

"Of course," she muttered as she slipped her arm into the crook of his elbow. Her eyes darted left and right, scanning the surroundings for any sign of danger. It felt good to walk again, as her muscles were stiff from the ride. The stares of both guards made the hairs on the back of her neck stand at attention as Cadmus led her between them and across the bridge. Mack and Luke followed behind, bringing up the rear.

As soon as they were across, a guard shouted "Up bridge!" and with a groan, the pulley system reeled in the rope and lifted the drawbridge back to its raised position. Lucy fought back a surge of nerves as she realized that there was no going back now.

They crossed the threshold of the castle and found themselves in a large stone atrium, where a bright red carpet led from the entrance across the atrium to a set of tall, intricate, carved golden doors. Lucy gasped. The height of the ceiling was dizzying. She released Cadmus' arm and turned in a circle, taking in the enormity of the atrium. Towering, color-drizzled tapestries adorned the circular walls, stretching from the floor to a hundred feet high. At the apex of the domed ceiling, a massive golden chandelier glittered far above, lit by the soft, gentle flickerings of a thousand candles. Lucy wondered how they lit the distant candle wicks.

"Greetings, Ms. Lucy Barnes! Welcome to Tropos Castle, home of his Highness Muttongale and the royal family," a well-dressed butler announced, taking Lucy by surprise. He had short cropped white hair and a matching, perfectly clipped bristled mustache. "Sir Cadmus, it's a pleasure as always." The butler bowed low, one arm swept behind his back and the other tucked in the fold of his waist.

"Milo, good to see you." Cadmus stepped forward and grasped the butler's hand in a firm handshake, clapping him on the shoulder.

"Well, thank you, sir. If I may, I have been instructed to show the Mapkeeper and her brothers to the Great Hall to be introduced to the royal family. If you will be so kind as to follow me..." He pivoted and floated across the room toward the golden double doors.

"I've never seen a place so magnificent," Lucy muttered to no one in particular.

Milo turned and smiled graciously, spreading his hands. "The palace is beautiful indeed, Ms. Barnes. It was built a thousand years ago during the reign of Lord Hammington the Bold. It is said he built the palace from the ground up for his wife, Lady Shirlet, whose loveliness is legendary. They say she was the most beautiful creature that ever lived." His eyes twinkled as he spoke. He reminded Lucy of her late grandfather, and this made her think of her father, bringing back the gnawing, consuming guilt. *He is probably worried sick about us at this very moment,* she reflected.

She missed him even more than she could have thought possible, and her heart ached at the thought of him alone in their home. Not just one, but all three of his children were gone, and he had no idea whether they were safe. Suddenly she regretted bringing her brothers with her. Though they had insisted on coming with her, it still felt selfish to Lucy, for they brought her great comfort. *Comfort that they could be providing to Dad instead of me,* she thought. The idea made her feel sick to her stomach.

Milo pushed open the heavy gilded doors, revealing two massive, identical spiral staircases. Cadmus held one door open while Milo held the other, standing stick-straight. The Barnes siblings stepped through the doors and waited at the base of the steps for further direction.

Lucy ogled the gorgeous, thick red carpeting of the stairs, which was inlaid with elegant floral designs in shades of violet and lilac. A dense, intricately carved wooden hand rail trimmed the bannister.

"Up we go, if you please, Ms. Barnes." Milo bowed and gestured with one hand for Lucy to proceed. She cringed, unaccustomed to this kind of treatment.

"Um, Milo, you can just call me Lucy." She smiled politely.

His eyes widened for an instant before his face relaxed into a kind smile. "Oh my, Ms. Barnes, I do appreciate your benevolence, but I must insist upon regarding you with the highest respect. After all, you are the Mapkeeper." Lucy glanced at Mack, eyebrows raised in uncomfortable disbelief. He shrugged, sharing in her surprise.

The eerie feeling of being the wrong person in the wrong place settled once again in the pit of Lucy's stomach.

CHAPTER 8

Despite the weight in her stomach and the tightness in her throat, she and Mack led the ascent up the wide staircase.

"It'll be up two flights to the Great Hall, Ms. Barnes," Milo directed from behind her.

They passed several enormous arched stained glass windows as they climbed. Abstract jets of colored light streamed in, bathing the room in blood red and egg yolk yellow. On the third floor Lucy found herself facing another set of heavy gold double doors, carved with the same detailed complexity as the set below. Milo and Cadmus quickened their pace to reach the doors first, pulling them open for their guests. Lucy's heart pounded in her chest as the doors opened. She had no idea what to expect beyond the double doors, but the presence of her brothers once again provided her with comfort. After a brief hesitation, they stepped into an expansive room with shiny white marble flooring.

"Ms. Barnes and gentlemen, I present to you the Great Hall." Milo bowed as the doors eased shut behind him. Cadmus gave Lucy a reassuring smile, his piercing blue eyes wrinkling at the corners.

Lucy's eyes were drawn across the room, where three thrones dominated the space, the largest in the center, flanked by two smaller ones. The thrones were perched atop a stepped platform overlooking the Great Hall, which included a massive banquet table. The royal family were perched in their thrones, expectant of their guests' arrival.

"Ah, good day, Ms. Lucy Barnes! What a pleasure it is to host the Mapkeeper and her two brothers in Tropos Castle for the very first time! My name is King Muttongale, and it is my honor to welcome you to Praxis." The king stood as he spoke. His height changed very little when he went from sitting to standing. He was one of the shortest men Lucy had ever seen! He sported a king's full regalia, with a bright red velvet cape and an eight-point golden crown. His wiry red beard extended two fists' length beneath his chin and matched his wild mop of red hair. "This is my wife, Queen Oleksandra, and my son and heir, Prince Puck."

The queen was stunning. She stood with graceful ease in a single, flowing motion. She was tall and slender, with soft dark eyes and long, smooth brown hair. A small silver tiara teeming with diamonds was combed through her hair, and a svelte, floor-length midnight blue dress cloaked her slender frame. "Good day, Ms. Barnes," the queen said in her melodic voice. "We are pleased and honored to host you. I trust these are your brothers?"

Mack stepped forward and bowed at the waist. "Good day my queen, my name is Mack Barnes and this is my brother Luke. We are Lucy's brothers." Lucy ogled her brother. He spoke as though he'd been accustomed to addressing royalty his entire life. *Good day?* Luke followed suit with a deep bow.

The queen smiled appreciatively. King Muttongale peered at Prince Puck and prodded him with an elbow. "Aren't you going to greet our guests, son?" The plump prince filled out his little throne quite well.

"Hello, guests." He pouted, his chubby arms crossed in a tight, thick twist across his chest. Lucy guessed he was about twelve years old. Strawberry-blonde hair hung over his forehead in strings.

King Muttongale chortled, throwing his head back and grabbing his round belly as it jiggled up and down. "Our prince is quite the little grouch this morning." He wiped a tear of laughter from the corner of his eye, but the queen's eyebrows furrowed with concern. Lucy looked down at her feet, uncomfortable. She could feel the burn of the prince's eyes—he was glaring at her. She released her breath with a soft hiss when Cadmus intervened.

"Your Highness, will we have the Ceremony of Light this evening?"

"Ah! Yes, thank you for reminding me, Cadmus." King Muttongale hooked his stubby thumbs into his leather belt. "Lucy, whenever Praxis acquires a new Mapkeeper, we have a tradition of introducing him or her at the Ceremony of Light. It is a grand festival and all the creatures of Praxis will be there to welcome you. The ceremony will be held tonight in Central Square in the village."

"I—I would be most honored, your highness," she stammered as she bowed. It was Mack's turn to give her a funny look. As soon as she heard herself speak, she knew her brothers would laugh at her choice of words. Nervous, she avoided making eye contact with her brothers and stifled an awkward grin.

"In the meantime, may I show you to your quarters?" Queen Oleksandra stepped forward, gesturing at the doors behind them.

"That would be lovely, your highness." Lucy met the queen's warm gaze with a smile of genuine gratitude.

"Cadmus, you will be our guests' personal escort throughout their stay," the King proclaimed. Cadmus bowed in confirmation. His long brown hair flipped over his forehead. Lucy looked away and noticed Mack watching her intently. She whipped around to follow the queen, who was already leading the way out of the Great Hall.

"Sir Mack and Sir Luke, please follow me. Your rooms are just down the hall from your sister's." Milo gestured toward the door.

Lucy heard the king give Prince Puck a halfhearted scolding as they left the room.

"How have you enjoyed Praxis so far, Ms. Barnes?" The

queen glanced over her shoulder as she led Lucy to her quarters.

"It is beautiful here, your highness! But I am still in shock at being selected as the new Mapkeeper. I have so much to learn," she confided. The truth was, she was *terrified* and vowed to find the first opportunity to figure out how to get out of this strange place!

Queen Oleksandra smiled. "It is beautiful indeed. You will learn in time, don't worry about that." She paused outside a set of wooden double doors with large gold handles and her smile disappeared. "But dark forces are stirring, Ms. Barnes. You must be very careful. We will not leave you unguarded."

"Why would anyone want to hurt me?" Lucy stopped, her chest tightening with fear. She had finally asked the question that had been haunting her since they'd arrived.

"There is plenty of time to talk on that later," the queen said, dismissing the question as she opened one of the doors and ushered Lucy in. Lucy's frustration was renewed, but she entered the chamber anyway.

Warm sunlight filled the large room, spilling in through a ceiling-high arched window. A canopy bed dominated the room, curtains tied around the bedposts. It was piled high with purple pillows and appeared tall enough that Lucy might have to perform a jumping dive to get into bed.

The knot in Lucy's stomach loosened as she admired the room. She'd never seen such a lavish bedroom! Lush red carpet with a gold pattern stretched to the corners of the room. A tall armoire sat opposite the window, and a smaller chest of drawers with a stool and a mirror was positioned next to the window, so the sunlight would illuminate whoever sat in front of the mirror. An overstuffed red chair with a matching ottoman occupied the far corner beside a red velvet cat bed, in which a fluffy white cat napped in the sun.

"Aww! Who is this little guy?" Lucy went to the cat, bending to pet it. The cat stretched, waking and beginning to purr at her touch. He was small, and soft as silk.

"That is Sir Wigginsworth, our trusty little companion. We have had him for six years now." The queen smiled.

Standing, Lucy peered into the bathroom. It joined the bedroom via a wide arched door on the wall opposite the bed. Walking in, she was overwhelmed by its magnificence. The floor and counter tops were adorned with gold-flecked cream marble. There were dozens of gold-knobbed cherry wood cabinets, polished to a soft shine. A massive four-legged bath tub with a complicated array of golden spouts sat at the far end of the room. At the near end was a large square shower with a frosted glass door. Lucy pulled open the door, peering inside.

"Whoa," she murmured.

The inside of the shower was tiled dark blue. An intricate gold swirl tile pattern circled the golden drain cover on the floor. There was another confusing array of gold knobs, spouts, and hoses mounted on the wall and dangling from the ceiling. One wall had a bench, and another was home to a half dozen nooks packed with an assortment of purple and pink soaps and rinses, a large wooden-handled scrub brush, and a poofy body lathering puff.

"You should have everything you need," the queen said with a smile. "However, should you require anything at all, Olivia will see to it." Lucy turned to see the queen place a gentle hand on a young girl's back, encouraging the shy girl to step forward. "Olivia, say hello to our new Mapkeeper, Ms. Barnes."

"Hello, Ms. Barnes," came her shy murmur. The girl looked to be about ten years old. She had long, dark hair and matching eyes. She was scrawny and wore a simple green dress beneath an apron.

"Hi, Olivia." Lucy smiled and extended a hand. The girl eyed it, uncertain.

"Go ahead, she wants to shake your hand, dear." The queen nudged Olivia forward. The girl slipped a limp hand into Lucy's and Lucy gave it a gentle shake, hoping to convey kindness with her smile. "Olivia will be your handmaid. She is at your disposal for the duration of your stay in Praxis." The queen smiled. "She lives here at the castle. Her mother Helda is a cook in the kitchens, and her father Quinn is our lead stableman. Her brother Pip will look after your brothers."

"It's a pleasure to meet you," Lucy said, smiling. Olivia nodded.

"Well, I'll leave you to get settled. Oh, and this is your

laundry chute," the queen added on her way to the door, pushing open an inconspicuous false panel in the wall. "I'll send Milo for you when it is time to go to the village for the Festival of Light." The queen floated out of the room, the door latch clicking behind her.

Lucy ran and dove onto the high bed, laughing. For a moment, her fears were forgotten. The bed was as thick and soft as it looked. She rolled onto her back and sighed, savoring the comfort. Her bed back home was a brick compared to this! She glanced over at Olivia, who still stood in the bathroom entryway, eyes agog.

"How old are you?" Lucy asked, propping herself up on one elbow.

"Twelve," Olivia replied, clasping her hands in front of her.

"Have you always lived at the castle?"

"No. When I was born we lived in the village. But my father was so passionate about horses that he trained to become a stable hand. He started out pitching hay, and now he is the head stableman for the royal family." She lifted her chin with pride.

"That's great! My dad is a boat mechanic." Olivia gave her a funny look. "I guess you don't have those here." Olivia shook her head. Her long, shiny hair swung back and forth.

Lucy dropped her head over the side of the bed and peered out the window upside down. She could see the stable in the distance. A boy was brushing a horse. Green fields stretched for perhaps a half mile, and then the hill ended with a sharp drop down to the village below. To the north, she could make out a large lake in the distance. She rolled onto her stomach and pulled the map out of her jeans pocket, unfolding it. The lake was marked Glacial Lake.

Olivia still stood in the doorway to the bathroom. "What did the queen mean when she said 'dark forces are stirring'? She seemed to think I would be unsafe if I'm not guarded." Olivia's eyes darkened.

"There have been many signs that something very, very bad is coming, Ms. Barnes. Here in Praxis, there is a legend passed down from one generation to the next about a great catastrophe that occurred over a thousand years ago. They say there were warning signs—natural disasters, tremors, and storms. A lot of people are on edge right now because we have been seeing some of the signs." Her voice descended to a whisper.

"Like what?" Lucy asked, riveted.

"Like last week, there was a tremor. The whole world was shaking. I was outside with Pip in the stable. The horses felt it coming first. They started to whinny and stomp, and we couldn't figure out why. Then the tremor came, and Pip and I ran and took cover against a wall. It was awful. Everything shook so hard I thought the stable would fall down on us! It felt like the world was ending." Olivia wrung her hands at the memory.

"Wow..." Lucy exhaled. Back home in Algid there were occasional snow slides, but never anything as awful as what Olivia had described. "What does legend say happened the last time all these signs occurred?"

Olivia's expression became solemn. "There is a dark magic in Praxis. It is ancient and capable of terrible power. The last time these signs happened was because the dark magic was being awakened. The wrong people came into possession of it—they called themselves the Wardens. They used it to awaken three terrible beasts: one from the sea, one from the mountains, and one from beneath the ground." Olivia shuddered. "The three beasts ravaged Praxis, almost to total destruction."

A leaden weight sank in Lucy's stomach and her palms began to sweat. Fearful of the answer, but knowing she had to ask, she whispered, "Who—who stopped the Wardens?"

Olivia gulped and took a deep breath. Looking Lucy in the eyes, she replied, "The Mapkeeper."

CHAPTER 9

That evening, they rode to town in a large horse-drawn carriage with the royal family. Lucy was squashed between Luke and Mack on a bench seat opposing Queen Oleksandra, Prince Puck, and King Muttongale, whose stubby legs didn't quite reach the floor. He bounced out of his seat each time they hit a rut in the road. Lucy couldn't make eye contact with Mack and Luke for fear of bursting out laughing at the sight of the bouncing monarch.

"Exquisite day outside," King Muttongale remarked, bracing himself against his two arm rests.

"It is beautiful!" Lucy agreed, leaning forward to gaze out the window next to Luke.

They were escorted by ten armed guards on horseback. Lucy thought it was all a bit excessive, but she enjoyed the carriage ride nonetheless. It was another first for her.

"The Festival will begin with our arrival, Ms. Barnes. I will step out with my queen and my boy..." He winked at Prince Puck. The prince rolled his eyes and shifted away from his father to face the window. "...and then I will introduce you and your brothers to the masses. You will be escorted on stage by your guards, and the ceremony will begin!" He spread his hands and grinned, unable to contain his excitement. His legs wiggled back and forth.

The carriage made a right hand turn onto a wide cobbled road labeled Central Sq. Promenade. Lucy's eyes bulged—throngs of villagers lined the street! They erupted into a roar of approval as the carriage made its arrival. Aproned women waved lace kerchiefs while men whooped and punched the air. Children darted to and fro amongst the crowd playing hide and seek or cheered from atop their parents' shoulders.

"Your highness, what is that massive fire burning up ahead?" Mack was leaning close to his window, peering toward their destination.

"Ah, the cauldron of fire! Each time a new Mapkeeper is chosen, the cauldron of fire comes alive. It is an ancient spell that even our most experienced maesters cannot decipher. The cauldron produces the likeness of the next Mapkeeper and spits it high into the sky for a fortnight. Today marks the final night, which is why it is time for the Ceremony of Light."

"Hold on. So you're saying there is a giant image of me made of fire?" Lucy leaned over Mack, straining to see.

"Get off me, sis!" Mack gave her a gentle shove. "I think

you can wait a couple more minutes to see it."

"Boo!" Lucy pouted, crossing her arms. Everyone laughed, but she couldn't stop an uneasy feeling from creeping into the pit of her stomach. It was strange that everyone was making such a big deal over her.

The crowds only thickened as they progressed down Central Square Promenade. Several minutes later they made a wide left turn and the road spilled into a circular town center fringed by tall, narrow A-frame storefronts.

"Central Square!" King Muttongale announced.

An immense clock tower dominated Central Square, four shops flanking it on each side. The storefronts were quaint and cheery, with colorful window shutters and round-topped wooden doors. The sidings were shingled, and cozy tendrils of smoke curled out of their crooked tin chimney pipes. Lucy squinted above the cheering crowd and read a hand-painted sign above the door out Luke's window to her right. "Emil's Clothier." Turning to peer out Mack's window, she gasped.

The town center was packed with people and in the center of it all, a fiery plume lit up the darkening sky. The fire formed the image of her own body! She could even make out the general likeness of her face and ponytail!

"Holy cow," she whispered. She could only stare.

"It's magnificent, isn't it?" Queen Oleksandra beamed at her from across the carriage.

Prince Puck yawned. "It's just the cauldron of fire," he muttered.

"I think it's amazing!" Luke murmured, leaning across Lucy to get a better view.

The cauldron was a thick black bowl the height of two men. It rested on a heavy stone cube and spewed its thick flame fifty feet in the air. Lucy's giant likeness stood holding the map in her left hand. From their vantage point, Lucy could see the left profile of her face dancing in the flames high above them. She noted that her fiery likeness seemed to exude a confidence that the real Lucy did not feel.

"All right Ms. Barnes, are you ready to meet the people and creatures of Praxis?" King Muttongale grinned and gestured toward the stage in front of the cauldron.

Lucy swallowed, rubbing her sweaty palms against her thighs. She was suddenly aware that she was still wearing jeans and a t-shirt. *Is that too casual?* She glanced at the queen, who dazzled in a deep purple silk gown with intricate white detailing and a gold sash.

"I guess I'm as ready as I'll ever be... Your highness, are you going first? What should I—" Before she could finish, one of their guards opened the carriage door and the royal family filed out. The deafening roar of the crowd and radiant heat from the fire poured into the compartment, causing beads of sweat to form on Lucy's temples. Mack looked back at his sister and shrugged. She wouldn't have been able to hear him over the din even if he'd said something. He hopped out of the carriage and followed the royal family through the human tunnel of uniformed guards. Luke patted Lucy's arm from behind, encouraging her to hop out.

She slid across the plush bench seat and plopped out onto the cobblestones, scurrying to catch up to her older brother. A row of stoic castle guards held back the cheering villagers, who were wild with excitement. Lucy caught glimpses of lit sparklers and heard the popping of crude fireworks from within the crowd. Someone howled—they must have been hit. Mack turned to grin at her. He waved to a group of teenage girls and they swooned, chirping and giggling in a gaggle. Lucy rolled her eyes.

Luke caught up and fell into step beside her. Lucy found herself once again grateful for her brothers' presence. Ahead, the king and queen were already climbing the short flight of carpeted stone steps to the stage. Prince Puck trailed behind, taking his time, gazing left and right with disinterest as he strolled toward the stage.

Lucy's stomach knotted in fear as she climbed the steps, her brothers flanking her. A red velvet carpet blanketed the wooden stage, and King Muttongale gestured for the siblings to sit in three gold-gilded wooden chairs. Prince Puck was already lounging on his throne. Queen Oleksandra stood by the king's side, waving at the crowd. As far as the eye could see, people and creatures filled the square and spilled into the street leading up to it.

The creatures! For the first time, Lucy took notice of the

different groups huddled together among the humans. None of them stood very near the stage. Toward the back of the crowd beside an alley that separated a store and a house was a large group of centaurs—they drew Lucy's eye first. She had read of them in many books growing up, but of course, in her mind, they had only been mythical beasts! They stood still and silent as they waited for the ceremony to begin, immune to whatever craze seemed to overcome the loud, exuberant crowd of people.

She would have continued to ogle them if not for the glowing group of dazzling women occupying the opposite corner of the square beside another alley. They had silken hair and translucent skin, and looked on with the same solemnity as the centaurs. Not a whisper was shared among them. A faint aura of light emanated from the group, giving them an ethereal quality. But what made them stand out the most was that each of them stood a full head taller than the tallest human!

A dent in the crowd somewhere in the middle revealed a huddled pack of waist-high gnomes. She could only see the back row of them, poking one other in the ribs and muttering amongst themselves. They were thick and squat, with braided beards and large noses.

A familiar face near the stage caught her eye. It was Cadmus, studying her with an inscrutable expression on his face. Unable to decide whether it was a good or a bad look, Lucy brushed the question away and focused on King Muttongale, who was holding out his short arms for silence. The din subsided and the people and creatures of Praxis settled until the powerful crackle of flames radiating from the cauldron behind them was the only sound.

One of the hooded castle maesters approached the king from the opposite side of the stage, holding a twig the length of a forearm. He took his time, moving with an air of grave purpose. His deep purple cloak shielded his face and dragged well behind him. With a flick of his wrist, the twig began to glow, a soft golden orb that illuminated the tip. The maester bowed and handed the glowing stick to King Muttongale, who thanked him with a hearty slap on the back. The maester flinched. Composing himself, he drifted off stage with dignity. Lucy's lips parted in an amused half-grin.

King Muttongale held the glowing stick beneath his mouth and his voice was amplified enough that the whole court could hear him.

"Good people and good creatures of Praxis! I come before you on this night to observe the Ceremony of Light, an ancient tradition that has been practiced by our ancestors for thousands of years. Most of us will only witness one or perhaps two such ceremonies in our lifetimes. With the exception of the Elves, of course." He gestured toward a group of thin, fair-skinned elves Lucy hadn't noticed before. They, like many of the other non-humans, stood in a quiet grouping on the outskirts of the crowd. "A momentous occasion indeed!"

The crowd erupted into applause. Lucy's stomach was somersaulting. She tried not to focus on the enormity of the crowd.

Instead, she stared at a charming little child clinging to her mother's skirt at the base of the stage. She sucked her thumb and stared back at Lucy with wide, innocent brown eyes. She helped Lucy momentarily forget that she was the focus of hundreds of eyes.

"Our last Mapkeeper served us well. He passed in peace and has been succeeded by Ms. Lucy Barnes, who joins us tonight to assume her rightful role among us!" Central Square resounded with raucous noise. Lucy's face flushed, making her hot and uncomfortable. She squeezed her abdominal muscles in an attempt to regain control of her flipping stomach. The king faced her and raised his arms as high as he could, grinning through his frizzy red beard. Queen Oleksandra smiled, her thin hands clasped in front of her. The din persisted.

At last, King Muttongale managed to quiet the people, waving his arms in a silencing motion. He stepped toward Lucy and handed her the glowing stick. Everyone's eyes were glued on the new Mapkeeper. Lucy hated public speaking, and this was by far the largest crowd she had ever encountered. Her somersaulting stomach dropped like an anchor with the realization that they expected her to make a speech.

Taking a deep breath, she held the stick a few inches from her mouth with a shaking hand and managed to utter, "Hi... my name is Lucy Barnes, and these are my brothers Mack and Luke." She gestured to her brothers, not quite knowing what else to do. The crowd beamed up at her, curiosity visible in every face. A profound silence hung in the air. The silence felt so dense and suffocating that she swore it was responsible for the trickle of sweat inching its way down her spine. "I uh—I just found out that I am the next Mapkeeper," she stuttered uncertainly. The crowd erupted in gleeful applause.

Grateful for the interruption, Lucy used the back of her hand to wipe a drip of sweat off her forehead. She glanced at her brothers, who smiled to show their encouragement. The applause died and the silence that followed seemed to imply that she should have more to say.

"I, uh... I'm really excited to be here. I don't know much of what my duties will include yet..." Sudden movements throughout the crowd caught her eye. On one side, the elves were shaking their heads and exiting through the alley. She glanced across to the other side of the crowd. The centaurs were leaving too. King Muttongale scurried over and snatched the stick from her.

"What—what Ms. Barnes means is that she is thrilled to be here, and will assume duties as Mapkeeper right away! In fact, she will hold a Council of Clans tomorrow evening in the Great Hall!" He pointed a chubby finger skyward for dramatic effect. The elves and centaurs stopped and turned at this news, cocking their heads in curiosity. One centaur hadn't moved. He was lean and muscular, with a sleek brown coat. He stood still and listened, arms crossed across his chest. The elves reemerged from the shadows and filed back into Central Square.

Lucy was certain that her face was beet red. She couldn't wait for this part of the ceremony to be over.

"That's right, a Council of Clans will take place tomorrow evening at sunset. At the council she will unveil her plan to save Praxis from disaster!" The crowd erupted with violent cheering. Lucy's heart thumped out of control. She looked at her brothers, but they shared her wide-eyed expression of shock—maybe even fear. She wiggled her fingers to make sure they were still there because she couldn't feel her limbs. Her breaths came fast and shallow.

Her attention was suddenly captured by a tall, thin man shouldering his way through the crowd without apology. Wisps of gray hair tufted his otherwise bald head and his long, pointed nose was visible even from afar. He hugged a black cape around himself as if disgusted by the idea of touching the people surrounding him.

A chest-high mop of auburn hair bobbed along behind him, bumping into everyone in its way. Whomever the hair belonged to was too short for Lucy to see their face. The thin man reached the front row as a hush fell over the gathering. His cold, calculating glare took Lucy aback. He studied her for a moment, glanced up at the burning image, then back at her.

"Hah!" he spat. "*This* is who the map chose as our bold and fearless leader? This scrawny *girl*? At a time when Praxis is in grave peril? The most serious threat to our existence in a thousand years and we are sent *this girl*?" He shouted the last sentence. The hairs rose on the back of Lucy's neck. She could feel the burn of his hostility from across the stage. The short redheaded man who had followed him through the crowd stood at his side, hands on his hips, scrutinizing Lucy with beady black eyes.

"Now, Bade, you must understand—" King Muttongale began, but the man cut him off.

"King Muttongale. You are an ornamental figurehead, useless to Praxis. The days of kingship are long gone. Now do us all a favor and go play in a corner or something." He shot a callous glare at the king, who bumbled, offended, but could muster no reply. Queen Oleksandra loomed over Bade and the little man, exuding a menacing air of authority.

"Bade, you will have your time to speak at tomorrow's meeting. Now be gone. We have a ceremony to complete—a thousand-year-old Praxis tradition that should satisfy even you, since you seem so absorbed by the past." Bade grinned up at the queen, pulling his cape tighter around his thin body. His freckle-faced friend lapsed into a fit of giggles.

"Ah, my queen, may I say that you are as enchanting as ever. And you are right. This will all be hashed out at the council meeting tomorrow. How insensitive of me to interrupt the ceremony. Rest assured, my voice will be heard." He grinned at her, shot a frown of resentment at Lucy, and with a swish of his cape, turned and shoved his way back through the crowd. His chortling companion followed along behind him, his auburn hair bobbing its way through the sea of people.

Murmurs of uncertainty rippled through the crowd. The Queen met Lucy's gaze with solemn reassurance, as if to say that everything would be all right. King Muttongale hurried to regain the momentum of the joyous ceremony.

"Ladies and gentlemen, it has been a privilege to introduce Praxis' new Mapkeeper, Ms. Lucy Barnes. Let the Ceremony of Light begin!" He and the queen turned in unison and looked up at the massive fiery image of Lucy, so the Barnes siblings did the same. The crowd oohed and ahhed as six shrouded maesters approached the great cauldron, arms raised, chanting in unison. The fire sputtered for a moment and then exploded anew, streaked with color. Purple, green, pink, and sapphire flames licked the darkening sky, even higher than before. The heat from the flames pressed down on them until Lucy had to shield her face. The sight was so spectacular that she almost forgot that she was on stage.

From somewhere in the crowd, the jovial sawing of a fiddle split the air. It was joined by two more, and the crowd sprang to life with dancing. Lucy saw the king and queen exchange a look of relief before pasting smiles back on their faces and settling into their thrones. Lucy was grateful to extract herself from center stage and relocate to her wooden chair. She wiped her sweaty palms across her pant legs as her eyes locked onto Cadmus' stare from the front row near the stage. She froze for an instant, and then averted her eyes, uncomfortable under his gaze. Why hadn't he moved away to dance like everyone else? Needing a distraction, she dove into a flurry of excited conversation with her brothers, rehashing the awkward moments of the ceremony thus far.

From the corner of her eye, she saw Cadmus swing a leg up on stage and hop up. He strolled across the platform and began to talk with the king and queen.

Central Square was alive, the music slicing through the

night air. Street-front pubs and restaurants were well-lit and buzzing with the flow of honeyed mead and elderberry wine. People whooped and laughed, and children shrieked and ran wild.

Lucy slid her hand inside her pocket in an absentminded probe. As she'd hoped, the map glowed warm at her touch. Somehow, this put her mind at ease. She noticed Mack staring at two of the tall, beautiful glowing creatures she'd seen at the start of the ceremony. The rest of their counterparts had left, but these two lingered at the edge of the alley. They stood side by side, whispering to one another and eyeing Lucy with solemnity. Mack was spellbound.

"You like the Bellaux, eh?" Cadmus appeared out of nowhere. Mack jumped, and then looked up at Cadmus from his chair with a slight air of suspicion.

"Bellaux?"

"Those two over there." Cadmus pointed. "They're called Bellaux. An all-female creature clan. They keep to themselves for the most part, but will protect the Mapkeeper at any cost. They live in the Tree of Virtue on the eastern edge of Glacial Lake. Very mysterious creatures."

"Wow..." Mack breathed.

"They're even capable of magic. They don't use it often, but it's said that the Bellaux are some of the most powerful creatures when called upon by the Mapkeeper for help. Of course, it's been years—before any of us were born—since their magic was used."

Cadmus glanced from Mack to Lucy. She still had one hand in her jeans pocket. She slid it out and folded her hands in her lap, realizing she'd been staring.

"How are you doing, Lucy? This is a lot to take in at once." He smiled, baring two rows of perfect white teeth. Lucy was determined to appear cool and collected.

"It is. I sort of don't know where I fit in yet, and I still have so much to learn." She wished her face would stop burning red.

"Well I want you to know that I'm here to help in any way I can. Not to add any pressure to your plate, but the truth is, if you fail, we all fail..." He smiled. "Wow. That did not come out how I intended. I mean, with that kind of attitude, how could you not feel pressure? I think I'm rambling. What I'm trying to say is—I'd love to show you around and help you get to know Praxis." He appeared hopeful. "If that's what you think will help," he added.

Lucy laughed, relieved that she wasn't the only one struggling for the right words. "I'd love that." She smiled up at him. Were her eyes playing tricks on her, or was he blushing too?

A heavy quake suddenly jolted them. Lucy gripped her arm rests for stability as a low rumble reverberated from the north. The townspeople cried out in fear and the fiddles screeched out a few off-pitch notes before going silent. Nervous murmurs rippled through the crowd. The ground continued to shake, though the intensity decreased.

Lucy looked up at Cadmus with wide eyes, her heart

pounding. She'd never felt anything like this before. *Was this one of the quakes that Olivia described earlier?* Cadmus was staring to the northeast. The king and queen were doing the same. In fact, all of Central Square stood, hushed and staring at something in the distance. Lucy followed their gaze past the castle and through the darkness, saw a red speck glowing on the horizon among the Dour Mountains.

"Cadmus, what is—" she began, but he raised a hand to stop her and cocked his head, listening. Lucy saw the king and queen exchange a wide-eyed look of fear. She watched Cadmus, desperate for answers. Her knuckles were white where she gripped the arm rests of her chair. He turned to face her, his mouth agape and his expression grave.

"I don't want to scare you, Lucy, but if I'm not mistaken, I believe that was Praxis' legendary, long-dormant volcano."

CHAPTER 10

* * *

The evacuation of Central Square was rapid and chaotic. Screams pierced the air. Children wailed and men shouted, herding their families home.

"No one alive today has ever seen, heard, or felt volcanic activity before. Nor have our parents, or grandparents, or great-grandparents," Cadmus explained to Lucy and her brothers on their hurried carriage ride back to the castle. "This is the stuff of legend—ancient secrets of Praxis that we all grew up hearing about!" Lucy couldn't seem to stop chills from running down her spine.

"You'll be safe at the castle," King Muttongale assured them. "It's on high ground, after all..." He gave a nervous chuckle, wringing his hands.

A strange, unexpected calmness come over Lucy as they approached the castle. It was as if she were removed from reality, somehow hovering above it all, a detached observer watching events unfold. The map hadn't stopped glowing with warmth since the rumbling began.

The quake had only lasted about a minute, and since then everything had remained calm. But all of Praxis was now holed away in a panic, hiding and fearing the worst.

Back at Tropos Castle, Lucy and her brothers huddled in the Hearth Room with the king and queen, Milo, Cadmus, Olivia, her brother Pip, and their parents Helda and Quinn. The rest of the servants and cooks were running about making preparations for the worst. Puck, as usual, remained in his room on the second floor with his attendants.

"I locked up the mares," Quinn reported. "They are all safe, with plenty of hay and drinking water. The stable hands are still out there—they refused to leave the horses alone."

"Very good, Quinn. You have done well." King Muttongale nodded. "Milo, collect reports as they arrive from the rest of the staff and let us know how preparations are coming along. But for now, stay here with us. We could use your good cheer."

"Yes, sir." Milo bowed.

Lucy hugged her legs, resting her chin on her knees. A thick red blanket was wrapped around her shoulders. They sat in a semi-circle around the hearth, where warm flames licked the edges of the massive brick fireplace. It was cozy and reminded her of home, which made her heart hurt. She thought of her father and her long-gone mother. Despite having just two or three vague memories of her, thinking of her mother brought Lucy great pain. Many times she had imagined what life would be like if their mother were still around: they would lie on the couch together and drink hot cocoa, her mother's arm wrapped around her like a blanket of warmth and love...

For a moment, everyone was silent as Lucy lost herself gazing into the flames, thinking about home and her parents. Suddenly the fire reminded her of the great blazing image of herself in Central Square. It had been snuffed out hours ago, signaling the official conclusion of the Ceremony of Light. Of course, the actual end of the ceremony had been forced when the volcano rumbled.

Queen Oleksandra's face was creased in contemplation. "More and more ancient warning signs are being realized. It's just like the legends said it would be," she explained to the Barnes siblings.

"What other signs were there?" Luke asked.

Cadmus sat across from Lucy, Mack sat to her left, and Luke was next to him, nearest the fire. Pip and Olivia huddled at their parents' feet sharing a fleece blanket. Helda and Quinn were nestled on a stuffed loveseat, and the king and queen reclined in cushioned, high-backed wooden rocking chairs.

"Oh, all kinds of things," the queen replied. "Quakes rattled the earth for minutes on end, many storms with powerful lightning and thunder came, bringing sheets of rain and hail stones as big as your head! Vast storms churned the Dark Sea, and of course, as you know now, volcanic activity. The extent of some of the disasters is lost to time, as is to be expected, so no one quite knows what we may be up against." The fire crackled as she hesitated. Lucy glanced at the solemn faces around the circle. "Up until now, no one was even sure if any of it was real," the queen continued. "For years, man and creature worked together hunting for the volcano without success. They explored the Dour Mountains high and low, including the miles of maze-like caves where the trolls live."

There was a brief pause, and Mack broke the silence. "What happened after all those disasters occurred?"

The king sighed and let his shoulders droop. He opened his mouth to reply, but Cadmus interjected.

"Your majesty, if I may, I can explain," he offered. King Muttongale eased back in his chair and smiled his thanks, gliding back and forth in his rocking chair.

Cadmus' electric blue eyes shone as he spoke. "Legend has it that over a thousand years ago in Praxis, one by one, these natural disasters began to occur. Each one was worse than the last, but the people tried to weather the storm. They hoped that if they waited long enough, whatever was causing the disasters would subside.

"Meanwhile, unbeknownst to the people, a dark magic was growing in power. The stronger this dark magic grew, the more powerful the disasters became. At last, it was discovered that a group of wizards known as the Wardens were manipulating the dark power, but by then it was too late. They had awakened three terrible beasts that devastated Praxis almost to complete destruction. If it weren't for the Mapkeeper, Praxis and all the creatures within it would have been destroyed."

The fire popped with such ferocity that Lucy jumped. She looked away from Cadmus and the others. She could feel everyone's eyes on her. Only Luke and Mack spared her their scrutiny. They understood her fear and lack of preparation for this enormous responsibility.

Cadmus continued, "The Mapkeeper was able to manipulate the map and defeat the three beasts and for that reason, the Mapkeeper is revered as a position of great heroism. Since then, there has been a Ceremony of Light for each new one. Many Mapkeepers have come and gone over the centuries. Some had very little responsibility during their tenure, while others achieved small acts of heroism, settling disputes and maintaining order among the clans. Our ancestors always said that each Mapkeeper is chosen for a reason. While some were more loved by the people and creatures of Praxis than others, all seemed to have particular characteristics that suited whatever problems arose during their tenure."

"Like Edmund Burrow, the nineteenth Mapkeeper, who realigned the foothills of the Dour Mountains to settle a territorial dispute among the trolls and the goblins," Olivia recited.

"Good memory, Olivia!" Helda rubbed her daughter's

shoulder.

"The trolls live in caves high in the mountains, and the goblins live underground in the foothills," Pip chimed in.

"Then there was Maximus Krieger, the twenty-fifth, who was able to negotiate peace between the Glacial Lake mermaids and the Bellaux, who live in the Tree of Virtue on the lake's eastern shore," Queen Oleksandra added. "That took years. He was a patient man."

"Each Mapkeeper discovers how to unleash the map's power in his or her own way," Cadmus explained. "No two have interacted with the map in quite the same way, and its magic only works for the person whose name is inscribed on the map."

Lucy pulled the map out of her pocket and unfolded it in front of her where everyone could see it. The firelight danced across the soft, beige parchment. *Lucy Barnes* was still inscribed in script in the bottom corner.

"Upstairs on the second floor you will find the hallway lined with portraits of all the Mapkeepers of the past, dating back to the third century PR. We track time based on the great rebuild of Praxis following the fifteenth Mapkeeper, who defeated the three beasts. PR stands for Post-Rebuild. Any records that existed prior to that were either lost or destroyed. You are welcome to go see the hallway of portraits later tonight if you'd like," King Muttongale offered. "Olivia and Pip can show you the way."

"Who was the fifteenth Mapkeeper?" Lucy looked up from

the map.

"Alas, his name did not survive him. We only know him as the fifteenth Mapkeeper. He perished in the process of defeating the beasts," the king said with a frown.

"How did he defeat the three beasts?" Luke asked.

Cadmus replied, "No one knows for sure, but legend has it that the king dispatched a great army to fight the beasts, but the entire army was annihilated! The beasts ravaged the town amidst the worst of the natural disasters: quakes, hailstorms, an erupting volcano, and even a massive ocean storm. Many people and creatures perished. Some were able to survive by hiding in the caves of the Dour Mountains or deep within Doldrums Forest. But even they were subject to terrible rock slides and a great forest blaze.

"When the beasts had demolished what was left of the forest and village, they refocused their attention on the castle. They climbed the castle hill, and were almost upon it when the fifteenth Mapkeeper unleashed the full fury of the map. It is said that he rode out of the stable on horseback at full speed toward the three beasts. In a blinding explosion of white light, he rammed straight into them, sacrificing himself but saving Praxis. The Mapkeeper and all three beasts were killed."

Lucy's mouth hung open and goosebumps sprang up on her arms. Cadmus continued, "To this day, a wide ring of trees remain leveled in that very spot. Nothing can grow where the white light touched. Records from that time state that the map disappeared without a trace that day and wasn't seen again until his successor arrived, map in hand."

"Do the Mapkeepers stay in Praxis their whole lives?" Mack asked. Lucy had been wondering the same thing. This question made her nervous.

"Some do," the queen replied. "But many do not. They are always free to come and go as they please. In times of peace, the royal family rules in their absence. The map calls them back when they are needed, and they always come."

Lucy glanced sideways at her brothers. They shared her look of confusion and disbelief.

"As you can see, Ms. Barnes, these are trying times. We all believe that it was no accident that you arrived when you did," the king commented. He peered down at her through his wiry red eyebrow hairs.

Lucy felt Cadmus' inquisitive gaze from across the circle. Uncomfortable and slightly aggravated, she ignored it by pretending to be absorbed by the map, tracing the edge of Glacial Lake with a finger.

"I can explain our history in greater detail if you'd like, Ms. Barnes," Cadmus offered. "I have studied extensively and am considered somewhat of an expert on the history of Praxis. If I can be of any assistance at all, please do not hesitate to let me know. I will be staying at the castle and am at your disposal." Lucy's heart constricted at his kind words. She met his gaze, and his eyes were sincere.

"Thank you, Cadmus. Your dedicated service is appreciated, as always," King Muttongale interjected. Lucy let her breath out, relieved. The influx of information was overwhelming, but she was grateful to be surrounded by such kind, welcoming people. *Maybe I can do this...* she thought, allowing herself to consider for the first time in earnest what it would be like to commit to being the Mapkeeper.

⁘

That night, the Barnes siblings descended the spiral staircase from their fourth floor apartments to the second floor with Olivia and Pip to see the hallway of Mapkeeper portraits. The hallway was long and wide, and the thick, ornate red carpet swallowed Lucy's sneakers with each step. They took their time, pausing before each gold framed portrait.

"Aodhan Orman, Thirty-Fourth Mapkeeper" was stamped on a gold plate mounted on the base of the frame. A muscular middle-aged man frowned back at them. Wiry salt-and-pepper hair and a trimmed beard complemented his gruff appearance. His skin was wrinkled and tanned, and intense dark eyes squinted from beneath a furrowed brow. He wore a simple white cotton shirt that bared his thick, hairy arms.

"So this was the previous Mapkeeper," Lucy said, touching the frame. "He looks a little angry."

"He was an intense person," Olivia agreed. She stood by

Lucy's side staring up at the portrait. Their brothers gathered behind them and stared at Aodhan Orman's portrait.

"What happened to him?" Luke asked.

"No one knows," Pip replied. He brushed his stringy dark hair out of his eyes. "He left about six months ago and never returned. Next thing we knew, Lucy's image was burning in the Central Square cauldron and we knew we had a new Mapkeeper." This gave Lucy the chills.

"How long was Aodhan Orman the Mapkeeper?" she asked.

"He had a short tenure—just a little over fifteen years." Lucy made a mental note that this aligned with what Mr. Quincy had told her. "Before him there was Edwin Frye. He was Mapkeeper even before our parents were born," Olivia replied. She led them to the next portrait. Edwin Frye was a round, jolly-looking man with a bulging belly and rosy cheeks. His smile was bright and his piercing green eyes squinted at them.

Lucy wandered past a dozen more portraits, examining each previous Mapkeeper. They were an eclectic bunch, no two alike.

"They are all so different," she mused as she strolled. "...but it seems like they're all men." She glanced over her shoulder at Olivia and Pip.

"Yes, they were for the most part. You are the second female. The first was the sixteenth Mapkeeper, in the first century

PR. Her name was Serafine." Olivia led Lucy to the far end of the hallway and pointed up at the second-to-last portrait. A tall, thin woman stared back with a serious expression. Her straight dark hair was pulled back in a banded braid. She wore a forest green hunting shirt and a shoulder bow and arrow sling. She had high cheek bones and dark, mysterious eyes. The portraits on this side of the hallway near the end were hand-painted and showed signs of their age. The frames were new and in good condition, but the portraits themselves had been restored over the years.

"Serafine is legendary for leading the rebuild of Praxis. She had the most difficult task ever faced by a Mapkeeper except for the fifteenth, of course. Without her, survivors would have remained spread out and uncivilized for a much longer period of time. They didn't want to rebuild or rejoin society after the destruction of their way of life. Clans were demolished, scattered, and terrified."

Lucy gazed up at Serafine, memorizing her face. *If I'm going to be the Mapkeeper, I'm going to do my best to live up to Serafine's legacy,* she decided. Taking and releasing a deep breath, she strode back along the opposite wall, perusing the other half of the diverse bunch who had each at one time been known as the Mapkeeper.

Alone in her room that evening, she studied the map and thought about what she would say at tomorrow's Clan Council. She thought about her role as Mapkeeper. Glancing out her window, the crescent moon was a large, brilliant white slice in the night sky. Her stomach clenched in a tight knot when she remembered that

Bade would be there. *What will Bade and the others say?*

CHAPTER 11

⁎

Lucy jolted awake to the harsh splatter of water against steel. Her heart pounded and she jerked upright in bed. Blinding rays of morning sunlight filtered through the white lace curtains framing the window.

"Oh gosh, I'm so sorry for waking you, Ms. Barnes." Olivia wore an expression of fear, frozen in the act of pouring a pitcher of steaming water into a steel wash basin.

Lucy put a hand over her racing heart. "Oh, good morning Olivia. Please, don't worry about it," she sighed, flooded with nervous relief as her heart rate slowed. "And please call me Lucy." She grinned, stretching her arms. She'd slept well in her oversized bed. She threw the heavy down quilt off, swinging her legs over the side of the bed and hopping out. Her nightgown was a comfortable cream silk garment.

"Here is some water for you to wash up. There are plenty of

clean clothes in the armoire." Olivia pointed across the room. "The royal family will be breakfasting in half an hour and have invited you and your brothers to join them in the Great Hall. Can I be of any further assistance?" She fisted the empty pitcher in front of her.

Lucy smiled. "No, you've already done more than enough, thank you Olivia. I'll just get cleaned up and be down for breakfast in a bit."

Olivia stepped out and Lucy picked up where she left off the night before, rehearsing in her mind everything she wanted to say at tonight's Council of Clans. Her stomach re-knotted itself in the familiar ball of anxiety.

"Good morning, Lucy!" Queen Oleksandra called across the Great Hall as Lucy approached from the spiral staircase. The queen sat in her throne at the head of the table, to King Muttongale's right. Prince Puck glared at a bowl of porridge steaming in front of him. Mack and Luke sat across from the prince, gobbling bowls of porridge, slices of bacon, and wedges of fresh fruit. They smiled up at their sister.

"I hope you don't mind us starting without you," the king quipped with a chuckle.

"Of course not! We don't wait for late-comers at our house either." Everyone except the grumpy prince chuckled as she slid into the seat next to Puck. Golden utensils gleamed in stark contrast to the dark, heavy wood of the long Great Hall table. The group was clustered at one end of the elongated table. She unfolded her maroon cloth napkin and laid it in her lap as a kitchen hand brought her a hot bowl of porridge. She thanked him and sprinkled some cinnamon on the porridge before scooping up a spoonful to let it cool.

"Did you sleep well?" the king asked.

"I did, thank you, your highness."

"You've got a big day ahead. Cadmus has volunteered to help you prepare as much as possible before the Clan Council if you would like." As he spoke, the Great Hall doors opened and Cadmus entered. He looked fresh, his hair still damp from a morning bath.

"Good morning, everyone!" he called with a wide smile and wave. He took the seat next to Luke across the table from Lucy.

"Ah, good morning Cadmus. Nice to see you. I was just telling Lucy that you'd volunteered your services to help her best prepare for tonight's council," the king replied.

"Of course I will." He dipped a spoon into his fresh bowl of porridge and stirred, looking up at Lucy as a lock of hair fell across his forehead.

"That would be great," she replied, tearing her gaze away and focusing on her food.

Cadmus reached out to one of the center platters and helped himself to a few cubed apples and some sort of sliced dark red-skinned fruit with a crisp, juicy yellow inside.

"Pip told me and Luke he'd show us the stable after breakfast," Mack said.

"Oh, wonderful! You'll love it. Have him take you for a ride if you'd like." The queen beamed.

The knot in Lucy's stomach returned as she realized that meant time alone with Cadmus. She stirred her porridge faster, steam pouring out of the bowl. She wasn't sure how she felt about being alone with him.

The rest of the meal passed with nearly everyone engaged in pleasant dialog, but the king and queen's attempts to include Puck in conversation were failures. The prince rolled his eyes and grunted answers to their gentle questions, shoveling food in his mouth like a starving animal. Lucy felt badly for the king and queen, but his behavior *was* slightly entertaining.

After breakfast, Cadmus took Lucy to the castle library on the fourth floor. It was very large, encompassing the entire fourth floor not already devoted to guest and servant quarters. Lucy had seen the dark wooden double doors in passing going to and from her apartment several times now, but had not known what was inside.

She gasped as she passed through the doors. It was magnificent! Ceiling-high wooden shelves lined every wall and were arranged in dozens of parallel columns across the expansive space. She drifted into the space, absorbing it with each deliberate step.

Cadmus grinned. "It's brilliant, isn't it?"

She smiled too, turning in a circle and seeing that the shelves even wrapped around above the doors they'd just come through! "It's stunning! I've never seen so many books in my life!" Tall ladders on wheels were scattered among the shelves. Lucy climbed halfway up the nearest ladder. "Will you give me a push?" She asked, her eyes glittering.

Cadmus burst into laughter, bending at the waist and grabbing his stomach with one hand. "Are you serious?" His eyes twinkled. "All right." He took the ladder in both his hands and gave it a smooth shove. She soared down the aisle, gripping a ladder rung with one hand and slapping book spines with the other. They were both laughing as she coasted to a stop.

"I'm glad you like the wheeling ladders so much. If you come over to this side of the library, you'll get a terrific view of the castle grounds out these windows." He pointed across the library to three large arched windows, leading her across the room.

"Wow," Lucy murmured, impressed at the view that extended for miles. The grass on the castle hill and in the pastures was so green from up here! She could see Pip leading her brothers to the stable in the distance. Beyond the castle hill, the village looked sleepy and cozy in the distance. There were no signs of the mass chaos that had taken place there last night. A few tiny figures walked the streets, but she couldn't make out their features from this distance.

Cadmus pulled out a chair and motioned for Lucy to sit at

one of the tables positioned next to the windows. He took the chair opposite hers.

"This library is fantastic. Is this where Praxis' records are kept?" she asked.

"Some are here, along with many old volumes from centuries past. But the most valuable ancient records are kept in the archive on the third floor near the Great Hall. It is kept under strict lock and key. Only the king, queen, Phestyr—the record-keeper—and I have access to the archives. The royal family entrusted me to access the archive under Phestyr's supervision to support my studies of Praxis' history. I became so fascinated and spent so much time in the archives that they allowed Phestyr to make me a copy of the key. Not long after that, I took over as clan leader for the people of Praxis. I have been the clan leader for three years," he explained.

"Is that why you live at the castle?" Lucy asked.

"Yes."

"What happened to the last clan leader?" she ventured.

Cadmus frowned. "The man who held my position before me became corrupted over the years. The power went to his head. He stole ancient records from the castle archives and was plotting an uprising. His intent was for the people to attack the creature clans and destroy them one by one. He has a vision of what he calls 'Pure Praxis', where humans are the only clan." Cadmus shook his head in disgust. "As soon as his journal was discovered, they threw him in the dungeon. He's been rotting there ever since. He is a madman."

"What is his name?"

"Fagen Swiltering. Let's hope you don't have to meet him any time soon."

The thought of a maniac imprisoned somewhere beneath them sent a chill up her spine. She pulled her loose cotton blouse tighter around her arms. She was dressed more like a Praxian today, though she was disappointed that her armoire hadn't contained any jeans or t-shirts. *At least these clothes are comfortable*, she thought. Her outfit included a pair of plain sand-colored riding pants and brown leather boots. A soft leather string secured her white blouse at the collarbone.

Lucy gazed out the window at the gorgeous scenery of Praxis. "This place is so beautiful and full of so many wonderful people and creatures. I'm not sure I will do it justice as Mapkeeper," she confessed.

Cadmus' eyes softened. "Really, Lucy? That's funny because I was thinking you're the best thing that's ever happened to Praxis." He smiled a genuine, eye-crinkling grin. Lucy's heart swelled.

"But I don't even know anything about this place! I don't even know who all the clans are that I'll meet tonight! I don't know how to use this thing yet—" she tugged the map out of her pocket.

"It's okay," Cadmus interrupted, holding his hands up and

signaling her to stop. "That's why I'm here to help you." Despite her severe misgivings, Lucy trusted him. "I'll start with the clans. You saw the Bellaux, the elves, and the centaurs at the Ceremony of Light. You might have seen the gnomes huddled in the middle of Central Square—they're easy to miss though. Pretty small." He grinned. "Some creatures don't interact with the rest of us, though. There are mermaids in Glacial Lake, trolls and goblins in the Dour Mountains, and kobolds in Doldrums Forest. They all keep to themselves, but they're still invited to the Council of Clans tonight. We'll see who shows up."

Lucy spread the map flat on the table between them. "Sometimes it glows and gets warm," she said. "And as weird as it sounds, I feel—I feel like I have some sort of connection to it." She made an uncomfortable face, embarrassed. Cadmus did not seem fazed.

"That's good! It's a sign that you are the rightful Mapkeeper. You must form a bond with the map and discover how to make it work for you. The map is a secretive thing. According to my research, Mapkeepers who tried to collaborate with others to unlock its power only delayed their ability to control it. It's something you must discover for yourself. Trust your instincts."

I want the map to work for me right now, she thought in frustration. How could she convince the Council of Clans she would be a competent Mapkeeper if she didn't even know how to control it yet? Cadmus' expression softened. His smile was kind and reassuring. Lucy took a deep breath and felt the map pulse with warmth beneath her palms. She allowed a smile to form on her lips too.

"All right, now let's talk a little bit more about the clans," Cadmus continued. "Each clan has its own idea of what kind of behavior is acceptable. The gnomes are gruff and blunt. They will tell you exactly what they're thinking, good or bad. They can be a grumpy bunch. Their leader is named Enzo.

"The Bellaux, led by Auriel, are calm and intelligent. They are good listeners and rational thinkers. It is hard to make a Bellaux angry, but if you do, you're going to have a bad day!"

On the map, the Tree of Virtue, home of the Bellaux, seemed like a large and lovely place to live—a stark juxtaposition of the Dour Mountains.

"The goblins are more difficult to deal with. They do not like compromise. They want everything done their way, every time. The head goblin is a cranky little creature named Glump. They live underground in the foothills of the mountains. The trolls live higher up in the mountain caves. They don't have a lot going on upstairs, if you know what I mean," he said, pointing to his head.

"They're massive and strong, and they will follow their leader without questioning. His name is Digby, and he is a ruthless leader. He will kill a member of his own clan if he is disobeyed!" Lucy's eyes widened. "I wouldn't expect Digby to show up to the council, though. The trolls only make occasional appearances in town, and that's often with the intent of disturbing the peace."

Lucy arched her eyebrows. The trolls sounded terrible! She was grateful they weren't expected to be at the meeting.

"Next there are the elves, who live in Doldrums Forest. Their leader is Adalia, and she possesses fierce loyalty to her clan. She also tends to be suspicious of other clans. She will compromise when necessary, but only if it will benefit the elves. The elves have been wronged throughout Praxis' history and have not forgotten it.

"The centaurs are led by Zadok, one of the kindest and most gracious creatures I've ever met. They also live in the forest and are almost as reclusive as the unicorns, but Zadok always attends Clan Councils. Their main goal is to foster peace among all the clans while maintaining their own secluded way of life. There are those within Zadok's clan who believe he interacts too much with the other clans, but as a whole, the centaurs respect and love him."

Lucy recalled the strong, serene centaur who had stayed behind at the Ceremony of Light when most of the others left through the alley.

"That covers all the clans," Cadmus said, counting in his head and ticking his fingers one by one to keep a tally. "There are other creatures in Praxis, but they either don't live in clans or don't participate in our society, like the mermaids in Glacial Lake or the forest kobolds."

Cadmus looked out the window beside them, and she followed his gaze.

"It's a beautiful land," she observed, mesmerized.

He smiled. "I love Praxis. Would you like me to show you and your brothers around town when they come back from the stable?" They glanced in the direction of the stable. Mack, Luke, and Pip were on horseback, galloping around the meadow. "*If* they ever come back from the stable," he corrected himself, laughing.

Lucy agreed. She and Cadmus left the library and parted ways. Before they went to the village, the king and queen had requested to speak with her in the Hearth Room on the main floor. As she exited one of the identical spiral staircases and turned to enter the Hearth Room, a sudden movement at the edge of her vision caught her eye. She whipped her head around in time to see the golden doors that led into the atrium click shut. *Who was that incredibly short person?* she wondered, having caught the slightest glimpse of the back side of an oddly-shaped figure slipping through the doors. She had no idea why this sighting made the hairs on the back of her neck stand up, but a strange chill of fear that she could not ignore ran down her spine.

CHAPTER 12

An hour later they were on their way to the village in the carriage accompanied by the familiar entourage of guards. When she met with the royal couple, Lucy had protested the need for armed escort, but King Muttongale refused to hear it. "Your protection is my top priority," he asserted, wagging a stubby finger. "I have instructed my head guard that they are to be by your side throughout your visit to the village. I won't compromise your safety, Lucy." Queen Oleksandra nodded her approval.

The carriage dropped off Lucy, her brothers, and Cadmus in Central Square, in the same spot as it had the previous evening for the Ceremony of Light. Lucy hopped out first.

"Look, Ma, it's the new Mapkeeper!" A young boy shouted, pointing and running toward her. Activity in the bustling town center came to a halt and the townspeople flocked to her. Cadmus put up both arms and held the people back. Mack appeared on her other side to help shield her from the crowd.

"Ms. Barnes! Ms. Barnes! What is your plan to stop the disasters that are happening?"

"Did you know you would be the next Mapkeeper?"

"Do you have the map with you?"

The pressure of the crowd pressed in on her, making her heart race. She could only hold out her arms in defense. To her relief, the guards dismounted and hurried to her side, forming a protective ring around Lucy, Cadmus, and her brothers. They prodded the townspeople back with the blunt ends of their sheathed swords.

At last, the eager throng began to disperse. Children hopped up on the edge of the stage, peering over the adults for a better view. Some people backed away or continued on with their errands, understanding that the Mapkeeper needed some breathing room.

"I think they're excited to see you," Mack declared with a laugh.

"I'm glad now that the king made us bring the guards," Lucy admitted. "That was a little overwhelming!"

"They'll get used to seeing you," Cadmus predicted. "We'll keep the guards close for today and we shouldn't have any more issues. In the meantime, let's get to seeing the town!" He led them toward the row of shops lining the south side of Central Square. The guards were on full alert, making sure no one came too close. But the guards couldn't stop dozens of curious eyes from following them across the cobbled circle.

"Emil's Clothier Shop," Luke read aloud the ornate hand-painted sign above the first shop they encountered. The street-level window had two mannequins—one dressed in the style of everyday men's work clothes that Lucy saw most of the townspeople wearing, the other a female figure clothed in a fine silk chartreuse dress.

"Emil is the town clothier. He's a very talented tailor. He can make any item of clothing you could ever need. He also makes and repairs shoes." Cadmus waved as they approached the shop. A small, dark haired man with thick glasses emerged. "This is Emil Poulsen."

"Ms. Barnes, it is my greatest pleasure to make your acquaintance." He folded in a deep bow then shook her hand in both of his. His dark, serious eyes appeared twice their actual size through his round bottle glasses. He craned his neck to look up from his vantage point a whole head shorter than her.

"It's very nice to meet you too, Mr. Poulsen," Lucy replied, smiling.

"Please call me Emil, and do let me know if you are ever in need of anything, Ms. Barnes. I am not just a clothier, I also specialize in leather goods—riding boots, saddles... you name it. It would be my honor to serve you." He bowed again, still cupping her hand.

Lucy smiled at Mack and Luke, uncomfortable with the

level of formality with which she was being treated.

"Emil, these are my brothers Luke and Mack."

"Nice to meet you, sir," Mack and Luke stepped forward and shook Emil's hand, towering over the little man.

"The pleasure is all mine, gentlemen!" He shook their hands with enthusiasm.

Cadmus clapped the little man on his dainty shoulder and they turned to face the row of shops encircling Central Square leading to the bell tower at the head of the circle. Their guards stood several paces away, deterring curious onlookers from coming too close.

A hulking, grimy man wearing a soot-encrusted apron stood nearby, peering around as if looking for something. He spotted them and his eyes lit up.

"Cadmus! I see you've brought Ms. Barnes and her brothers out to town. How do you do? I am Vasyl Demir, the village blacksmith. I'd shake your hand, but mine are always filthy, and I'd hate to be responsible for mucking you up," he smiled a slow, easy grin that reached all the way up to his tired eyes.

"Very nice to meet you, Vasyl." There was something about this exhausted, stringy-haired behemoth that Lucy liked right away. He rested against a large sledgehammer on his left side, one massive hairy arm extended and braced against the tool. In a flash, two small black creatures appeared, squealing and flitting in circles around Vasyl's tree-trunk legs.

"Whoa, there kiddos, there you are!" Vasyl stood upright, reaching down and grabbing each sooty child by its head. "I was looking for you!" The whites of their teeth and eyes were in stark contrast to their grubby faces. "These are my young ones, Skew and Nell. Slow down, kids, and say hello to our new Mapkeeper."

"Hello, new Mapkeeper," the little gremlins echoed in unison before sprinting back inside the shop. Vasyl chuckled.

"I apologize for their rudeness, Miss Lucy—may I call you Miss Lucy?" His soft brown eyes were hopeful.

"Of course, Vasyl. And your children are adorable."

They continued on, meeting a number of villagers this way. An elderly man named Hamlin Buell hobbled up to greet them. He was a reedy, white-haired man, all spectacles and teeth. His bony hand felt knobby and cold in Lucy's grasp. She worried she might break his frail arm off his body if she shook it too hard.

"Ms. Barnes, it is a pleasure to meet you..." Hamlin squinted at her through the narrow lenses of his spectacles. "...a pleasure indeed. It has been many, many years since Praxis has had a female Mapkeeper, you know," he added, wagging a long finger at her. "This," he gestured over his shoulder to the three-story building behind him, "is the library of Praxis. You are welcome here any time. Cadmus has spent many hours here poring over my books, haven't you, young man?" He winked at Cadmus.

Cadmus chuckled. "You're right, Hamlin. The castle library

127

is wonderful but limited in what it has to offer. Hamlin's collection was crucial for me to develop a complete understanding of Praxis' history. And Hamlin himself is a very valuable resource. He knows more than anyone else in the village of Praxis' history."

Hamlin's white-blue eyes clouded, gazing into the distance. "Ah, yes. There are dark forces afoot, Ms. Barnes. We must all be very, very cautious. Both in where we go, and in whom we trust." His cloudy eyes sharpened and locked on hers. "There are those who wish you harm, Ms. Barnes. Choose your companions with the utmost care."

Lucy shuddered. Hamlin's warning replayed in her mind, even after Cadmus placed a gentle hand on her shoulder and led her away from the old man.

"Cadmus, what did Hamlin mean by that?"

"Don't worry about that now. There will be a time and place to discuss it." His curt reply took her by surprise. "This is the town hall." He pointed at a plain brown shingled building with square windows. It was three stories high, like most shops in Central Square, but it appeared dark and deserted.

They reached the top of the circle and stood at the base of the bell tower. Lucy looked up, and its sheer height made her feel like an insignificant speck on the cobblestone. It was made of rough-hewn gray stone, and the clock face high above was gold with large black numerals. Lush green ivy wrapped its way up the clock tower, hugging the stones so that it appeared to be a part of the rock.

They continued their little tour around Central Square toward the matching row of shops bordering the northern side of the circle. A heavy, red-faced man in a bloodied apron stood outside the first shop. The front window of his shop boasted large rump roasts and various cuts of meat hanging from butcher's twine.

"Hello, Cadmus!" the large man roared.

"Hello, Arnold," Cadmus replied. "This is Lucy Barnes, our new Mapkeeper, and her brothers Mack and Luke."

"Glad to meet ya, Ms. Barnes. I'm Arnold Brawne, the town butcher. I run the shop with the help of my son Fritz." He gestured to the crude hand-painted sign tacked above the door that read "Brawne & Son Butchery."

"It ain't much, but it keeps a roof over our heads and it sure keeps us fed!" he grabbed his swollen belly with both hands, threw his head back, and roared at his joke.

Lucy and her brothers joined in laughing, more out of surprise than amusement at the joke.

"Come on back any time for a good meal," Arnold offered.

"Thank you Arnold. It was nice to meet you." Lucy smiled and continued on. The next shop sign read "Maerwynn's Artifacts." The run-down structure appeared to be closed and shuttered.

"I'd bet Old Maerwynn has already turned in for the day,"

Cadmus explained. "She is a widow, and she runs the shop by herself."

They were met by a tall, thin man in a buttoned vest outside the second shop from the end. Beside him stood a very short woman with curly brown hair.

"Hello, Rolf," Cadmus called. "Lucy, this is Rolf Schuman and his wife Bernie."

"How do you do," Bernie and Rolf shook each of their hands. "We are so pleased to have you, Ms. Barnes. The last Mapkeeper was just so strange—"

"Bernie, don't bring that up now," Rolf interjected. "That's no way to greet our new Mapkeeper. Ms. Barnes, we just would like you to know how thrilled we all are to have you here."

"Well, most of us, anyway," Bernie corrected her husband, putting her hands on her hips.

"Bernie! Don't give the nice lady the wrong idea. Ms. Barnes, you'll be hard-pressed to find anyone who isn't ecstatic about your arrival in Praxis. You're the third Mapkeeper for Bernie and me, and we couldn't be happier." He reached down low and put an arm around his wife, hugging her to his hip.

"Thank you, Rolf. That is such a relief to hear," Lucy smiled.

A sudden rumbling noise startled them all. A huge black cloud moved across the sky, where a moment ago only the warm, bright sun had been. The map began to quiver. She slipped a hand into her pocket and touched it, feeling its warmth.

"Oh, my!" Bernie exclaimed. "Isn't that an odd-looking cloud?"

It swirled and roiled, expanding as it swept toward them from the northwest. It now covered half the sky. An audible crack of lightning split the sky beneath the monstrous cloud. Children across Central Square screamed and scrambled into their mothers' arms. The townspeople scattered, running for cover.

Cadmus put a hand on Lucy's shoulder and turned to Mack and Luke.

"Quick, follow me!" He ran toward the last building in the row of shops. Lucy had enough time to read "Alewife Inn" on the crudely painted sign above the door they were running toward before the cloud moved overhead and a dense curtain of rainfall engulfed Central Square. They made it through the door after just a few seconds of running through the downpour, but it was enough that they were all drenched. Lucy wiped her face, breathless, and Luke shook his mop of wet hair, flipping it out of his eyes.

"Jeez!" Lucy exclaimed, shaking a sheath of water off her arms. The castle guards followed them and stood under the awning outside the inn, scraping water off their sleeves and hats.

"Welcome to Alewife Inn," a husky female voice crooned from behind them.

Lucy twisted, squinting at the stocky woman standing behind them through the dim light. She had a round face and a shock of thick red hair tied back in a large, dense bun.

"Cadmus, how are you?" she crooned, brushing past Lucy and extending a hand toward him. He took her hand and smiled with good grace, still wiping water from his brow.

"Miss Marla, always a pleasure," Cadmus replied.

She scoffed with offense. "How many times do I have to tell you to just call me Marla? Come on in, now. You're soaked! That rain sure came out of nowhere, didn't it? Here, I've got a prime table for you." She took him by the elbow and led him away. Cadmus shrugged, looking over his shoulder and beckoning the Barnes siblings to follow.

"Marla, this is Praxis' new Mapkeeper, Lucy Barnes, and her brothers Mack and Luke."

"Oh, so you're the new Mapkeeper!" Marla turned to Lucy as if seeing her for the first time, seating them at a wide booth table near the edge of the restaurant. The first floor was a restaurant and pub, lit by occasional hanging lanterns and rickety candlelight chandeliers. Heavy wooden tables with bench seats lined the walls of the establishment, and taller round tables with stools littered the rest of the room. "Nice to meet you," Marla stated, turning her attention back to Cadmus.

"It's been ages since you've stopped by!" she complained, unfolding a napkin into his lap and handing him a menu. "What have you been so busy with?" She leaned up against a wooden column beside him.

"I've been spending a lot of time at the castle," Cadmus replied. "Marla, if it's not too much trouble, can we please have four hot mulled meads?"

"Oh, of course! How rude of me, let me go grab three more menus for you kids." Marla bustled off into the shadows toward the bar.

"I think she's got the hots for you, Cadmus," Mack grinned.

Cadmus chuckled, looking down at his hands. "What can I say?"

Lucy found herself relieved that Cadmus was so disinterested in Marla. She shook the feeling off, irritated that she even cared. She wanted to focus on the rainstorm and what it might mean.

"So this type of sudden storm isn't a regular thing?"

"Not at all. Typical weather in Praxis is very moderate," Cadmus replied. "I'm sure a lot of people will be speculating that it's somehow connected to the volcano action yesterday."

Marla returned with two overflowing glass steins of steaming mulled mead in each hand. The drinks were garnished with long, hook-tipped cinnamon sticks and curled orange peel shavings. Lucy's eyes lit up.

"These look amazing!" Luke exclaimed.

"Just give me a holler if you need anything," Marla said, tossing three more napkins onto the center of their table before strolling to the far corner to serve two dark-clothed figures whose faces were indiscernible in the shadows. They wore all black with hats pulled low over their brows and leaned over their table, whispering to one another. Lucy couldn't help but notice they kept glancing over toward her group.

"Cadmus, who are they?" she asked, flicking her eyes over his shoulder in the direction of the mysterious strangers.

"I thought you might notice them," he replied, his lips forming a grim line. "I'm not sure. I saw them when we came in. I know almost everyone in town, but I've never seen those two before."

"They keep looking over here and whispering," Luke added.

"Try not to stare," Cadmus warned. "I can't promise they're not dangerous men. We need to be careful. Times are changing fast, and we have to keep our guard up." He squeezed the handle of his stein. "I don't want to scare you, but this could be very serious." His knuckles were white with strain.

Lucy lifted her stein and took a big swallow of mead. The tangy-sweet liquid fizzed on her tongue and warmed her body from the inside out as it traveled down her throat to her stomach.

"The mead's delicious," she remarked, welcoming the distraction from the knot of nerves that had formed in her stomach.

"Yeah, it's the best," Cadmus agreed, taking a sip.

"Have you been able to make any progress with the map?" Luke asked.

Lucy dug it out of her pocket and spread it open on the table between them. It was still warm and pulsing with a subtle glow.

"Not really. I've kept it with me day and night, and it glows and gets warm like this every so often. I pull it out when I feel the warmth, but nothing else happens. I haven't been able to make it colored again like I did back in Algid. Now I'm not even sure that I had anything to do with that... maybe it was just random." She smoothed her palms across the map, wishing she had more control over it. The others leaned in, taking a closer look.

"I've done a lot of research on what each Mapkeeper did to make the map work for them. The complicated part is that no single method worked for more than one Mapkeeper. Each had to find his or her own unique way to manipulate the power of the map."

"What are some examples?" Lucy asked.

"One Mapkeeper had to hold it between his palms and close his eyes, using deep breathing and meditation. There are some stranger methods, too. One Mapkeeper had a pet ferret that he loved so much that he wouldn't allow it out of his sight. To unlock the map's power he had to be holding his ferret in one hand

and holding the map out in his other." Lucy lifted her eyebrows in surprise. "Without the ferret, the map was a useless piece of parchment for the Mapkeeper!" Mack and Luke burst out laughing.

"I want a pet ferret!" Luke proclaimed.

"One thing I can say after my research is that the key to unlocking the map's power seems to be found in emotion. Each Mapkeeper's temperament had something to do with how they interacted with the map. For example, the seventeenth one was a fiery man prone to angry outbursts. He was the one who unleashed the map's power by channeling his anger and crumpling it up! When he was angry, he was most effective."

"So if she figures out what emotion she identifies with most, it'll put her on track to figure out how to use the map," Mack offered.

"I think so," Cadmus agreed.

"Well then it's got to be sassiness," Luke joked. Mack and Luke cracked up. Lucy rolled her eyes.

"Can you guys please be serious for two minutes?" The map was still warm and glowing. "I'm not sure which emotion I feel the strongest connection to. I'll have to think about it." A long, deep rumble was followed by a blinding flash of lightning outside. "Cadmus, in your studies, did you ever come across anything about the map glowing and warming up?"

"Yes. It is said to react not only to the Mapkeeper's

emotion, but also to stirrings in the magical forces in Praxis. Because so many years have passed without much incident in Praxis, many Mapkeepers didn't have the opportunity to utilize the map to its full extent. But those who did were said to know that something was stirring before it happened because the map gave them clues."

"Like it's doing now," Mack said.

"Right," Cadmus replied, his expression grave. His eyes darted toward the strangers in across the room again.

Suddenly, the door to the inn crashed open, the pummeling sound of the downpour filling the restaurant. A very short silhouette was illuminated against a flash of lightning behind him. The visitor moved inside and hopped up onto a stool at the bar. It had the torso and head of a man, with the legs and horns of a goat. The Barnes siblings' mouths hung open.

"I take it you've never seen a satyr before," Cadmus chuckled, taking a sip of mead.

"No, I have not." Lucy was still staring at the creature as he placed an order at the bar. The satyr whipped around and locked eyes with her. She averted her eyes, but it was too late. He'd seen her staring. Despite having never seen a satyr in her life, there was something vaguely familiar about the strange little creature. He hopped down, hoofs clopping against the stone floor as he made his way over to their booth.

"Well, well, well. If it isn't Cadmus takin' the new

Mapkeeper out for a bite on the town," he sneered, crossing his hairy arms and leaning against the column next to their table. His horns grew out of his hairline above his forehead, ribbed with a slight curvature. He stood about chest-high to an average man, with coarse brown goat hair and a matching mop of hair on his head. His nose was long and hooked, and he had small, beady brown eyes. "Ms. Barnes, welcome to Praxis. I hope you like impossible challenges, because what you've got ahead of you is just that."

"Rhys, that's not true," Cadmus objected.

The satyr threw his head back and belly laughed, letting out a boisterous cackle. The dark-clothed men in the corner had stopped talking and were watching.

"Let's not fool ourselves, Cadmus! And not the new Mapkeeper. Our charming lady Mapkeeper!" He crossed his arms again and glanced toward the bar. The gruff-looking bartender was holding a small aluminum cup and gesturing toward Rhys.

"Well gentlemen and madam," he accentuated, curtseying toward Lucy with excessive emphasis, "I must go. I am needed at the bar. Pleasure to make your acquaintance. I'm Rhys. You'll be seeing me around." He twirled around on his hoofs and strutted back to the bar, his plump rear end and little tail bobbing with each step.

"He's not always so crass," Cadmus grinned, apologetic. "He's cranky, and he's never been one to make a good first impression, but he's not all bad."

The strangers across the restaurant resumed their whispered conversation as Marla poured dark ale into their glasses from a tin pitcher. Rhys hopped back up onto his barstool and took a swift swallow of whatever was in his tin cup, twisting sideways to glance across the room at the strangers.

Lucy drained her glass. Following suit, Cadmus tipped his back and tossed a few coins on the table, scooting off the bench.

"Shall we?" he asked. He waved at Marla, who was bumping a swinging door open with her hip across the room, arms full of dirty dishes. "I'll have the guards send for the carriage."

Mack wiped his upper lip with the back of his hand and scooted out of his seat. Luke was finishing his last gulp. Lucy glanced at the stranger as Cadmus made his way to the entrance. One of them whispered something to the other, who looked at Lucy. The lip of his hat cast a shadow across his face, but a shaft of light from a nearby lantern crossed his face as he turned. Goosebumps formed on her arms. Beneath the dark hat, a pair of yellow eyes watched her.

CHAPTER 13

***

Juices from a tender leg of lamb dribbled down Luke's chin. Lucy grinned and leaned across Mack to poke Luke on the shoulder, motioning for him to wipe his chin. He shrugged and complied.

"It's good!" Luke explained with a sheepish grin.

Lucy laughed. Her younger brother could be so goofy sometimes!

They were seated around the long banquet table in the Great Hall. It had been several days since their trip to town, and Lucy had spent much of her time poring over the map in anticipation of tonight's Council of Clans.

Lucy tried to relax, but despite the warm, pleasant atmosphere, her nerves were holding a full-on riot inside her stomach, and her hands were keeping up a faint but constant tremor. She did her best not to let her shaky hands cause her fork or knife to clatter against her dinner plate.

All over the banquet table, dozens of golden goblets brimmed with apple cider, mead, and effervescent spring water. The guests shared from platters of roast duck stuffed with apples and spices, slow-cooked lamb chops drizzled in mint sauce, hazelnut rice pilaf, pan-seared mushrooms and steamed greens, hot rye bread with spiced butter, pumpkin ginger brulee, and fresh fruits. The warm glow of flickering candlelight pooled on the thick, polished oak tabletop. Fiddles and tambourines provided jolly background music.

To Lucy's right, at the head of the table, Queen Oleksandra sat beside King Muttongale. Across from Lucy was Cadmus, in the king's right hand position. Beside him were Auriel and Odessa, the Bellaux representatives. Next was Zadok, who reclined atop a cushion designed for centaurs to dine at the table. Beside him sat Glump, the brooding goblin representative. Glump spoke little and ate voraciously. Adalia, the leader of the elves, sat at the far end of the table beside Prince Puck, who occupied the head table position opposite his parents. As usual, the prince's expression reflected his disgust at being compelled to be present.

Enzo, the leader of the gnomes, sat to Prince Puck's right. Next were Rhys, then Bade, then Luke, Mack, and Lucy. The Council of Clans was underway. Lucy tried to calm her nerves, letting the warm apple cider glide down her throat into her stomach, warming her from the inside out.

So far, conversation had been cordial enough, although several members of the council had made it clear that the superb fare was not the driving force behind their attendance. Glump and Bade spent most of the meal glaring at one another across the table, Glump gnashing aggressive portions of steaming lamb meat off the bone with his razor-sharp teeth. Bade ate with surgical precision, knifing diminutive morsels into his mouth and wiping his lips with his napkin after each bite. Rhys ensured that Prince Puck's end of the table remained lively, bombarding disinterested Enzo and polite, amused Adalia with his emphatic stories.

"Pass that pitcher of mead this way, Lukey-boy!" Rhys roared from the other end of the table, thrusting his empty mug into the air.

Luke obeyed, laughing at the satyr's overbearing demeanor. Bade leaned away from the sloshing pitcher with distaste, refusing to pass it. Luke reached over him, supporting the full pitcher with both hands.

"That's my boy, a very good lad!" Rhys thundered, reaching across Bade to slap Luke on the back and accepting the pitcher. Bade rolled his eyes and sighed with supreme irritation. Zadok caught Lucy's eye and smiled, and Odessa shook her head.

"He'll never learn when enough is enough," she observed.

"I think he's funny," Luke shrugged, spooning pumpkin brulee into his mouth.

"He adds a healthy dose of character to the bunch," the

queen agreed, chiming in. "And he's the one member of the Council without a clan."

"Is Rhys the only satyr in Praxis?" Lucy cocked her head to one side.

Cadmus nodded. "He is a dying breed, as I like to remind him from time to time," Cadmus winked at Rhys across the table. Rhys shook his full mug in pretend anger.

The king and queen laughed and bantered with the clan leaders like old friends, and Cadmus caught Lucy's eye and smiled on more than one occasion. She blushed and chastised herself for being caught staring, focusing with intensity on stabbing a piece of glazed sweet potato with her fork.

Zadok seemed to be the calm, unifying force among them. Seated at table's center, he was congenial and warm, with kind eyes and an open mind for others' opinions.

Lucy noticed a shift in Mack's behavior as soon as Auriel took her seat across from him. He fumbled his silverware trying to unfold his napkin, sending all three pieces clattering to the floor.

So much for Mack being the smooth, coordinated one, Lucy chuckled to herself. Auriel graced her older brother with a kind smile. Lucy watched him stutter through several minutes of forced conversation, fishing for the right thing to say.

"So Auriel—may I call you Auriel?" Mack's eyebrows arched as he folded his hands in his lap.

Auriel laughed, a melodic tinkling of tiny bells. "Of course you may. You must." She smiled. *Her smile that could melt all the snow in Algid*, Lucy thought. Like all the Bellaux, she was gorgeous. Her smooth, light brown hair framed eyes as clear and blue as Glacial Lake. Her cheekbones were high and her lips were two perfectly formed pink pillows beneath a button nose.

Mack let out a nervous chuckle. "I've been wondering: what is it like to live in the Tree of Virtue?"

"It is paradise for us," Auriel began. "We live in harmony with all the creatures of the tree, and the tree provides us everything we need—the bark is crispy and rich in nutrients. It tastes like your sweet potato," she gestured to the brimming bowl of candied sweet potatoes between them. "The leaves are abundant and succulent, full of vitamins and proteins. The tree also produces red berries, crunchy brown nuts, a sweet syrupy nectar, and thick golden honey that comes from the seasonal blooming of little white blossoms."

"It sounds amazing!" Mack's mouth hung open, entranced.

"Well, it is—but we do not allow any other clan creatures into the tree. Just the Bellaux and the woodland creatures who call it home. We share the tree with many such creatures—squirrels, song birds, and owls, to name a few."

To Auriel's right, her dark-haired sister Odessa nodded in an absent, distracted manner. Lucy noticed she kept shooting nervous glances toward the other end of the table. Something seemed to be bothering her.

When everyone had finished eating, servers cleared away the dishes and the pitchers were topped off. King Muttongale cleared his throat to silence the chatter.

"Leaders of Praxis, we have gathered tonight with the very important purpose of discussing the way ahead for Praxis in this time of great significance. As you all know, this is Praxis' Mapkeeper, Ms. Lucy Barnes." He gestured to Lucy. "We owe her our complete allegiance and support. Together, we must unite to defeat the dark forces that would destroy us!" He popped to his feet for emphasis, but only became shorter upon extracting himself from his plump, cushioned throne.

Bade rolled his eyes, leaning back in his chair and rubbing his forehead. Low chatter broke out among the guests.

"Why is Bade here if Cadmus is the people's clan leader?" Lucy whispered to Queen Oleksandra.

"He is permitted to attend because he claims to represent the interests Digby, the leader of the trolls. Of course, we would rather a human attend than Digby—he's a massive brute," the queen confessed, leaning in close. "Of course, there are those who question whether Bade represents the interests of the trolls, or has his own agenda..." she trailed off as the king clattered a spoon against his golden chalice, calling for attention.

"Let the Council begin! We will open with some words from Ms. Barnes." He hopped back up onto his throne, his bejeweled crown tipping askew on his head.

Lucy gulped. Her palms were sweaty as she pushed back from the table to stand.

"Good evening," she began, battling back the flurry of nerves that was whirring in her stomach. "As his highness said, I'm Lucy Barnes, the new Mapkeeper of Praxis."

Everyone was watching her. She swallowed hard, and then continued with her premeditated speech. "I didn't know I would be Mapkeeper, or even what that was, until just a few days ago." Her brothers smiled, reassuring her. She clasped her hands in front of her, realizing that they were shaking. "But I am here, ready to do whatever it takes to bring peace to Praxis. I look forward to learning from each of you. I don't know much about Praxis yet, but I am very willing to learn, and I am becoming more proficient with the map each day. Thank you for your attention," she trailed off, sliding back into her chair with a huge sigh. Her hands were shaking more than ever. She stuffed them into the pockets of her pants.

Across the table, Cadmus gave her a soul-melting smile of reassurance. Tears of relief and appreciation sprang into her eyes. Cadmus stood and broke the silence.

"Thank you, Lucy. Know that we all look forward to working with you as well to find the best solution to our current situation here in Praxis." He squared his shoulders, facing the rest of the table. "You elected me head of the Clan Council, and as such, I will direct the progress of the meeting from here on. The floor is open for dialogue regarding the recent disasters that have stricken our land." He sat down, leaning forward with one arm on the table.

Adalia rose to speak first. She was petite, with cropped white-blonde hair that swept across her forehead in a smooth flat layer. Her green eyes were a brilliant contrast to her unblemished ivory skin, even from all the way across the room. Her ears were large and pointed, somehow lending her an aura of wisdom. She spoke with precision and clarity.

"Fellow clan leaders, I think we all recognize the signs of what is happening in Praxis. Our clans have existed in this land for thousands of years. We've all been passed down the legends of old detailing the disasters which came close to overcoming our ancestors. It is clear that we are in the middle of the same progression of events. The fifteenth Mapkeeper was able to defeat the three legendary beasts before they destroyed the castle—this time, we must not wait until the bitter end to find a way to squelch this dark magic."

"And how do you propose we do that?" Enzo cut in as he stood. Standing, he was a hair taller than Rhys, who remained seated beside him. His pale blue eyes flashed with passion beneath thick black eyebrows. All of his features were small and squashed with the exception of his ears, which were large and positioned low on his head. His trimmed, straight black beard was peppered with flecks of silver and white that traveled up his mutton chops, becoming more frequent and outnumbering the dark hairs in his sideburns. He had a helmet of straight black hair that seemed to grow at a vertical angle from his scalp, forming a rectangular covering atop his head.

He slammed his little hands on the table. "We've got a brand new Mapkeeper who has no experience with handling the map!" he cried, gesturing at Lucy in frustration.

Lucy's face burned. The council erupted in arguments. Everyone had an opinion, and they all wanted to share it at once. Only Zadok was silent, arms crossed in thought as he listened to Odessa and Rhys try to shout over one another across the table. Bade and Adalia were engaged in a similar cross-table debate, while Enzo and Glump leaned so far over the table toward one another, only the short distance between them seemed to hold them back from a physical confrontation. Across from Lucy, Cadmus was engaged in a debate with Auriel.

"Enough!" the king cried, smashing his chalice onto the table, sending mead sloshing all over the table and into Cadmus' lap. King Muttongale didn't notice. "We'll never get anywhere arguing like a bunch of children!" Rhys was pulling Enzo back into his chair. Zadok placed a calming hand on Glump's shoulder, but the goblin threw it off in irritation.

"Don't touch me, horse man!" Glump growled.

"If we can't hold a civilized discussion, we will send you all away!" the king shouted. His meek voice was not intimidating, but the group quieted nonetheless.

Bade, silent up until now, stood and lifted his chin with an air of superiority.

"I think what we all need to focus on is how Ms. Barnes intends to help us. After all, isn't she supposed to be the one who can defeat these so-called dark forces?" His stubble-encrusted upper lip curled in a sneer as he glared in Lucy's direction. A warm rush of blood saturated her face. Cadmus stood, rescuing her from the daunting chore of defending herself.

"Lucy will continue to work with the map to figure out how to make it work for her. In the meantime, we need to discuss ways our clans can best prepare for future disasters. The people in the village have already begun reinforcing their roofs with hard wood, and are storing up extra days of food and supplies just in case. Should any clan's home be destroyed, they will find refuge in the Town Hall."

Auriel and Odessa let out sighs of relief. The Tree of Virtue was massive and thick-trunked, but it was only one tree.

"I speak on behalf of Digby and the trolls," Bade announced. "They will not run from natural disasters. Should their caves be destroyed, they will come down from the mountains and take whichever dwelling suits them. They are not concerned with the wellbeing of the other clans. But perhaps if that child—" he gestured toward Lucy, "learned how to use her map, we wouldn't be having this conversation in the first place," he spat.

Lucy felt the heat rise to her face again. Furious, she shoved her chair back and spread the map on the table.

"I have already begun to develop a bond with the map and am well on my way to learning how to make it work for me," she declared, believing most of her claim to be true. She jabbed the map with a finger for emphasis.

Without warning, the Great Hall began to shake with force, rattling utensils and clattering plates. Lucy grabbed onto the heavy table for support. A moment later, the shaking faded away as dust drifted down from the ceiling, coating the hushed group in a thin layer of powder. Lucy slowly lifted her gaze to discover the eyes of everyone in the room fixed on her. She swallowed hard, unsure if she had caused the quake, or if it was a matter of chance that it coincided with her forceful poke of the map.

Arguing broke out among the leaders once again.

Suddenly, a resounding crash exploded somewhere behind Lucy, and the chandeliers far overhead extinguished. At the same time, the doors to the Great Hall burst open and a rush of cold air extinguished the tabletop candles. With what little light was left and her eyes being maladjusted to the darkness, Lucy couldn't see a thing! Her heartbeat began to thunder in her chest, her instincts telling her she was in danger. There were groping hands and confused muttering. She found Mack's arm beside her, clinging to it in the darkness.

A sickening thud came from somewhere to her right.

"Mack, what's going on? Can you see anything?" she whispered, her voice quavering as she clung to her brother's arm.

"No, I am just starting to be able to make out silhouettes," he replied, his voice shaky.

A female voice screamed—a high-pitched scream of genuine horror. The hairs on the back of Lucy's neck stood up as the faintest puff of air dusted the back of her neck, as if someone had just exhaled directly behind her. She whirled around, her heart thundering in her chest, but could see no one through the darkness. Her breaths came in ragged, terrified spurts, her eyes straining against the shroud of darkness.

"Pardon me, excuse us," Milo's voice joined the chaos from somewhere across the table. She turned around to see him lean across the table, his face illuminated by the glow of a lit candlestick. He lit five more, making his way along the table top. Farther down the table, several servants did the same.

To her immense relief, at last a dim glow hovered over the table, illuminating the frightened faces of the clan leaders. Milo used his candlestick to light a portable lantern, and then scurried to the king and queen's end of the table. There was a great scuffling of chairs and footsteps. In the dim light, Lucy saw a form that appeared to be Queen Oleksandra bent over something on the floor.

The chandeliers overhead flickered back on, illuminating the hall. A servant heaved the Great Hall doors closed, and all was still. Each guest stood around the table behind or near their original seats.

Lucy gasped, clapping a hand over her mouth. Queen Oleksandra and three servants knelt over a body. King Muttongale lay unmoving on the floor, blood gushing from a gash on his head.

CHAPTER 14

Heavy sheets of rain and furious lightning shredded the sky in the distance.

"Whoa, it's getting dark outside!" Luke leaned back, staring upward.

"Let me see," Lucy leaned over him and peered out the window. Colossal black clouds roiled overhead, making swift progress toward them from somewhere over the Dark Sea. A thick bolt of jagged lighting split the sky, making apparent landfall somewhere between them and the sea.

After a quiet, gloomy breakfast, Cadmus, Lucy, and her brothers had departed the castle by carriage, hoping to find Zadok in Doldrums Forest to discuss the previous night's events. He was the one clan leader they all agreed could be trusted, though Mack had voted for a visit to the Tree of Virtue to see the Bellaux.

They made it down the Royale Byway without incident.

"That lightning bolt was huge!" Lucy's eyes widened and she sat back, allowing Luke to have another look. A disconcerting blow of thunder exploded as thick drops of rain began to splat against the roof of the carriage.

Cadmus' lips were set in a thin line. Rain began to hammer the roof as he slid open the panel separating the passengers from the driver. "Take us to the satyr's hut," he ordered. The crack of reins and an abrupt whinny preceded a jolt of speed. "We need to get to shelter. There's no way we're crossing the valley with this storm closing in," he rubbed his forehead and peered out at the sky, now blanketed in darkness.

Rhys' hut was a faded brown shingled A-frame structure on a ridge overlooking Glacial Lake. The ridge boasted a distant view of Pernicious Landing, which was spitting sea foam as powerful waves slapped its craggy rocks. Exiting the carriage, they dodged raindrops as they ran to the hut. Four of Lucy's guards remained huddled in the carriage outside, but two had insisted on accompanying her inside the hut and now flanked the door, keeping a watchful eye on their charge.

"How is the king?" Rhys asked as he passed around flimsy, mismatched tin mugs of hot tea.

"He hasn't come out of it yet," Cadmus' brow furrowed. "The castle maester fears he has slipped into a coma."

Lucy winced with sadness not just for the king, but also for the queen, who hadn't left his side since the previous night's attack. The queen had maintained remarkable composure throughout the ordeal. She'd shared her thoughts with Lucy later, fearing that whoever wished harm to a king as virtuous as King Muttongale no doubt had evil intentions. Though they'd searched the guests before they left the castle, neither weapons nor suspects were discovered.

"I fear this is just the beginning," she had confided. "You must be vigilant, Lucy. Do not let your guard down for even a moment. There is a traitor among the clan leaders, and now no one is safe—least of all you, my dear." She'd placed a hand on Lucy's arm. Her concern affected Lucy to her core. *Is this what it might be like to have a mother?* she wondered. The sudden thought had sent physical pain shooting through her heart.

"It's a shame. These are dicey times we're living in," Rhys grunted as he joined them around the cramped table, squatting onto a low wooden stool. "Did you know there's a whorl forming?"

"I saw it from the castle turret this morning," Cadmus confirmed, his lips set in that familiar, grim line.

"A whorl?" Luke scratched his head as he accepted a tin mug of tea.

"A giant whirlpool in the Dark Sea. Legend has it the same thing happened last time." Cadmus had swept his damp, matted hair to one side when they'd come inside. His long, dark eyelashes were exaggerated in the ever-changing candle light and his cheeks were flushed berry red. He took a gulp of tea and flinched. "Ouch, that's hot!"

"What'd you expect?" Rhys muttered, swallowing a large mouthful of the scalding liquid without wincing. "I first spotted the whorl from my ridge this morning," the satyr grunted.

Lucy warmed her hands on the lopsided tin mug. She gazed down into her cup. The liquid was black, with flecks of tea leaves floating on the surface. *This doesn't look very appetizing*, she thought.

Mack stood and went to the thick-glassed window on the cabin's northern wall, peering through sheets of rain in the direction of the Dark Sea. "Still can't see much through this downpour," he reported as a flash of lightning lit up the sky.

The map had grown warm in Lucy's pocket, so she slipped it out and held it beneath the table. Somehow, it brought her a sense of comfort.

Through the rumble of thunder that trailed the lightning, a different noise became perceptible. *Thump. Thump. Thump.* Lucy glanced around the table. The others perked up—they heard it, too.

"What was that?" she tightened her grip on the map beneath the table.

"What was what?" Rhys replied, hopping to his hoofed feet and grabbing a dish rag off the kitchen counter, busying himself wiping the round wooden tabletop. He bumped mugs and the solitary tall, lumpy candlestick as he scrubbed the grimy rag across the table.

"That thudding noise during the thunder—didn't you hear it?" Cadmus' eyes narrowed.

"You're not used to storms. It was probably your imagination," the satyr snapped.

"But I heard it too," Luke protested. "It was a thumping noise."

Rhys whipped around to face Luke. "Well I didn't hear it, so what do you want me to do?" he barked. Cadmus glanced at Lucy, raising his eyebrows in surprise. There was a momentary silence.

"You seem pretty rattled, Rhys. Is everything okay?" Lucy watched him, waiting for his reply.

"Yes, yes, everything's fine," he spat, exasperated. "Let's just finish our conversation about the whorl before I decide I need something stronger than this tea to drink." He squatted back onto his stool. A dribble of sweat snaked its way down his temple and buried itself in his bushy eyebrow.

Mack and Luke exchanged a look of surprise, and then raised their eyebrows at their sister. Lucy shrugged.

"Like Cad was saying," Rhys began, nudging Cadmus with his elbow, "the whorl also formed back during the era of the fifteenth Mapkeeper. It grew so large that it swallowed up the creatures of the sea. Everything on and under the sea was sucked into its vortex and thrust into the depths. Ships, too." He shuddered, clasping his mug. "This added to the chaos in Praxis. See, some clans rely on fish from the Dark Sea as a source of sustenance. The humans and elves are skilled fishers and if they snare a big enough load, they trade with the gnomes and centaurs for spices, roots and vegetables, or other useful items."

Lucy pressed the folded map against her thigh, savoring its warmth. The rumble of distant thunder heightened the ominous tone of Rhys' tale.

Luke stood to take a closer look at a high wooden shelf, upon which were perched numerous vials and bottles. Purple, green, and clear liquids, mysterious powders, miniscule bone fragments, slimy eel eggs, rotten pumpkin seeds, and dozens of other bizarre supplies filled the mismatched glass vessels. Faded labels, each in some stage of peeling away, identified the contents of each container.

"What's all this stuff?" Luke crossed his arms as he squinted to read the labels, fascinated by the collection.

"Those," Rhys boasted, "are the stock of an alchemist-extraordinaire. I mix Praxis' highest quality draughts, tonics, and poultices. Among my supplies you will find exotic ingredients like tongue of boar, limproot, snagglemarrow powder, sclera juice, shadow moss, and lizard oil."

"No horn of unicorn, I hope?" Cadmus cocked his head.

"Of course not, that's illegal," Rhys scoffed, shifting in his seat. "Everyone knows that."

The thumping noise returned. The three muffled thuds seemed to emanate from somewhere within—or was it beneath the cabin? All four guests glanced at one another, their curiosity obvious.

"Rhys, there it is ag—" Cadmus began.

Rhys leapt from his stool in agitation. "The rain let up. It's time for you to move on." The satyr corralled them out of his cabin. "Mind your own business for once, Cadmus. I'm sure you all have important things to take care of, and I have matters of my own to attend to." He ushered them to the door and shoved them outside into the lazy post-storm drizzle.

Luke hesitated, the last one to leave the cabin. Lucy glanced back and thought she saw him saying something to Rhys as she was rushed into the carriage by her guards. Rhys' beady eyes shifted to meet hers, and he waved Luke away, slamming the door behind him.

CHAPTER 15

They skirted Glacial Lake on their way to Doldrums Forest. Lucy peered through the gray light at the large, dark body of water. She could make out Rhys' hut on the ridge across the lake. She wondered if he was watching them—*what business did he have to attend to?* His strange behavior baffled her.

"There are mermaids in the lake," Cadmus noted, gazing out the window.

"Are they peaceful?" Luke asked.

"They prefer to be left alone. They want no part in the affairs of land creatures, and they don't take well to being disturbed. But in my research, I did find notes mentioning the interactions of several past Mapkeepers with the mermaid queen. She was said to be reasonable enough. She is the oldest of all the mermaids—at least two thousand years old by my estimate."

"Did she help them?" Lucy asked.

"In one instance that I found, yes. A massive flood threatened to wash out the entire valley and the eighteenth Mapkeeper went to the mermaid queen for help. It was in the mermaids' best interest to preserve Glacial Lake because the flood was devastating their fragile underwater ecosystem. It had rained for a month straight and was showing no sign of letting up. The Tree of Virtue was a third of the way swamped by floodwater, and the creatures of Doldrums Forest were running for higher ground, encroaching on the territories of the trolls and goblins.

"The mermaids are rumored to hold special powers over the weather. The queen mermaid saturated the map with a fair weather blessing and the Mapkeeper released it into the skies. The rain stopped, and over time, excess floodwater dried, returning Praxis to its natural balance."

"She saturated the map with a blessing?" Lucy scratched her head, fascinated.

"The record I dug up in the archives said that she was able to somehow transfer her blessing to the map. I've deduced that as a magical object, the map is capable of receiving and storing both blessings and curses. The caveat is that only the Mapkeeper has the ability to release those blessings or curses. Of course, the map has also been known to generate its own magic."

Lucy gazed out the window, allowing her mind to drift as she stared at the dreary, rain-soaked valley. She hoped wild storms like the one that passed through today wouldn't become a regular occurrence. She didn't care to meet the mermaid queen if she didn't have to.

Doldrums Forest materialized through the mist ahead of the carriage, shadowy and thick. The dirt road they followed continued into the forest, but narrowed as it breached the trees. The guards who accompanied them on horseback had to fall in ahead of and behind them as there was no longer space for them to ride abreast the carriage.

They entered the forest and were engulfed by trees on all sides. Strange squawks and hoots echoed through the dark, hollow spaces between the tall trunks. The forest air was colder, shaded beneath the high leafy canopy. Mack leaned against his window and peered up.

"These trees are massive."

"Doldrums Forest has thrived for many centuries. A large part of it burned in the Great Fire about eight hundred years ago, but over time it regrew and expanded."

"What lives here?" Luke asked.

Lucy ignored the eerie sensation that from somewhere in the darkness, they were being watched. A chill ran down her arms and she rubbed the goosebumps away.

"The elves and the centaur clans live deep in the woods. Kobolds are mischievous little creatures that play tricks on travelers and wanderers. They are good-natured, though, and will come to the aid of someone in need. There are unicorns within the woods, but they are very rare. I have never seen one. People try to avoid the forest as much as possible. It's not... safe," he revealed, his eyes narrowing.

Lucy frowned and watched tree trunks pass as they drove deeper into the forest.

"Do the guards know where to find Zadok?" Luke asked, uneasy.

"The centaurs' residence is a large cavern called Abodox. I told the guards to take us there. It shouldn't be much farther now," Cadmus replied with a grim smile.

Just then, the carriage jerked to a rough stop. One of the guards' horses behind them let out a sharp whinny.

"What's going on?" Lucy tensed, clenching her fists.

"Everyone get down!" Cadmus ordered. "Stay low, and keep quiet." He leaned to peer out the carriage window. A sudden chill seeped into the carriage, permeating Lucy's bones. Her heart pounded as she crouched on the carriage floor, crammed between Mack and the sideboard. Cadmus' arm rested against her back. Despite her alarm, his touch was reassuring. She focused on keeping her breathing steady and quiet.

"Do you see anything?" Mack whispered to Cadmus.

"I don't see any of the guards..." he trailed off. His face went pale. "Who's driving the carriage?" he wondered aloud as he threw the carriage door open and jumped out.

"Cadmus! Don't—" Lucy started to reach for him but he had already slammed the door behind him. A tense moment later, the carriage leapt forward. The Barnes siblings scrambled back onto the bench seats and looked out the windows. Lucy's heart caught in her throat and a numb void of terror materialized in her stomach when she saw what was outside. They sped past the bloody carcasses of three guards and their horses. The guards had been beheaded.

"Ahh!" Lucy looked away, crying out in disgust and sorrow. Mack put an arm around her and hugged her against his side. The image of a bloodless face, dull eyes, and a mouth hanging wide open burned in her mind's eye.

"Who would do this?" Luke cried in revulsion, his eyes wide with horror and face pale as a sheet.

Lucy steeled herself, physically bracing to force the nausea back down into the depths of her abdomen. She peered out the window again, this time paying close attention to their surroundings. In the deepest recesses of the woods, almost out of sight through the thicket, she thought she glimpsed three figures in long, black-hooded robes.

"There! Way back in the forest, do you see those things in dark robes?" She pointed.

Mack leaned past her, but they were going too fast. They flew through the forest, leaving the gruesome scene behind. A shiver ran down her spine. An instant after she'd seen the hooded figures, they were gone.

CHAPTER 16

⁂

The carriage cruised to a halt in front of a tall, deep rocky cavern. Cadmus leapt from the driver's seat and opened the carriage door, helping Lucy out. Her pale hand shook as she gripped his hand and hopped down into the dirt. Dry leaves crunched underfoot. Her brothers hopped out after her and swung the carriage door shut.

Zadok emerged from the torch-lit depths of the cavern entrance tunnel flanked by two other centaurs. He smiled when he saw them, though his companions' stern expressions were far less welcoming than their leader's.

"What *were* those things back there?" Mack asked Cadmus, looking over his shoulders in both directions, his eyes still wide with distress.

"I'm not certain, but I have an idea," Cadmus replied, his tone foreboding. His face was drawn and pale.

"Friends," Zadok called, extending his arms, "welcome to Abodox, home of the centaurs. I see you survived your journey through Doldrums Forest unscathed so far." He smiled.

"Not quite, my friend," Cadmus replied. "We were attacked not far back along the path. Our six armed guards and their horses were killed."

Zadok's expression fell and his demeanor changed. His companions assumed a tense, defensive posture wielding their spears and squinting as they scanned the forest.

"Come inside," Zadok urged, beckoning them toward the cavern. He scanned the forest with his clear blue eyes as his guests hurried past him into the tunnel. The centaurs were tall and strong, with sleek, muscled haunches. Lucy noted that her height was in line with Zadok's abdomen as she passed him. She felt safer among these strong creatures.

The long entrance tunnel leading to Abodox was cold and damp, lit by flickering torches mounted to the moist rock walls. They came upon a thick iron gate blocking off the rest of the cave, which expanded in height and width as it deepened. One of Zadok's companions performed a series of twists and jabs on an intricate forged iron lock and the latch released with a moan.

Zadok held the gate open for the others and passed through last, locking the gate behind him.

"Welcome to Abodox," Zadok announced, "the home of the centaurs."

The tunnel opened onto a rock ledge overlooking a vast cavern descending into blackness far below. Sporadic flickering torches dotted the stone walls along a carved footpath that spiraled along the walls into the depths of the cavern. Dim lighting revealed dozens of chambers hewn from the rock along the pathway. The quiet hum of overlapping conversations echoed off the stone walls, softening the cold gloom of the place.

"Come, we will sit in my chamber and talk," Zadok motioned, leading the way down the gentle sloping path to the first compartment, where he gestured them inside.

It was spacious, with enough torches and candles to provide a warm glow of light. Zadok pulled string hammock seats off a high shelf and attached them to ceiling-mounted hooks. Cadmus, Lucy, Mack, and Luke each sank into one of the hanging woven pods. Luke and Mack grinned at one another, delighted by the amusing contraptions.

Zadok settled on one of six long, thick silk cushions designed for equestrian comfort.

"Thank you for your hospitality," Cadmus said, running a hand through his hair.

"It is my pleasure." Zadok was polite as ever though his expression remained rigid. "Please tell me everything you saw back on the trail."

Cadmus hesitated, glancing at Lucy as though unsure whether he should disclose his suspicion.

Lucy took the opportunity to speak up. "Our carriage came to a sudden stop, and Cadmus got out and took the reins," she replied. "When we passed, we saw our guards decapitated and their horses dead beside them."

"Cadmus, when you were outside the carriage, did you see..." Zadok trailed off, his eyes wide with concern.

"I'm not sure what I saw, but I think it was several figures robed in black," Cadmus answered. "Most of them were on the outskirts of the scene by the time I got out, and I was in a hurry. The air was icy cold—*too* cold. I knew we had to get out of there, and *fast*. As I hopped up into the driver seat and grabbed the reins, I saw one of them. It was still bent over one of the guards..." He looked away and rubbed his forehead with one hand, distraught. Lucy hated to see him so upset.

"Please go on," Zadok encouraged. "It is essential that you tell me everything."

"It—whatever it was—was... was w-wiping his blood off a blade," he stammered. "It looked up at me as we drove by, and I couldn't see eyes or a face. Just blackness inside the hood. It was awful," he finished, running a hand through his hair as if to wipe the memory from his mind.

Zadok's frown deepened. He rubbed his chin, deep in thought. "How many of these creatures did you see, Cadmus?"

"At least four."

"I saw a few of them, too," Lucy added. "Just for an instant in the distance, half-covered by the mist."

"I fear the worst," Zadok confided, his brow furrowed in concern.

"I know." Cadmus shook his head. "I do too."

"What?" Mack asked.

"That the Wardens have returned," Zadok muttered with a grimace. Noting the puzzled looks on the Barnes siblings' faces, he explained. "The Wardens are the authors of a dark magic. They created the map long ago with good intentions, so the map itself is not tainted. The ancient Wardens' intention was for an outsider—someone pure of heart—to restore the natural order to Praxis in times of conflict and when dark forces stirred." Cadmus nodded as the centaur explained the history of the map.

"But over time, their ancestors became jealous of the Mapkeeper. They wanted that power for themselves, so they began to work against the Mapkeeper. They isolated themselves from all other creatures in Praxis and for hundreds of years, no one saw or heard from the Wardens."

"Until the fifteenth Mapkeeper," Lucy predicted.

"Correct. They were growing their powers and developing a dark plan. They craved the destruction of our way of life, and the awakening of the three beasts almost brought them success." The wall-mounted candles flickered, shadows dancing across the chamber. "In a twist of ironic justice, the map—the original Warden creation—was the downfall of their plan."

"And now you fear they are back again? And possibly the cause of all the disasters that have been happening?" Luke deduced, running a hand through his hair in thought.

"Right." Cadmus nodded. "I've been mulling the possibility over in my mind for a few weeks now. I just didn't think it was possible! The Wardens were rounded up and killed after the fifteenth Mapkeeper sacrificed himself to defeat the three beasts. It is said that they made sure there was not a single Warden left to continue their dark work."

"Wardens or not, those things were *not* human," Lucy remarked, a chill running down her spine at the memory of the hooded figures. "Wait—Cadmus, those two people we saw in the shadows at Alewife Inn—you don't think they were..."

He sighed and nodded, his cornflower blue eyes appearing a darker shade of sapphire in the candle light. "It's possible. I'd never seen them before, and we never got a good view of their faces. I'll have to go back and talk to Marla to see if she got their names or saw their faces."

"What happens if the creatures in the woods are Wardens?" Mack asked.

"I don't know, but we've got to hold out hope that they're not. The Wardens' brand of magic is very powerful. It would be difficult to overcome. As the king's alchemist, Rhys has developed a few quality potions to counter dark magic, but the ultimate burden would fall on you, Lucy. Only the map is powerful enough to defeat them."

Lucy swallowed, placing a hand over the outline the map formed in the pocket of her riding pants. She was beginning to like the Praxian clothing she'd been provided. Her tan riding pants, brown shin-high boots, and breezy elbow-length blue shirt were comfortable and practical. To her disappointment, the map was not warm. She clenched her teeth.

"All of the clans will have to band together," Cadmus mused, rubbing his chin.

"You know the centaurs will be on board." Zadok gave a curt nod.

"I never doubted you, my friend," Cadmus replied with sincerity. "It's the other clans I'm worried about—the elves and Bellaux will be wary, and the goblins will be difficult. Of course the trolls will not cooperate, and Bade will no doubt find a way to manipulate his relationship with Digby to his advantage."

Zadok sighed. "We must do our best to form a united front and hope that the others will follow. My greatest fear is that it may take a catastrophe for some clans to come to their senses and join us... but by then it may be too late." His blue eyes were clouded with worry.

"I'll need to train," Lucy added, "but I will make the map work for me. I'll also need to work on a few practical skills if I'm to be of any use—riding, swordsmanship, and archery."

"We will train too," Mack added. "I'm a decent rider, and Luke is pretty smart. I'm sure we can help the cause somehow."

"Great." Cadmus nodded. "We're going to need all the allies we can muster."

"I'll hold a meeting with my top advisers tonight and lay the groundwork for our united front against the Wardens." Zadok crossed his arms. "Until proven otherwise, we must assume the Wardens are back. Waiting for them to surprise us is too risky." Cadmus nodded in agreement.

"As you know," Zadok continued, "most of my centaurs don't hold humans in the highest regard, but I will ensure their priorities are set straight. You'd better get going. It's getting late, and you can't be out in the forest after dark. I'll send four armed escorts to provide you safe passage to the forest limits."

"Thank you, Zadok." Cadmus pulled himself out of his hanging chair to shake the centaur's hand. "You are a true friend."

"The feeling is mutual." Zadok smiled, returning the firm handshake and clapping Cadmus on the shoulder. "Ms. Barnes, gentlemen, it was a pleasure to see you. I hope we meet again soon."

"Thank you, Zadok." Lucy stood and shook his hand. As she did so, one of the two centaurs who had accompanied Zadok to greet them outside Abodox earlier galloped at top speed into the chamber.

"Zadok," he gasped, breathless. "You've got to come right away! It's Odessa, the Bellaux. She just arrived at the gate in the tunnel. She's injured. It seems the kobolds guided her here—she's in a very bad state. Blood everywhere."

Zadok leapt up. "Excuse me, I must go. Axel, send four armed guards with our guests to the forest's edge."

"Yes, sir," Axel replied.

"Is there anything we can do to help?" Mack asked, fists balled in frustration as Zadok thundered out of the room.

"It's best we get moving." Cadmus put a hand on Mack's shoulder. "The sun will be setting soon, and we can't be out in the forest after dark."

"He's right." Axel's tone was stern. "We leave right away, or not at all."

CHAPTER 17

٭

In the days that followed the terrible encounter in
Doldrums Forest, Lucy, Mack, and Luke fell into a routine. They
did not leave the castle grounds again for several days, instead
taking time to practice the skills they lacked—skills that were
taught to most humans in Praxis from a young age. The siblings
spent most mornings practicing riding, archery, and
swordsmanship with Pip and Quinn at the castle stables. Lucy
spent several hours each day alone with the map, memorizing its
details and testing her abilities. She practiced deep breathing and
twisted her mind in ways she'd never done before in an attempt to
learn how to best connect with the map.

In the castle library one evening, Lucy spread the map out
on a table and stared at it, hoping something new would stand
out... some obvious detail she'd overlooked all along. But she
couldn't rid her mind of horrible images from the bloody scene in
Doldrums Forest. The headless guard, dead horses, cloaked

figures in the shadows, and Odessa's bloody, unconscious body in the cavern tunnel haunted her. She shook her head, desperate to rid herself of the terrors.

A sudden hand on her shoulder made her start.

"Ahh!" She leapt out of her chair, wheeling about. "Oh Cadmus, you scared the living daylights out of me!" She gasped, holding a hand over her drumming heart.

"I'm sorry." He smiled, amused. "I didn't mean to sneak up on you. I just wanted to check in and see how you're doing. Any luck with the map?"

"Not at all." She sat back down, flustered. "I just can't seem to figure out what I'm missing."

"Have you thought much about the Council of Clans when you made the castle shake by jabbing the map?" He slid into the chair across the table from her.

"Do you really think I caused that?"

"I do." He held her gaze. "Lucy, I've done a lot of research on past Mapkeepers, and I've been watching you since you arrived in Praxis to try to help you. I think when you become passionate about something, the map reacts to your emotion."

Absorbing his theory, she nodded. It seemed to make sense.

"Think about it—Bade tried to humiliate and belittle you, but you believed you were worth more than that. You defended yourself in front of an intimidating group of leaders without thinking twice. That was something you had strong feelings about. You were passionate!" His bright blue eyes were lighter than usual, reflecting the sunlight that filtered in through the massive library windows. She couldn't hold his gaze—it was too intense. She worried that her heart might leap out of her chest with joy at his strong presence and belief in her.

Sudden color flooded the map in a swirling vortex. Vigorous life and motion animated the images on the paper. Tiny townspeople buzzed about in the village, mermaids skimmed the surface of Glacial Lake, and wild horses stampeded across the plain outside town where the Barnes siblings had first crash-landed in Praxis. Two trolls clubbed at one another in a brawl in the Dour Mountains, a rabble of rocks clattering down the mountain. Lucy was captivated by the animated, vibrant colors saturating the map, her eyes darting from scene to scene.

When she looked up, Cadmus was still staring at her. She blushed, realizing what the sudden animation of the map implied. Embarrassed, she pushed back her chair and stood on impulse.

"Hey," he said, coming around the table to her. He took her by the shoulders. "It's okay, you don't have to be ashamed... I feel it, too." He met her gaze, his handsome smile making her weak in the knees. He leaned in and closed his eyes, his soft lips brushing hers. She melted into him, her arms holding on to the firm muscles of his upper back. He moved his hands up to her head, weaving his fingers through her hair and kissing her faster. For a moment, her whole world consisted of his soft, smooth lips and fervent kiss.

"Ahem..."

They jerked apart, glancing in the direction of the voice. Milo smiled from across the room. "Pardon the interruption, Ms. Barnes, but the queen requests your company in the king's chamber." The butler's eyes twinkled.

"Oh, of course, no problem at all," Lucy stammered, pulling away from Cadmus and attempting to smooth her ruffled hair. Her face was hot. She knew it was as red as a chokeberry. She snatched the map off the table, mortified.

"See you later," she mumbled to Cadmus as she hurried across the room, unable to make eye contact with Milo. She glanced up at him as she passed and saw him wink at Cadmus. Her cheeks burned.

⁂

Two armed palace guards waited for Lucy outside the library. They escorted her past a half-dozen more on their way up to the king's chamber on the fifth floor.

"Your majesty." Lucy bowed as she entered.

Queen Oleksandra glanced up from her chair next to the king's bed. Her cheeks were hollow, her eyes dull and sunken. "Hello, Lucy, please do come in."

"You look unwell, your majesty. Have you slept much in the past few days?"

"Oh, I'm fine, but thank you, dear. I just can't bear to leave my husband's side. He'll awaken soon enough, and I want to be by his side when he does." Dark circles beneath her eyes belied her. "I'm sure you are worried about Odessa after what happened in the forest. I received word that she is recovering under the protection of the centaurs. She can't remember what attacked her, only that it was sudden and unexpected."

Lucy cringed. "What was she doing in Doldrums Forest? I thought Bellaux rarely left the Tree of Virtue."

"That's what everyone wants to know. She claims she can't remember." The queen's brow furrowed. "But tell me, Lucy, how are you doing?"

"I'm fine, just a little frustrated with trying to figure out the map, that's all," Lucy confided.

"Understandable." The queen smiled. "Keep your head up, dear. I believe in you." Her eyes reflected her sincerity. "And I want to encourage you to go out amongst the villagers and get to know them. Their support will be crucial to your success. They are good people and will rally behind you. Tomorrow is the Blossom Jubilee, an annual celebration marking the blooming of thousands of tulips in the fields outside town. There will be music, dancing, and Central Square will be stunning, dressed for the occasion."

"I appreciate your kind words, your majesty. I will plan on going to town for the festival and mingling with the people."

"Under armed guard, of course," the queen insisted.

Lucy smiled. "Yes, your majesty."

"You saw what happened to the king," she murmured, stroking his forehead. "Goodness knows none of us are safe these days... least of all you, my dear." She appeared to age before Lucy's eyes, the yoke of responsibility heavy upon her shoulders.

"I promise I'll be careful, your majesty."

"Thank you, Lucy. Now go and get some rest. We all need rest..." she turned back to her husband and stroked his red hair. Lucy bowed and backed out of the room, which she realized was stuffy and dark upon reentering the hallway.

Her guards were waiting just outside the room, patient as ever, and followed her all the way to her bed chamber.

"Is it really necessary for you to accompany me everywhere I go inside the castle?" Lucy asked over her shoulder.

"Queen's orders, miss," one of the guards chirped. "We're happy to oblige. After all, there could be a traitor among us. Now's not the time for takin' chances, miss." They posted up, one on either side of the door to her chamber. Lucy smiled but shook her head, unaccustomed to being fussed over. She unlocked her door using a lever lock key, then slipped the key back into her pocket, entered her chamber and latched the door behind her.

Letting out a deep sigh, she jumped up onto her high, soft bed, alone at last. She gazed out the window and saw Mack and Luke practicing swordsmanship with Pip outside the stable. Lucy was eager to join them but knew she had to focus on the map first.

Sir Wigginsworth hopped onto the bed and rubbed his soft body against her shoulder, his tail brushing across her face.

"Well hello, Sir Wigginsworth. How have you been? Has Olivia been taking care of you?" She stroked the cat, eliciting a soft purr. Sir Wigginsworth looked at her, cocked his head, then pranced to the edge of the bed and leapt off. He scurried to the bathroom door and began to scratch it, meowing in agitation.

"What's wrong, Sir Wigginsworth? Do you want to go in the bathroom?" She got up and opened the door. Sir Wigginsworth ran inside the moment it was wide enough to allow him through. Lucy grinned, amused by his urgency.

"Why are you so antsy to get in—" She froze mid-sentence as she peered into the bathroom. A bloodied uniform jacket she recognized as belonging to one of the guards who'd been killed in the forest hung from a vanity light atop the main mirror. A bronze pocket watch on a long chain hung from the adjacent vanity light, a lock of hair tied to its face with a piece of twine.

Across the mirror, in messy script, the message *"Everything is not as it seems. The dungeon holds the answers you seek"* was scrawled in—blood? Lucy did not dare step closer to investigate. Her heart seized up as if constricted by a tight cord, her pulse rattling her whole body and thumping in her ear canals.

Transfixed by the horrific scene, she couldn't stop herself from reaching up to the back of her head and patting her hair, feeling the length of the strands. Her eyes were glued to the lock of hair tied to the pocket watch. It was brown and wavy. Her breath caught in her throat when she found what she was feeling for. A chunk of hair was snipped short at the back of her head.

CHAPTER 18

⁎

The map grew warm in her front pocket. Images of the Wardens and the murdered guards flashed across her mind's eye.

"Sir Wigginsworth, come!" she demanded.

The cat meowed and pranced across the bathroom tile to her side. She slammed the bathroom door shut and leaned against it, adrenaline pumping. Her mind raced—*am I alone in my room? Is one of my guards working for the Wardens? Is the queen safe? Are Mack and Luke safe? Where is Cadmus?*

The solitude she had been enjoying a just moment ago now terrified her. But the thought of surrounding herself with people was equally unnerving. The possibility that anyone could be a traitor eroded her confidence in her alleged allies.

Her heart continued to pound, threatening to leap out of her chest. Now more than ever, she was thankful her brothers had accompanied her to Praxis. At least she knew she could trust them. Reason prevailed over her whirlwind of emotions and she considered her options. *I won't be able to escape my room without the guards tailing me.*

Remembering the laundry chute Queen Oleksandra had shown her, Lucy summoned her courage and acted on an impulse plan. Scanning the room again, half-expecting to discover someone watching her, she pushed open the hidden entry to the chute and slid inside. It was dark and steep. Holding her breath and squeezing her eyes shut, she folded her arms over her face to protect herself and let go, sliding into the blackness below.

She shot down the chute like a toboggan on ice, eyes closed and heart racing. Seconds later, she popped out of the chute and skidded to a stop along a dark stone floor, her landing cushioned by a mound of dirty laundry that clung to her as she slid.

Breathless, she wrinkled her nose at the sour smell, but disciplined herself to remain still. All other senses deferred to her hearing as she listened. Her heartbeat drummed against her brain and her eyes took their time adjusting to the darkness. Somewhere in the room, the splat of a drip was steady and soft. Nothing else stirred. She counted to sixty as she lay in stillness, willing her thunderous heartrate to subside and anticipating the noise of an enemy close at hand. None came.

Thump. Thump. Thump. The thudding of her heart was the only noise vibrating her eardrums.

At last, her vision accommodated the darkness and she

slowly pushed herself to her feet atop the pile of dirty laundry. As far as she could tell, she was alone. A small set of steps led up to a barred and bolted wooden door wrought with iron bars. Based on its positioning, she assumed it led to the outside. Against the adjacent wall, three large woven baskets brimmed with balled-up sheets and clothes. Next to them were six smaller baskets stacked with neat, folded linens and garments. Lucy crept across the room to the wall opposite the wooden door, where an open arched entryway spilled indistinct gray light into the space.

Based on the amount of time she'd spent sliding down the chute, she guessed she was either on the main floor or beneath it. Despite an innate fear of the unknown and her surging adrenaline, she hoped she was in the dungeon beneath the castle. Whoever painted the sinister message on her bathroom mirror was no friend, but curiosity still gnawed at her. Lucy wanted to know what secrets the dungeon held. Cadmus had mentioned that his predecessor was imprisoned there, but aside from that, she knew nothing about what may await her should she stumble upon it.

Edging up to the arched entryway, she peered around the corner. A dim, empty service hallway stretched in both directions, a closed wooden door sealing each end. She decided to try the right side first. She crept down the narrow passage and twisted the cold iron knob. It was locked. Tiptoeing to the opposite end, she was rewarded when the second door opened at the slightest touch.

The door let out a loud creak, which reverberated through the torch-lit stone tunnel beyond. Lucy froze. Her heartbeat in her ears was thunderous in contrast with the hollow silence that followed the creak. Certain that someone would appear at any moment, Lucy braced herself. The seconds ticked away and she found herself alone with the flickering torchlight.

She moved forward into the cold tunnel, unable to make out how far it stretched ahead. A carved hollow in the stone wall materialized on her left side, opposite a torch. She gathered her courage and peered into the deep recess. It was a barred cell.

"You must be Lucy Barnes," a low, scratchy voice rasped from within.

Lucy jumped back in surprise, squinting into the hollow to discern the prisoner. He made it easier for her by scuffling from the back of the cell up to the bars. Gripping one bar in each skeletal hand, the man ogled her with chilling black eyes and a yellow-toothed grin. His black hair was matted and thin, and his face was sharp-edged with bones and bristling with mangy scruff. Lucy cringed at the sight of him.

"I thought I might be meeting you soon," he continued.

"Who—who are you?" Lucy asked, finding her voice. She glanced left and right. There was no one else in sight.

"The guards are probably off sleeping somewhere," the gaunt prisoner muttered. "Lazy, worthless dimwits. Ah, but how rude of me." He grinned, tucking his chin in mock humility. His crazed black eyes seemed to swallow her in their soulless scrutiny. "I am Fagen Swiltering, the rightful leader of the people of Praxis. I'm sure by now you've met Cadmus, the imposter who my foolish people appointed as their leader following my wrongful imprisonment."

"I know him," Lucy stated, taking a step back to put more distance between her and the dreadful man.

"You see, I was accused of conspiring against Praxis. In reality, I am the only one with the sense to do what's right for Praxis. I have a vision I call Pure Praxis, where all evil is eradicated and the people can live in harmony with nature." He raised a claw-like hand. "You'll notice that the other clans do nothing but cause problems for the humans. I was the first leader of the people to stand up for our clan! I had a plan to make Praxis a beautiful place where we never had to live in fear again..." He trailed off, his eyes unfocused, as if contemplating some far-off vision.

"I see," Lucy murmured, uneasy. "Well, it was good to meet you Fagen. I must be going now." She started to turn.

"Wait! There's more. You would be very, very interested to meet the man imprisoned just over there." He pointed to the cell next to his, breaking into a wide grin and letting out a maniacal laugh. The throaty cackle echoed off the shadowy stone walls, reverberating down the tunnel and back to her ears, overlapping with previous echoes. The auditory effect was unnerving.

Shuddering, Lucy indulged her curiosity and peered into the cell beside Fagen's. It too was shrouded shadow. She could make out a larger figure huddled in the back corner. "Hello?"

"Hello," a deep voice replied. The man stood and lumbered to the front of the cell, stepping into the flickering torchlight. He was tall and thick, with tree trunk thighs and hands the size of bread loaves.

"Hello." Lucy's reply was meek and felt insubstantial as soon as it left her lips. Fagen had stopped laughing, but she could still hear his raspy breathing. He was listening. "My name is Lucy Barnes, and I'm the Mapkeeper of Praxis. I was told you might be of interest to me."

The prisoner's glossy eyes were deep and sad, and his face was vaguely familiar. Noting his broad, hairy arms, another memory was triggered. She was sure she'd seen this man before.

"Oh, nice to meet you," he intoned without emotion.

"Um, well, may I ask who you are?" she prompted, wringing her clasped hands. The feeling of utter vulnerability was creeping over her, leaving her nerves on edge.

His look of dejection deepened. He stared at the cold, rocky floor as though contemplating the answer to her question. "Well, I guess you could say I am Aodhan Orman."

"That's it! You were the thirty-fourth Mapkeeper! I knew I recognized you from the wall of portraits. But doesn't a Mapkeeper have to..." She trailed off, unsure of how to phrase her question.

His glazed, chestnut brown eyes met hers. Like an unstitched cloth puppet with some of its stuffing yanked out, the man's build was smaller and less brawny than it had been in the portrait.

"Die before turning over to a new Mapkeeper?" He finished her question and sighed. "Yes, that is true. That's why I am only "kind of" Aodhan Orman."

"I'm confused," Lucy admitted with a clipped, nervous laugh. She glanced left and right, paranoid that someone might pop out of the shadows and attack her.

"Understandable. I guess you'll want the whole story, then." He seemed to possess a peculiar lack of emotion.

"If you don't mind." Unlike Fagen, Aodhan did not frighten her. She found herself pitying him.

"I am not the original Aodhan Orman. The original Aodhan Orman is in fact, deceased. He passed away in your world, as I'm sure you have been told. I am a replica of him. His genetic double."

Lucy's mouth fell open in surprise. "You're his clone?" Her brow furrowed and the man nodded. "But how—"

"I don't know how it happened. My head was bagged and I was dragged straight to this cell. I couldn't tell you who did this, or how. Or why," he added, his brown eyes sincere. "All I know is what I've overheard."

"Oh, wow," Lucy whispered. Fagen let out a high-pitched giggle. "Do you share Aodhan's memories?" she ventured.

"No," he replied. "I am a shell of a person," he stated in his matter-of-fact way. "While I have found that I possess the education and knowledge he had, I do not share his memories or emotions."

Lucy took a moment to let this revelation sink in. "If Aodhan was cloned, there may be others..." she thought aloud, scratching her head.

"I've had the same thought. I can tell you that as far as I know, the crazy man in the cell beside me is the only other prisoner in this dungeon."

"Who are you calling crazy?" Fagen barked. Lucy ignored him. Her instincts told her that Aodhan's clone was trustworthy.

"Hey, when did you slugs become so chatty?" a deep voice called from the darkness down the tunnel. Lucy whipped around and sprinted back the way she'd come, away from the voice.

"Ooh, the guards are coming, the guards are coming!" Fagen chanted, dissolving into a hysterical fit of giggles.

Lucy didn't stop to look back. Heartbeat racing, she sprinted back to the laundry room and up the stone steps, yanked the brace bar off the door and threw her shoulder against it. In an explosion of dust, the door shuddered open and she spilled out into a patch of dirt.

The sun glowed crimson on the evening horizon. Coughing, she picked herself up and shoved the door closed before running across the grassy field toward the front of the castle. The disturbing blood-red message on the mirror wouldn't stop running through her mind: *"Everything is not as it seems. The dungeon holds the answers you seek."*

CHAPTER 19

Central Square was abuzz with people and creatures in celebration of the Blossom Jubilee the next week. Shops were adorned with strings of bright flower buds and paper lanterns clung to lamp posts and eaves. The happy humming of conversation and laughter resonated throughout the town.

"The weather cooperated," Cadmus remarked, smiling up at the cloudless sky.

Lucy stood in the midst of it all, absorbing the cheer of the Blossom Jubilee. A group of fiddlers and an accordionist harmonized a cheerful jingle outside Emil's Clothier Shop. Women flitted to and fro wielding woven baskets brimming with tulips, offering the long-stemmed flowers to anyone who crossed their paths. Red, yellow, crimson, pink, and white flowers were everywhere.

"They're beautiful!" Lucy gushed, accepting a handful of

stems from a grinning curly-haired woman she recognized as Bernie Schuman.

"I guess the Blossom Jubilee is pretty cool," Mack admitted.

Arnold Brawne and his son Fritz had set up a stand outside their butchery, where they were cooking delicious-smelling meats over an open grill and selling skewered meat lunch plates. Lucy's mouth watered at the tantalizing aroma, but they'd already eaten lunch at the castle before coming to the festival. The queen had insisted, saying they couldn't chance someone trying to poison Lucy. Lucy was incredulous that she was in such imminent danger, but the queen wouldn't take no for an answer.

Now they wandered Central Square flanked by six armed guards. Lucy wasn't sure she'd ever get used to their constant presence. She was itching to tell her brothers and Cadmus about the message on the mirror. It wasn't a conversation she wanted to have in a public setting, but she was determined to find time to fill them in as soon as possible.

"Look, they're playing a game." Luke pointed to a group of children tossing a ball to one another in a circle. Beyond the children, Lucy saw Odessa and Auriel enter Central Square, their height making them impossible to miss. They were arm in arm, deep in conversation. Mack's attention was diverted right away. Lucy grinned to herself.

"There's Auriel and Odessa." Cadmus pointed. "Let's go see how Odessa is recovering. I'd also like to hear what she has to say about the encounter."

"Agreed." Lucy nodded.

As they made their way across the cobbled courtyard flanked by their entourage of guards, Odessa caught sight of them and redirected her sister to meet them.

"Odessa, how are you?" Cadmus reached out to give her a warm hug.

"Much better, thank you Cadmus." She had a raw slash across one cheek, and bruising that peeked out from under a scarf tied around her neck. Lucy noticed a smattering of bruises on her forearms as well. "These events must be kept private, if you would be so kind. Please don't tell anyone who doesn't need to know. In fact," she murmured, "let's go to the edge of Central Square where we can speak with privacy." The Bellaux sisters led their group to the edge of the courtyard.

"That's better," Odessa continued. "I'm sure you are wondering what happened in the forest."

"We were pretty concerned," Lucy replied sincerely.

"Yeah," Mack chimed in, glancing at Auriel.

"To tell you the truth, I'm not sure what attacked me or how I ended up in Abodox," Odessa confessed. "I have a vague memory of the kobolds guiding me, but I was so weary... so out of it... one moment I was walking along the edge of the forest, and the next I woke up at the entrance to the cavern."

Cadmus frowned. "You're sure you can't remember anything else? Not a single detail about what attacked you or how? I ask because we were attacked, too." Odessa and Auriel's expressions were grave but unchanged at the news.

"We heard," Odessa replied. "Zadok and Axel backfilled me after you left. I ended up spending the night in Abodox because by the time I had my wits about me, it was after sunset. And we all know you can't travel in the woods after dark."

"Did you get a glimpse of whatever attacked your group?" Auriel asked.

"They were dark hooded figures—I saw at least four of them, but there may have been more. They killed six of our armed guards and their horses. We escaped to the centaurs' cavern where Zadok offered us refuge."

"Wow..." Odessa whispered. The sisters appeared ill at ease.

"I thought Bellaux didn't go near the forest?" Luke asked the question that had been gnawing at Lucy's mind.

Odessa and Auriel exchanged an uncomfortable look.

"In general, we don't," Auriel affirmed.

After an awkward pause, Cadmus asked the obvious question. "So were you doing anything that may have caused you to be targeted, Odessa? I don't question your motives, I only want us to work together to defeat whatever is lurking in Doldrums

Forest. The more information we can compile, the better off we'll be."

"I know." Odessa brushed a silken lock of brown hair back from her fine cheekbone. Her clear blue eyes were troubled. "I was just out for a walk, enjoying the scenery. I know I shouldn't have gone near the forest, but I did." She glanced at her sister with guilt. "I'm sorry for it. It won't happen again."

"All the Bellaux are on edge," Auriel continued. "Odessa and I came to town not just for the Jubilee, but to see you and discuss what happened. We want to work together to defeat whatever those—things are. The others have been directed not to leave the Tree of Virtue."

"Well, I'm glad you came, and it's good to see you are doing better, Odessa," Cadmus replied. "You were in... quite bad shape when we saw you."

"Hello, all!" Enzo approached the group with a one of his fellow gnomes. Lucy noticed Odessa freeze, a flash of apprehension crossing her eyes before she forced a smooth, relaxed expression.

"Hello, Enzo. Hello, Bartimus." Cadmus greeted them.

"Ms. Barnes, brothers of the Mapkeeper, Cadmus, Odessa, and Auriel, good day to you all." Enzo appeared to be in a much friendlier mood than he had at the Council of Clans. "What brings you all together for a sideline discussion?" he quipped, grinning at Odessa.

Lucy and Cadmus' eyes met, alarmed that Enzo seemed to know that something was wrong with Odessa.

"Oh, just talking about what a great day it turned out to be for the Blossom Jubilee," Auriel fibbed.

"Oh, is that all?" Enzo pried, clasping his stubby hands behind his back and feigning innocence.

"Yes, that was all." Cadmus crossed his arms, frowning.

Something wasn't right between Enzo and Odessa, Lucy decided. She would talk that over with her brothers and Cadmus later. Glancing around, she caught a glimpse of Rhys skulking across the courtyard. He sported his usual ill-tempered grimace. No surprise there. *But why does he keep glancing over his shoulder at us?*

"We must be going now," Odessa muttered, staring at the ground. "It was nice to see you all, as always. Enjoy the Jubilee." Arms still linked, the beautiful sisters disappeared through an alley beside Alewife Inn. Mack scowled.

"Well isn't that a shame." Enzo's observation reeked of sarcasm.

"What's your issue with them?" Mack challenged the leader of the gnomes.

Enzo's eyes flashed as he whipped to face Mack. "None of your business, boy! Just know that many things are not as they appear to be in Praxis. More to the point, many *people* are not who

195

they appear to be," he corrected himself. "All I know is that the gnomes will fight tooth and nail against whatever dark forces are stirring.

"Everyone knows that beyond the Dour Mountains, the Dark Sea stretches on and on, and a distant shore has never been discovered. And beyond the meadows to the south lies the driest of wastelands, its endpoint unknown. Praxis is the only fertile, habitable land that we know of in our world. We must protect our homeland." He pounded a thick fist against his palm. "Cadmus, when the clans unite, count us in." He whipped around, clapped Bartimus on the back, and the two creatures strutted away on their stubby legs.

"Arrogant little guys," Mack observed, irked.

"That is for sure," Cadmus agreed. "But at least they're on our side."

"That's the most important thing right now," Lucy agreed. "If we're fighting each other, how can we fight the Wardens if they have, in fact, returned?" The thought sent chills down her arms. "Let's go mingle with the townspeople," she suggested, hoping to lighten the mood and enjoy herself for a bit.

"Just when I thought the quality of our company had gone downhill," Mack commented as they caught sight of Bade and his smirking sidekick marching toward them.

"Well, well, well. If it isn't the wonderful new Mapkeeper and her devoted entourage," Bade leered, pulling his cape close to his body as he joined them. His little companion chuckled. "They don't look too happy to see us, do they, Hobart?"

"No, they don't!" The short, freckle-faced man grinned.

"It's time to stop playing games, Cadmus." He looked right into Cadmus' eyes, his thin clumps of gray hair blowing in the light breeze. "You are ill-equipped to lead our clan if you think the best way to defend Praxis is to go around to the other clans begging for assistance. Further, your reliance on this girl's ability to wield the powers of the map is disturbing. It's time to grow up and face the facts." Bade leaned closer, eyes locked on Cadmus. "If you don't start taking a serious approach, there will be consequences."

"Are you threatening me, Bade?" Cadmus shot back, not backing down.

"I will do what needs to be done to protect our clan. And if you won't, so be it."

Bade whirled around and stormed off, his cape cascading around Hobart and tenting the little man inside. Hobart clawed at the silk, ripping it off his head and shaking his mop of curly red hair, trotting after Bade. The odd pair disappeared into the crowd of people.

Lucy struggled to control her anger. "Those two are infuriating!" She balled her hands into fists.

"I know," Cadmus agreed. "But don't let them get to you, Lucy. There's no point. We have our allies. Whatever Bade and Hobart are planning, we can't let it interfere with what we need to do."

"Yeah, and I bet Bade is just trying to scare us because he's jealous of Cadmus," Mack agreed.

Lucy tried to allow the music and sunshine to warm her mood, but dark thoughts and uncertainty plagued her mind. They wandered Central Square, attempting to enjoy the afternoon. No one noticed Luke was missing until nearly sundown.

CHAPTER 20

"I just don't understand where he could have gone," Lucy repeated for the third time, frustrated and desperate.

She sat next to Cadmus and across from Mack in the carriage, riding back to the castle. They'd searched for Luke until sunset, covering the whole town and even venturing into the fields outside town. No one had seen him. Their armed guards were a wreck, blaming themselves for letting him out of their sight.

"The Queen will fire us all," one of them had predicted.

By sundown, they'd called off the search and decided to head back to the castle.

"Luke's smart. He can take care of himself," Mack said in an effort to comfort his sister. His grim expression told her he was thinking the same thing she was, though none of them dared speak their fear aloud—could anyone really defend themselves against the Wardens? What if he was kidnapped... or worse?

The carriage bumped its way uphill along the Royale Byway toward the castle. They did not speak again until they disembarked at the castle drawbridge. Pip was walking toward them from the stable, haggard from a long day's work.

"Hey! I'm hungry, how about you lot? I wonder what Mom is cooking tonight." His good-natured chatter died when he noticed the looks on their faces. "What's wrong?"

"You haven't seen Luke, have you? We lost him today in Central Square. We haven't seen him in hours," Mack replied.

Pip's mouth fell open. "Oh, man. No, I haven't, I'm sorry."

Weary, Lucy took Cadmus' arm and walked across the drawbridge into the atrium. The hundreds of candles in the golden chandelier high above them were already lit in anticipation of sunset. Yet instead of the usual cheerful glow, Lucy found the dancing shadows on the round stone walls to be disturbing. The thought of her little brother in the hands of those creatures was nauseating.

"We don't know anything for sure yet, just remember that." Cadmus placed a gentle arm around her shoulders as they passed through the massive golden doors and trudged up one of the two matching wide spiral stairways. Lucy leaned on the carved wooden hand rail.

"Let's take ten minutes to wash up and then meet back in the Hearth Room," Cadmus suggested. Lucy and Mack agreed, parting ways on the fourth floor, each flanked by three guards.

Lucy was relieved to find Olivia waiting for her outside her room. She wasn't sure she had the courage to go back in there alone after the discovery she'd made in her bathroom. She found her room and bathroom spotless.

"Did you clean up in here?" she asked Olivia.

"Yes." The girl nodded. "Is it to your liking?"

"Oh, of course. Thank you so much, Olivia. But—when you cleaned, did you find anything, umm... unusual?"

Olivia seemed puzzled. "No, should I have?"

"No, no, I'm just—I'm just on edge with all the weird things that have been happening, that's all." Lucy chose a soft wool sweater out of her armoire and pulled it on over her head.

"That's understandable," Olivia sympathized. "I can't imagine how worried you must be about Luke. I overheard you talking about him being missing when you came in."

Lucy forced a grim smile to show her appreciation for the young girl. "Thanks, Olivia."

⁖

Helda brought three steaming mugs of sweet peppermint tea to the Hearth Room where Lucy, Cadmus, and Mack sat on the floor atop piles of cushions and blankets. Lucy was still chilled despite her oversized wool sweater and fuzzy socks. She pulled a fleece blanket tighter around her shoulders, thanking Helda as she accepted the large mug of tea.

"We'll have to reassume the search in the morning," Cadmus began. "I stopped in and spoke with the Queen. She has granted me permission to enlist the help of half the castle guards. We'll have them span the valley and even Doldrums Forest." The fire crackled, its light dancing in his eyes. His expression was one of deep concern. His presence comforted Lucy.

"I'll be up before dawn, ready to ride as soon as the sun rises," Mack said.

"Me too," Lucy agreed. Her heart ached at the thought of her missing brother. Helda had offered them bowls of beef stew, but they'd turned it down, unable to stomach food in their anxious state. Lucy hugged her knees, letting the warmth of the mug seep into her body through her hands. It was just hot enough to hold without burning her hands. The almost-painful heat was a welcome distraction from her troubled thoughts.

"There's something I've been meaning to tell you," she began, meeting Mack's and then Cadmus' gaze. "Yesterday around this time, when I went back to my room after meeting with Queen Oleksandra, I found something awful in my bathroom." They were rapt. "Sir Wigginsworth, the cat who lives in my room with me, was scratching at the bathroom door and making a fuss, so I let him in. Inside I found the jacket of one of our guards who was killed in the forest, and a message written on the mirror in dark red—it looked like blood." Cadmus and Mack ogled her, as shocked as she'd been upon discovering the mess.

"*What?*" Mack cried, "What did it say?"

"It said '*Everything is not as it seems. The dungeon holds the answers you seek,*'" she replied, bracing for the reprimand she knew was imminent. They would both be upset she hadn't told them sooner.

"Lucy, why did you wait so long to tell me?" Cadmus cried in disbelief, dropping the blanket he'd been clutching around his shoulders. "This is crucial! Was there anything else in the bathroom?"

"Yes," she continued, "there was a bronze pocket watch dangling from one of the vanity lights over the mirror. And there was a lock of hair tied to it with a piece of twine." She pursed her lips with guilt for not telling them sooner. In speaking it aloud, she realized how dangerous the situation sounded.

"What kind of hair?" Cadmus asked.

"Brown hair, slightly wavy," she admitted, clutching the spot on the back of her head where a lock of her hair was snipped short.

"Oh, no. You've got to be kidding me..." Cadmus covered his mouth with one hand, and then crawled around her to see the back of her head for himself. "*Your hair* was tied to the pocket watch? But how did they..." he trailed off, speechless.

"And you *slept in your room* last night?" Mack asked,

incredulous.

"I know, I know, it was stupid of me," Lucy admitted. "Really stupid. In fact, saying this all out loud makes me realize just how crazy I was. But at the time, I just didn't think it all through. And I had Olivia in there with me, plus my armed guards outside the door."

"Yeah, but someone had to get *inside* your room to write that message on the mirror and leave that stuff there. Lucy, this is bad."

"I know. But wait, there's more. I slid down my laundry chute because I was afraid someone was in the room with me—and I wanted to check out the dungeon without being seen going down there. Turns out the laundry room is on the same level as the dungeon." She grinned. Cadmus and Mack were not amused. "Anyway, I found the prison cells."

"You met Fagen," Cadmus anticipated.

"Yes, and there was one other prisoner. I think that was the one the message was referring to."

"There are two prisoners in the dungeon? I only knew of Fagen..." he rubbed his chin.

"Brace yourselves for this one," she warned. "It was a *clone* of Aodhan Orman, The thirty-fourth Mapkeeper!" No one spoke for a moment as her revelation sunk in. "I know. I couldn't believe it at first either. But it's true, I recognized him from the hall of portraits upstairs. He is a little thinner, but otherwise identical to

Aodhan. He said he doesn't know who cloned him or how, and that he doesn't share Aodhan's memories, just his intelligence. His only memories are of time spent in the cell in the dungeon next to Fagen. Fagen is crazy, by the way."

"Unbelievable..." Cadmus breathed. "This changes everything, Lucy. I think we may have a traitor within the castle walls. We've got to stick together from here on out. We can't trust anyone but the four of us. You, Mack, Luke, and me. Until we can figure out who is behind this." The mention of Luke's name was a painful reminder of their current predicament.

With a loud bang of the Hearth Room doors, Pip burst into the room and ran toward them, tumbling onto a pile of pillows in exhaustion.

"It's Luke—he's here!" he exclaimed, gasping for air.

CHAPTER 21

"I'm sorry, I'm so sorry," Luke repeated. They were all seated around the fire now—Lucy, Cadmus, Mack, Luke, Pip, Olivia, Helda, Quinn, Milo, and the queen. She'd made an exception and left King Muttongale's side to hear the story of what happened to Luke.

Relief had swept over Lucy like a tide of warmth when she'd embraced her younger brother ten minutes before. She had stifled a sob, unable to speak for several moments.

"I had no idea I would get separated from you guys or that you'd be so worried. It was thoughtless of me to go off with my new friends," he apologized. "I met them while you guys were talking to old Hamlin. They were two guys and a girl about my age, and we got to talking. Next thing I knew, you guys had moved on and I couldn't find you anywhere. So I accepted an invitation to go back to Grace's house for dinner. I am so, so sorry for all the worry I caused you all. I feel awful about it."

Mack smiled. He had chastised Luke at first, but now a knowing smile crossed his face. "Grace? I bet she's a pretty girl, huh, Luke?" he and Cadmus broke down in laughter. Luke blushed, defensive at first, but he soon broke down in laughter too.

Everyone else joined in, and the intense tension of the evening dissolved as they laughed together, warm and comfortable in the glow of the fire. In that moment, Lucy's heart soared.

※

Lucy was relieved when Mack insisted they all sleep in the same room from then on. Milo made accommodations for Mack and Luke's beds to be moved into Lucy's room since it was the largest. She slept in discontinuous fits, slipping from one bad dream into another. She was being hunted and chased through Doldrums Forest.

She rose before sunrise, unable to fall back asleep after a horrible dream in which the Wardens had brutally murdered her brothers. Mack and Luke's beds were set up on either side of hers. They both lay in tangled messes of sheets and blankets.

She made her way to the window and plopped down on the window seat to watch the sun rise. The first rays illuminated a heavy haze that clung to the valley and atop Glacial Lake. The resulting effect was a gray-orange glow. Praxis was still and quiet. The morning birds did not sing, and the horses in the stable across the field below made no noise. The air was heavy and still. The usual morning breeze was absent today. Leaves on the trees surrounding the castle property hung motionless. The stillness troubled Lucy.

At last Mack stirred, then sat up, stretching. Luke woke with some prodding, and soon the Barnes siblings were showered, dressed, and on their way to the stable to practice riding and archery.

The morning's stillness and the gray-orange haze persisted. Lucy wore a light jacket as she bounced up and down on her mare, practicing guiding the horse by its leather reins. Luke trotted behind her, while Mack urged his steed ahead at maximum speed. After two hours of riding, improving her form under Pip's expert tutelage, Lucy was feeling quite comfortable in the saddle.

Next, the Barnes siblings practiced archery at the range behind the stable. Lucy found she was not a natural archer, though with concentration and practice, she had shown great improvement. After many days of practice, Lucy was finally comfortable with the feel of the bow in her hand. She improved her speed, moving from draw, to load, to shoot in a single fluid motion. Mack, of course, was already nailing the bullseye as often as not. Luke proved to have a steady hand, and surprised himself with his own precision and accuracy.

When the sun was straight overhead in the sky, Lucy's stomach began to growl. She backfilled Luke on her discovery in the bathroom and her trip to the dungeon as they walked back to the castle for lunch.

Helda prepared a broiled meatball soup and served it with fresh baked bread and honey-glazed roasted vegetables. The

Barnes siblings scarfed their food, ravenous after a long morning outdoors. Though Cadmus joined them, the queen did not. Instead, she insisted upon taking her meals in the king's chamber. Lucy was beginning to worry about her.

"How were your riding and archery lessons?" Cadmus asked, pulling a chunk of bread off the loaf and mopping out his soup bowl with it.

"Great!" Lucy glowed as she recounted the morning, describing their new skills.

"That's wonderful! I have no doubt you are all quick learners. I've been doing some digging this morning while you were out," Cadmus revealed. He lowered his voice and leaned over the table so they could hear him. "I paid a visit to the dungeon, and Fagen's was the only occupied cell." His eyes narrowed. "I don't doubt that you met Aodhan Orman's clone, Lucy, but he must have been relocated. The guards claimed Fagen has been the castle's sole prisoner for over a year. Fagen went berserk when he saw me, shouting and screaming, so I was in and out of there as fast as I could.

"I also paid a visit to Queen Oleksandra this morning. The king's condition hasn't changed. I advised her to hold another Council of Clans as soon as possible. We can't wait for the Wardens to make their next move before we unite. We must come up with a plan together, or they will succeed in dividing the clans."

"What did she say?" Luke asked.

"She agreed. She sent messengers to deliver the word to the clan leaders just an hour ago. They will be invited to arrive at the castle at six o'clock tonight. I'm hoping this council proves more productive than the last one," he finished, taking a swig of sparkling pear cider.

"This time, I'll be ready," Lucy assured him.

※

Rhys was the last one to show up for the Council of Clans that evening. He burst through the Great Hall doors, distracted and frazzled—one eyebrow was singed and he couldn't seem to focus. He took his seat at the table between Bade and Enzo and across from Glump. They had all selected the same seats they had occupied at the last council. The tensions among the clan leaders were tangible. Lucy took a deep breath, steeling herself to be firm and resolute. From across the table, Cadmus smiled at her, making her feel strong.

Queen Oleksandra sat alone at the head of the table. King Muttongale's chair remained unoccupied as a symbolic tribute. Her face was thin and drawn, with dark bags drooping beneath each of her eyes. Her silver tiara combed her dark hair back so that it fell long and straight down her back. She wore a fitted deep purple silk gown.

"Rhys, we're glad you made it. The castle cooks have prepared a beautiful feast for us to enjoy, but first, we have urgent business to discuss. As we all know, Praxis is in grave peril. We can now say with near certainty that the Wardens have returned." A hush fell over the group. Lucy knew this, but hearing it spoken aloud underscored the urgency of the situation. "The Wardens are powerful and cruel. They will stop at nothing to gain control of the map and destroy us. The time has come for us to unite for the protection of our land and of all creatures of Praxis."

"Well, then, let's go around the table and see who's in," Bade interjected. "Let's see who's onboard and who isn't." He grinned at Cadmus, who was seated to the queen's right.

"I'm in." Cadmus' reply was firm.

Odessa and Auriel looked at one another then said in unison, "The Bellaux are in." Lucy found herself glancing at Enzo to gauge his reaction. He was smiling at Odessa. Lucy caught Odessa's eyes for a moment, but the Bellaux averted her eyes.

In his strong, deep voice Zadok stated, "The centaurs are in."

To Zadok's right, Glump rolled his eyes. "The goblins will protect Praxis. But we're not going to do any sort of team-building, happy-go-lucky type nonsense, so don't even try—"

"Are you with us, or against us, Glump?" Bade challenged.

Glump sighed, propping his hairless green head up with a claw-like hand. Scratching the inside of one of his long, pointed ears, he muttered, "We're in." His permanent sneer widened.

Adalia was quick to confirm, "The elves will join the alliance of Praxis." Her sharp green eyes flashed.

From the head of the table opposite the queen, Pip rolled his eyes, chewing on a bread roll with disinterest as the eyes of everyone around the table skimmed from Adalia, past him, and came to rest on Enzo.

"The gnomes will fight," Enzo declared, thumping the thick wooden dining table with a fist.

Rhys shrugged as the collective eyes of the clan leaders fell upon him. "Of course I'll do what I can to support, not that a single satyr will be of great use to the kingdom," he growled. Lucy leaned to peer past Mack and Luke, curious about Rhys' singed eyebrow. He took a large swig of hot mulled mead, clattering his metal goblet back on the table.

Bade was next, seated to the right of Rhys. "The trolls won't be easy to convince, but I'll do my best," Bade stated, pressing his long, thin hands together in front of him. "They will prove very useful to us in battle. They may not be the most intelligent creatures, but we all know trolls are ferocious in a fight."

"We will fight alongside you too," Mack stated.

"We've been learning riding, archery, and swordsmanship," Luke added.

Lucy felt the eyes of the group fall on her. She was the only one who hadn't yet sworn loyalty to the alliance. Forcing back a sudden surge of nerves, she stood to address the group.

"I too, have been practicing riding and archery, but I have also been practicing controlling the power of the map. I believe I have discovered the key to make it work for me, though I still have some tweaking to do." She pulled out the map and laid it out on the table before her, then clasped her hands in front of her.

Bade growled, brow furrowed over his dark, angry eyes. "Some tweaking to do? What does that mean, Ms. Barnes? Can you use the map, or not?"

In the pause that followed, she could hear her heart pounding in her ears. Cadmus opened his mouth to speak—likely about to defend her—but Lucy wanted to fight her own battle this time. "Yes, Bade, I still have some tweaking to do. But I know that I can unlock the map's power, and that's what matters."

"*That's it?* You don't have anything substantial to report? No quantitative progress?" Bade spread his arms in a gesture of disgust. Blood rose in Lucy's face. She focused, redirecting her embarrassment and anger to the map on the table before her. She would show them what she could do.

Tearing her focus away from her surroundings, Lucy began to trace her finger along the castle moat, a slow circle at first, then faster. The clan leaders were silent as they watched her. Faster and faster, she traced the moat in circles around the base of castle. The map infused with color and began to grow warm, swirling with animation and color, more alive than ever before.

The distant sound of rushing water from outside the castle walls permeated the Great Hall. Adalia and Zadok jumped up and rushed to a window, peering down at the moat below.

Wide-eyed, Adalia reported, "It's moving! The water is churning and flowing!"

Lucy did not allow the clan leaders' gasps to distract her. Channeling her emotion, she pressed hard as her finger reached the front side of the castle and traced a line straight up to one of the windows of the Great Hall, jabbing at the window.

With an earsplitting crash, a wall of water exploded through the stained glass window above Adalia and Zadok, surging into the Great Hall. Chaos ensued as the clan leaders jumped onto the table, toppling goblets and clawing at one another to avoid being swept off their feet by the violent, churning current of knee-deep water.

Her intense focus broken at last, Lucy jumped onto the table just in time to avoid being engulfed by the torrent of water. Mack and Luke were perched on the table beside her, mouths hanging open as they ogled their sister.

"Did you know you could do that?" Luke asked, eyes agog.

"I, uh, uh, whoa. I mean... um, I guess I thought, uh... no!" Lucy's heart was racing. The queen was standing on her chair, encircled by a tight throng of armed guards. The guards were knee-deep in water, clinging to her chair and one another to avoid being knocked down by the unbridled current.

A trio of guards clung to the table's edge just behind Lucy as well, ordered to protect the Mapkeeper at all costs. After the last council of clans, the queen wasn't taking any chances.

Zadok's reaction was swift when he saw the mass of water outside the window. He'd snatched Adalia up as though she weighed nothing and moved the side of the window, pressing up against the stone wall as the deluge of water broke through the glass. He shielded Adalia from the shower of glass when the window exploded.

Now the leader of the elves was thanking Zadok, helping him pluck out small shards embedded in his bare back. Everyone else ogled Lucy, shock written on their faces. She turned to gauge Cadmus' reaction. Crouched in a squat atop his chair, Cadmus' eyebrows were arched in genuine astonishment. When their eyes met, he broke into a wide smile and began to chuckle.

"You did it, Lucy! That was incredible!" Lucy smiled, his excitement rubbing off on her. He reached across the table and grabbed her hand, raising it high in the air. "Clan leaders, I believe now there will be no doubt as to whether Ms. Barnes is able to control the map!"

"*Unbelievable!*" Milo exclaimed from across the room, ankle-deep in the dirty pool of water. "This will be no small task to clean up." With a snap of his fingers, a team of castle employees appeared and began to mop up the water, wringing their mops into steel pails. "But it's nothing we can't handle, your majesty," he assured the queen.

Queen Oleksandra was helped down from her chair by one of the guards. She refused their offers to carry her so she wouldn't spoil her shoes. "Nonsense, it's footwear. It's meant to become dirty." She laughed. Her eyes sparkled with life and Lucy realized it was the first time she'd seen the queen smile since King Muttongale's attack. "Lucy, that was... shocking! But brilliant! You have exceeded our expectations, and in such a short amount of time. I have no doubt you will prove a legendary Mapkeeper."

Reaching over the table, the queen took Lucy's hand in both of hers. With a sobering, glassy-eyed sincerity that sent chills down Lucy's spine, the queen leaned toward Lucy and whispered, "Now, please do be *careful*, dear."

CHAPTER 22

"You were amazing last night!" Cadmus gushed, smiling broadly. He and Lucy walked together across the field outside the castle toward the row of trees beyond the stable that lined the cliff overlooking the valley. Lucy was elated, dizzy with excitement that she'd proven Bade wrong the night before. She'd shown that she could manipulate the power of the map in a big way.

"I didn't even know what I was going to do until it was happening," she admitted. "I just felt like if I channeled my emotion and focused about what I wanted to happen, I could use my touch to make it happen. And it worked!" she looked up at him, grinning.

"I have complete faith in you, Lucy. It won't be easy, but with all the clans onboard with the possible exception of the trolls, plus your mastery over the map, I think we'll have a good shot at not only defending ourselves, but at wiping out the Wardens for good."

They reached the tree line and broke apart to pass on either side of a tall evergreen. A short walk through the narrow yet dense plot of trees lining the cliff brought them to the edge, shielded from sight of anyone in the castle by the trees.

The view took Lucy's breath away. It was mid-morning, and the sun dappled the Dark Sea with dancing splats of golden light. The same light glistened off the milder waves of Glacial Lake, making it shine like a gemstone set in the middle of the soft green valley. The Tree of Virtue on its eastern shore appeared healthy, laden with a variety of colorful fruits and flowers. Beyond that, Doldrums Forest loomed dark as night.

Lucy could just make out the path they'd taken across the valley along Glacial Lake leading into the forest. She shuddered at the unwelcome memory of what she'd seen within. Across the valley, the Dour Mountains lorded over the valley, imposing as ever.

She inhaled the crisp, clean air, filling her lungs to capacity and holding it for a moment before releasing it. It was renewing. To the west, almost out of sight beyond the cliffside, Lucy could make out Rhys' hut on its outcropping overlooking the valley. She wondered if he was inside, concocting some fancy new potion.

"It's a gorgeous day." Cadmus crossed his arms and leaned against a tree trunk.

"It is," Lucy agreed. "It's hard to imagine that anything is wrong in Praxis when you see it from way up here. Everything seems so peaceful."

"I know."

They were quiet for a moment, soaking in the natural beauty of the land from their incredible vantage point.

"You know, the map doesn't just pick anyone to be its keeper." Cadmus faced her. "The original Wardens ensured that the map would only select keepers who were brave and pure of heart. Worthy of the position. You may not know it yet, but you're more courageous than you think. You shouldn't worry about what lies ahead. You will be equipped to handle it when the time comes." He took both of her hands in his, stepping closer. "And I'll be by your side the whole time," he added, looking into her eyes. Her heart hammered against her chest.

"I appreciate that, Cadmus. You don't know how much your support means to me. Thank you." She was entranced by the depth of his dazzling blue eyes. She leaned toward him at the same time as he leaned in toward her. His lips seemed to draw hers in like magnets, and she began to close her eyes as they came together, an instant away from a deep, passionate kiss. The map began to glow warm in her front pocket, but she was too engrossed to pay it any attention.

It wasn't until she was falling that she realized something wasn't right. Cadmus' warmth faded with an odd sluggishness from her hands, and all she could see was white—blinding white.

CHAPTER 23

*

Her hard landing was cushioned by something soft and cold. Blinking her eyes open, the first thing she noticed was the map in her pocket. It was hot—hotter than she had ever felt it! She snatched it out and tossed it to the side, where it fizzled for a moment, fine wisps of steam rising around it. The world came into focus around her and she became aware that she had landed in a large drift of snow.

Lucy shook her head and pushed herself into a sitting position with a groan. Her backside was tender from the fall. *What happened? Where am I?* Tall evergreens loomed high above her. The scene was familiar...

With a stab of panic, she realized where she was. She could just make out the tree line in the distance. Beyond it, the vague outline of a familiar single-story cherry log cabin peeked through the trees. She picked up the map, which was now cool to the touch, and slipped it back into her pocket, pushing herself to her feet and dusting snow off her pants and backside. She winced, irritated by the minor injury.

"Ahh!" She grabbed her head with both hands in exasperation. She pivoted in a quick circle, assessing her surroundings again just to be sure. With a groan, she admitted to herself that she had been transported back to Algid.

⁎

A dozen different thoughts vied for Lucy's attention as she made her way toward her house, cutting through the woods and keeping to the outskirts of town. How had this happened? What if she couldn't get back to Praxis? What if someone saw her? What time of day was it? She knew she needed to return to Praxis as soon as possible. They needed the Mapkeeper *now*. She formulated a plan on the fly as she trudged through the pristine, shin-deep drifts.

She slipped into her father's house, undetected as far as she knew. Of course, in the small town of Algid, one never knew who might be peering out their living room window, snooping on the neighbors for lack of anything better to do.

Luckily, her father never bothered locking the back door. Crime wasn't a problem in Algid, and the Barnes family didn't have much worth stealing anyway. She slipped inside and discovered that everything was as she'd left it. This did not surprise Lucy, as her father didn't spend much time at the house.

Breezing through the living room, she checked the clock in

the kitchen. 2:54. It was mid-afternoon. Her father would be hard at work at the shop, in the middle of reassembling an outboard motor or replacing an old oil filter. She needed to hurry—she was anxious to get back to Praxis.

Grabbing a duffel bag, she pulled open the chest of drawers in her room and stuffed it with a pair of jeans, a long-sleeved shirt, a sweatshirt, underwear, wool socks, a thick woolen hat, and waterproof gloves. She hurried back to the kitchen, where she slapped together two peanut butter sandwiches, bagged them, and stuffed them into the duffel.

Will Dad notice four slices of missing bread? She wondered as she rinsed and wiped the knife, putting it back in the utensil drawer and mopping the excess water out of the stainless steel sink with a rag. She filled her favorite stainless steel canteen with warm tap water and screwed on the top. In a cabinet in the living room, she grabbed a flash light and two spare batteries, adding them to the bag and zipping it closed.

Touching the outline of the map in her front pocket for reassurance, she slipped out the back door and grabbed the birch twig broom that Peter always left leaning against the back porch rail. High-stepping backwards away from the house, she swept over her footprints, masking them with a tousled layer of powder. When she was as far from the house as she dared to venture with the broom, she gave it a hard toss, sending it crashing against the side of the house. Wincing at the clatter, she looked around. Nothing stirred, so she turned heel and raced for cover among the woods, the duffel bag slapping against her thigh.

"Lucy! Lucy!"

She whipped around. Her father stumbled out the back door, striding toward her with such desperation that the deep drifts caused him to misstep and stumble.

"Lucy, oh sweetie, I missed you so much! Where were you? Where are your brothers? I've been worried sick!" He suffocated her in a long embrace.

Tears welled in her eyes and slipped down her cheeks as she hugged him back.

"Dad," her voice cracked.

"Where are you going? Come back inside!" He put an arm around her shoulder and led her back toward the house.

"I want to, Dad." She allowed him to lead her as she wiped her cheeks with the back of a hand. "But I have to go back to Praxis." She did a quick scan to make sure no one was in earshot. "There's a map, Dad, and it's a portal to another world. It took me and the boys to a place called Praxis, and they need my help!" she whispered.

Peter's eyes divulged his apprehension as he held the back door open for her.

"I don't know why I transported back to Algid." She set her duffel bag on the floor. "But I was going to try to get back to Praxis as soon as possible." She traced a circle on the floor with her foot. She couldn't meet her father's eyes.

Peter sighed. "I don't know what to say." He scratched his beard. "Are the boys all right?"

"Yeah, we're all fine. I know it sounds a little crazy, but just trust me. We have friends in Praxis and they will keep us safe."

The front door burst open with a startling bang.

"Move in!" A helmeted Commune guard with a large semi-automatic weapon held the front door open as he waved four more guards across the threshold.

"Ahh!" Lucy screamed as she jumped behind her father, who pushed her behind him.

"Lucy, run!" Peter directed, pointing to the back door.

She flung the door open and sprinted, pumping her arms. Her heart thundered in her chest. Hearing no one in pursuit, she paused halfway to the edge of the woods and looked back, still able to see through the open back door.

"Lucy, keep running! They took your mother, Lucy! Come to the Capital and find her! We'll be together again!" he screamed as four guards dragged him through the house and out of sight. Three more guards were making their way through the house toward the back door. She knew they would hunt her. She was their prey.

Lucy heard herself whimper as she whipped around and sprinted into the woods. She knew this part of the woods better than anyone, she realized, settling into a fast but rhythmic pace.

She needed to use that to her advantage. She cut left, then right, hurdling fallen trees and blasting through patches of supple saplings. She could hear the Commune guards shouting to one another in the distance behind her.

At last she came to the ravine known only to her, her brothers, and Drew. It was their secret hideout. She leapt over a large tree trunk and hopped between two patches of dirt to avoid leaving footprints. She slid down the snowy slope, making a clumsy landing in a crevice sheltered by thick, leafy fallen boughs. She scooted beneath the boughs, which provided a canopy that hid her from sight from above.

The guards' footsteps pounded nearer and nearer. They ran in step, their boots tramping in unison. They reached the point where she'd hurdled the fallen tree and the rhythmic stomping ceased. Lucy held her breath.

"Which way, sir?" a deep voice demanded. There was a minor shuffling of boots.

"This way!" came a gruff reply. The boots tromped eastward, fading as they ventured farther from Lucy's position.

Lucy put her head down and held her breath until the only sound was her heartbeat thudding in her ears. She allowed herself to breathe again, icy air funneling in and out of her lungs as tears trickled off her chin, dotting her pants with moisture. She didn't know how long she sat like that, but when she considered it, she sensed that it must have been quite a while.

Without meaning to, she pulled out the map and unfolded in her lap. It was instinctive. She didn't know why she'd done it, and she didn't care. She could barely process coherent thoughts, though her mind cleared slightly when she noticed a few of her tear drops had splattered against one of the bottom corners of the map. *What is that?* She leaned closer to inspect the partial imprint that had suddenly become visible through the moisture-saturated parchment.

Trod trod trod. She suddenly became aware of the distant, slow rhythm of footsteps. It was growing louder—someone was coming. She wiped her cheeks and folded the map, stuffing it back in her pocket. Then she froze, remaining as motionless as possible. *Did the guards split up to search for me?* The unknown individual drew nearer, closing in on her secret spot. Her heart raced as her mind whirred with terrible possibilities.

She held her breath when the footsteps paused. A thump signaled that whoever it was had just hopped over the fallen tree! Despite the cold, Lucy's palms began to sweat. Though her lungs began to burn, she dared not breathe. *Trod trod trod.* Three footfalls were all the warning she had before a body slid down the side of the ravine, skidding to a stop a mere arm's length from her concealed location.

CHAPTER 24

Lucy peered through the branches of her hideout, nerves on edge, ready to jump up and run. Instead, she was hit with a wave of relief when she recognized her visitor. She let her breath out with a whoosh.

"Drew?" She parted the branches and crawled out. He leapt out of his skin.

"Whoa!" He scuttled away from her, sliding on his back side and kicking with his feet. "Lucy! What the... where have you been?"

In spite of herself, Lucy chuckled, wiping tear streaks from her cheeks. "Sorry for scaring you," she whispered, grinning. "It is so good to see you. But listen—before I explain anything, we need to go back inside the hideout." Her eyes narrowed. "There are Commune guards looking for me."

Drew's eyes darkened. He held back the branches as she slipped inside ahead of him, and then followed her inside. He settled against the rocky embankment across from her.

"Hey!" She beamed, thrilled at the unexpected chance to see him.

"Were you at the Capital? And where are your brothers? Everyone at school has been talking about it." He pulled his legs up, clasping his hands around his knees.

"Drew, I really want to tell you everything, but I'm so afraid..." Her eyes welled up again and she glanced through the barrier of limbs, scanning for signs of movement outside their sanctuary. "They took my dad!" Her voice cracked.

"Oh my gosh!" He grimaced, his face distorted with emotion. "I'm so sorry, Luce!" He crawled across the base of the ravine beneath the tree limb shelter and scooted up beside her, putting an arm around her.

"I came home and was telling my dad everything when all of a sudden, five Commune guards burst through our front door and grabbed him. I ran, but when I looked back, my father cried out that my mother was taken too..." Her voice cracked again. She drew in a ragged breath, holding back a torrent of tears. "...and that she's in the Capital. He said to come to the Capital and we'd all be together again, but..." She paused, unable to go on without breaking down in tears.

"It's okay if you can't tell me," he insisted. She looked into his brown eyes, which were framed by stray locks of tousled hair. Her chest tightened as she realized how much she'd missed him. "I am so sorry, Lucy. Please know that I'm here for you, no matter what."

She drew in a shuddering breath, calmed by his presence. Her mind spun with conflicting emotions: fear of the Commune guards, terror at what they might do to her father, desperation to return to Praxis, and elation to be with Drew. "I'm a mess," she confessed, wiping a tear away. "I feel like my life is spinning out of control!" He nodded and tightened the arm he'd draped around her shoulders, his dark eyes filled with concern.

"Do you want to come back to my house for a little while?" Drew offered. "I was just coming out here to be alone and think. This is kind of my hideaway... and home base, of course, when Mack and I are adventuring or hunting in the woods." He grinned, flashing his handsome smile.

"I would love to, but I can't be seen," she replied, her breathing steadier now. "I'm not supposed to be back in Algid right now. In fact, I'm leaving again as soon as possible." Her heart constricted, sensing his disappointment. "Not that I don't want to spend time with you," she bumbled, trying to explain without revealing anything of substance.

"It's okay, I understand." He squeezed her in a one-armed hug. "You don't have to explain." Despite his kind words, his eyes revealed his dejection. Guilt and frustration seared through her like a white-hot spear, making her chest constrict. Overwhelmed, she didn't realize the ravine sanctuary around her was fading until she felt the familiar falling sensation.

CHAPTER 25

* * *

She landed with a painful thud in the same field as when she'd first transported to Praxis. She lay there for a moment, exhausted with emotion. She allowed the pain of the fall to radiate from her back side up to her neck and down her legs, feeling it without reacting. She didn't have the energy to acknowledge it. Without emotion, she noted the heat of the map burning inside her pocket. She just lay on the grass, splayed out in pain, trying to focus on the darkness of the inside of her eyelids instead of the anger, sorrow, confusion, and fear that wrenched her heart.

After several minutes, she sat up and opened her eyes. She could see the clock tower and the thatched roofs of houses in the distance. Beyond that, from its lofty hill, Tropos Castle loomed over the village. She sat for a moment, alone in the middle of the grassy field. Her roiling emotions dwindled into a flat-line sensation of dullness. Sighing, she willed herself to stand and acknowledge that she had responsibilities to fulfill. She began to trudge in the direction of the village.

A train of new thoughts troubled her, adding to her list of fears. *Why did the map take me home to Algid? What if it happens again?* She entered town at the opposite end of the road from Central Square, trudging down the cobbled street past charming shingled houses toward the clock tower.

Her pensive state of mind fizzled as an unsettled feeling washed over her. It was broad daylight, but not a single soul walked the streets of town or peered from a window. In fact, she realized with a chill, all the windows were shuttered and all the doors were closed. She glanced around, slowing her pace. Something wasn't right.

Suddenly fearing for her safety, Lucy slipped between two cottages and found a spooked horse tied up in a back yard. She pulled a thick riding blanket off a peg and threw it over the horse's back before untying the animal. Its eyes were wide and wild as it pawed the dirt.

"Whoa, girl. Easy," she cooed. She didn't bother trying to find the horse's owner to ask permission to borrow it. In addition to the intuition that she needed to get to the castle as soon as possible, she could tell that no one was around. The village was a ghost town.

She unlatched the waist-high wooden gate. *I'll send the horse back fed and watered later*, she reasoned as she mounted the jittery animal.

"I hope my riding lessons at the castle pay off," she muttered to herself. Tugging the reins, she guided the horse out of its pen and wedged her heels into its sides, urging it into a gallop across the meadow toward the winding Royale Byway that led up to Tropos Castle.

She did not encounter a single soul as she sped toward the castle. The apprehension that she could be attacked at any moment grew with each passing minute. She urged the horse onward, pushing as fast as she dared without risking exhausting the poor thing before she reached her destination. At last, she rounded the final bend in the road and emerged from the tree-lined road. She allowed the weary steed to slow to a trot as she crossed the field in front of the castle.

Shielding her eyes from the sun, she squinted toward the stable. There was no sign of Pip, Quinn, or any of the other stable hands. The castle drawbridge was raised in its usual upright position above the moat. Helmeted guards stood watch on either side. Relieved to see human life at last, Lucy willed herself to relax a little bit, though her nerves were still taut with foreboding.

"Who goes there?" One of the guards challenged her as she trotted to a halt across the moat.

"Lucy Barnes, Mapkeeper of Praxis," she responded with confidence. *Do they not recognize me?* she wondered.

The two guards exchanged a glace. The one who had addressed her continued, "What are the names of your two brothers?"

"Mack and Luke," she answered with a twinge of uneasiness. *Why are they testing me?*

The guards nodded and lowered the drawbridge, which moaned in protest. A single stable hand scampered out from within the castle and took the reins from Lucy as she dismounted.

"I borrowed this fella from someone in the village," she began to explain, but was cut off by the wide-eyed boy.

"I'm sorry, miss," he interrupted, "but I've got to hurry. There's no time to lose!" He hopped up onto the tired horse and dug his heels in, taking off toward the stable.

Lucy shook her head in confusion, hurrying across the drawbridge and through the atrium's gold doors, which were guarded by two more sets of armed sentries. *Where is everyone?* she thought with a chill of uneasiness.

She rushed to one of the wide spiral stairways, leaping up the steps two at a time. To her irritation, four guards tailed her.

"Where is the queen?" Lucy called over her shoulder.

"She's still in the king's chamber, Ms. Barnes," one of the guards stated.

Lucy ran all the way up to the fifth floor, grateful that she was in good enough physical condition that she didn't need to stop to rest. The guards struggled to keep pace in their heavy armor. She did not slow to wait for them at the top landing, jogging straight to the king's chamber and pounding three times on the door. A golden peep-hole plate slid aside and a magnified eyeball ogled her from within.

The thud of a deadbolt and the click of a latch signaled her acceptance. She hurried past four more guards, her chest heaving. The queen jerked around at the sudden noise.

"Queen Oleksandra!" Lucy exclaimed, flooded with relief at the sight of a familiar face. The queen's eyes were dark and sunken. She looked thinner than when Lucy had seen her last. *Has she even left the king's side?*

"Lucy," the queen murmured as she reached out to her, the sleeve of her robe falling to her elbow to reveal a thin, pale wrist. With her other hand, the queen clung to the king's limp hand, which poked out between bed sheets. "Oh Lucy, I'm so sorry. I'm so, so sorry." The queen's face crumbled in sorrow, her brow furrowing and her eyes pooling with tears.

"What is it, your majesty?" Lucy fell to her knees by the queen's side, grasping the queen's free hand in both of hers. "What happened?" Her mind raced, trying to stay ahead of a growing sense of panic. The queen's skin was dull, reflecting the gray light of the shadowy, stuffy room. King Muttongale's ailment seemed to fill the room like a dismal haze, permeating the corners and swallowing everything and everyone in the vicinity. It was as though the queen was becoming part of the chamber.

The queen lifted her downcast eyes to meet Lucy's. They shone as a tear dripped down her hollow cheek. Her voice wavered and broke as she whispered, "They're dead. They're all dead."

CHAPTER 26

Lucy's stomach dropped. "*Who* is dead, your majesty?" she demanded, tugging on the queen's hand, terrified to her core of the answer.

Queen Oleksandra's eyes were dripping now, steady rivers of tears that flowed down her cheeks, slipped under her chin, and dampened the collar of her robe. Lucy fought back an upwelling of panic in her throat.

"The villagers, the elves, the centaurs, the Bellaux... they're all dead, Lucy." The queen rocked back and forth as she spoke, her knuckles white against her vise grip on Lucy's hand. A gaping hollow of shock formed in her stomach.

"The Wardens launched a massive attack before daybreak. First, they slaughtered the elves under the cover of Doldrums Forest. The poor creatures never saw it coming," she muttered, her voice catching like gravel in her throat.

"It is rumored that before the army of Wardens were discovered by the castle sentries, they came upon and killed a group of centaurs on patrol in the forest. They emerged from the forest like a solid black line, an army so large they are believed to outnumber the humans two to one. They made their way across the valley to the Tree of Virtue, which they burned to the ground. They killed so many... so many Bellaux..." the queen's mouth hung open as she stared into space for a moment, losing herself in the mental images conjured by her own words.

"I am told the Warden army was so great that it spanned the entire valley," she continued after several tense seconds. "There were still Wardens marching out of the forest as the Tree of Virtue was being burned, clear across the valley near Glacial Lake."

Lucy's heart thundered as she processed the information, her mind working at lightning speed. She willed her overactive mind not to leap ahead. She needed to let the queen finish, even as she struggled to control the rising nausea in her esophagus.

"It was worse than a nightmare. They marched into the village, where people were in a frenzy. They used dark arts to kill... the people had no chance to defend themselves. No chance to survive. Meanwhile, the castle was making preparations to defend itself. We sent a large contingency of guards to defend the villagers, but by the time they made it to town it was too late. The massacre was over and the Wardens had retreated back across the valley and were disappearing into Doldrums Forest."

"Your majesty," Lucy interrupted, taking advantage of a pause in the story. "This is such terrible, awful news, and I cannot express how sorry I am that I was not here to help. I am so, so sorry." She looked the queen in the eye, both of them crying rivers of tears now. "But your majesty," Lucy whispered, "what about my brothers and Cadmus? Where are they?" Her voice trailed off, weakening as she spoke the question whose answer she most dreaded.

"Oh, Lucy, I'm so sorry." The queen burst into massive sobs, the force heaving her shoulders. Lucy felt as though she'd been punched in the gut. She fell back to a seated position, staring at the queen in disbelief. "They—they went out with the guards," Oleksandra sobbed. "They were so brave, Lucy. They had their bows and quivers, and they dressed in armor from the castle armory before they set out. But... they never returned." The queen wept and clung to her husband's limp hand.

Lucy's mind raced. "Your majesty," she began, talking over the sobs, "certain things don't seem to add up. When I walked through town, it was deserted, but there were no signs of a struggle, and no bodies. When the Wardens killed the guards in the forest, it was a gruesome killing. How did they manage to slaughter so many people without spilling any blood?"

The queen wiped her bloodshot eyes and squinted at Lucy, her sobbing slowing as she listened to the Mapkeeper.

"And another thing—if the Wardens want to take control of Praxis, why would they attack the elves, the centaurs, the Bellaux, and the people, but stop short of raiding the castle? Why would they retreat after attacking the village?" Her heart was still pounding in terror, but she was certain that the queen didn't have the full story. "Your majesty, if I may ask, who reported all these things to you?"

The queen's sobbing had stopped. "Well, my personal guards, of course," she replied. "Are you suggesting that they lied to me?" The queen's tone was not indignant, but fearful.

"I don't know, your majesty. All I know is that the story doesn't add up. Something is wrong—I can feel it—but I've got to get the full story before I act." Lucy stood, touching the outline of the folded map in her front pocket. "And the truth is, your majesty, I don't know who to trust anymore."

Glancing at the guards who stood watch at the entrance to the chamber, Lucy took off running in the opposite direction across the room.

"Hey!" one of the guards called.

"Wait! We're under strict orders—"

Before he finished his sentence, Lucy slid feet-first into the laundry chute across the room, glancing back at Queen Oleksandra as she disappeared into the chute. The queen's mouth fell open in shock.

Lucy felt sorry for the woman, but she knew she had to get out of there. She was certain that the queen would be dead by now if that was what the Wardens wanted. The fact that she was still alive meant she was most likely safe as long as she remained at the king's side, which Lucy had no doubt she would.

This chute was longer than the one she'd slid down from her own room, and just as dark. She spilled out into the familiar laundry room in the castle basement. This time, there was no time to lose. The guards would be coming for her. At this point, she was certain of only one thing: that she could not trust anyone within the castle.

Scrambling to her feet, she ran to the little wooden door that led outside. The brace bar she'd removed last time she was here had been replaced. Yanking it off, she threw her weight against the door like she had done before. She managed to ram it open on her first try, falling to her knees in the dirt. Jumping to her feet and slamming the door shut behind her, she took off running toward the grove of trees behind the stable where she had almost kissed Cadmus.

Tucked behind the safety of the tree line, she allowed herself to catch her breath. *I have to keep moving*, she thought. The guards would find the brace bar on the floor of the laundry room and know she'd made it outside. Not knowing where to go next, Lucy pulled out the map, hoping it would help her think. She needed to come up with a plan.

To her surprise, it was warm and glowing. She scanned the map. The village was deserted, but the castle was abuzz with little cartoonish guards trotting the halls in pairs. They were searching rooms—*looking for me*, she thought with a prickle of fear. Queen

Oleksandra was labelled beside King Muttongale's bed, right where Lucy had left her. That was no surprise.

Prince Puck was in the dungeon with six guards. Lucy hesitated, considering what business he might have in the dungeon. It struck her as an odd place for the prince to be found.

Desperate to find her brothers or Cadmus, she continued scanning the map. Rhys was in his lab beneath his hut, mixing a vial of something green with a flask of something purple. It fizzled, little cartoon bubbles bursting above the beaker. Trolls roamed the Dour Mountains, dragging clubs behind them, and a few gnomes were harvesting some sort of crop near the foothills. When she scanned Doldrums Forest, her eyes lit up and her heart began to race. Cadmus, Mack, Luke, and Zadok were huddled around a table together in a chamber inside Abodox!

CHAPTER 27

∗∗∗

I have to get to the cavern, she thought desperately.

Her brothers, Cadmus, and Zadok were the only ones she
believed she could trust. She scanned the map one more time,
searching for Wardens. There were a lot of different creatures in
the centaur cavern, she realized. But the Wardens were nowhere to
be seen on the map. Folding it up and returning it to her pocket,
Lucy trotted toward the stable under cover of the tree line.
Bending at the waist, she slipped out from the trees and crossed
the short distance to the stable, using it to block her from the view
of anyone in the castle. She entered through the back gate, which
was always open.

"Hey, what do you think you're doing?" Quinn shouted
from across the stable as Lucy grabbed the reins of the nearest
horse.

"Quinn, it's me—Lucy! I need to borrow a horse. I'll bring it back as soon as I can, I promise!" She rushed the horse out of its stall, threw a saddle on its back, and mounted it in a single swift motion.

"How do you know my name?" Quinn demanded from the middle of the stable, hands on his hips, blocking her exit. "I've never seen you before in my life, and you're not about to steal one of the castle's horses on my watch."

A chill ran down Lucy's spine once again. Something had changed since she left Praxis—she could sense it everywhere she went. Quinn would have remembered her, she was certain.

Pip peered out from one of the other stalls where he was re-shoeing a mare, his brown hair falling in strings around his eyes.

"Pip! It's me, Lucy. Tell your dad it's me, Pip, please! I have to go, it's urgent!" she pled with the young boy, but his stare was blank.

"How does she know my name, Dad?"

Lucy's blood went cold. They really didn't recognize her.

"Let's go!" she shouted, digging her heels into the horse's sides and flicking the reins.

"Gah!" Quinn bellowed as he dove out of the way of the galloping horse. "You won't get away with this!" he called after her. Lucy looked over her shoulder as she urged the horse across the field. Quinn was scrambling to his feet.

Leaning forward, she urged, "Come on, old girl, I need you to run like you've never run before!"

She blazed down the Royale Byway into town, traversing the grassy field behind the village instead of the paved roads. Slipping between two shingled houses, she crossed a street and emerged on the western side of town, galloping toward Rhys' hut. She didn't dare slow the horse, certain that Quinn or the guards would be tailing her soon. She thundered past Rhys' hut and down into the valley, skirting Glacial Lake as she pressed on toward the forest. She stole a glance over her shoulder. No one was following her yet.

She allowed the horse to rest, slowing to a trot. As far as she could see, she was alone in the center of the valley, not a trace of life stirring anywhere. Beside the path, Glacial Lake rippled, unsettled in the stiff, icy wind that blew off the Dark Sea to the north. With a shiver, she rubbed the horse's neck in gratitude as she scrutinized her surroundings. All her senses were heightened in her state of unease. Across the lake, she noted with horror that the Tree of Virtue was indeed reduced to a smoldering stump. She clapped a hand over her mouth. She'd been halfway convinced that the queen had been wrong about the Wardens, but this was proof of at least part of the story she'd told.

She continued across the valley without incident, though her utter solitude was concerning. *Shouldn't I have come across someone by now?* The horse walked now, the impressive, dark trees of Doldrums Forest looming just ahead. Every instinct told Lucy not to enter the dense, gloomy woods, but she had no choice.

She had to reunite with her brothers and friends. She became suddenly aware that she'd neglected to arm herself with a weapon before leaving the castle. *I'll be helpless if I am attacked*, she thought, cursing her own lack of foresight.

The forest closed around her as if clamping her in. She let her head fall back, amazed at the sheer height of the forest canopy. The air was cold and motionless in the shadows of the great trees. Strange scuttling noises and occasional low hoots were the only indicators of life around her. Lucy shivered, tightening her grip on the reins.

She pulled out the map and confirmed that the main path led to the centaur cavern. She was comforted to see the map was still animated, and that her brothers and Cadmus were still in Abodox with Zadok. The cavern was located off the path ahead—all she had to do was stay on this trail to get there.

Minutes passed, and nothing changed. The trees flanking the path all looked identical. Twice more she checked her map, tracking the progress of the little animated Lucy on horseback making her way toward the cavern. Reassured, she carried on.

The trail was wide but well-traversed. Between scanning her surroundings and checking the map, Lucy was careful to remain on the path. When another fifteen minutes passed and the scenery hadn't changed, her anxiety increased. The woods were darker now, and colder. She pulled the map out again, and to her dismay, discovered that according to the map, she hadn't moved since the last time she checked her progress. Her stomach sank.

Something wasn't right.

"Giddyup." She heeled the horse into a gentle trot. A bush quivered nearby—*just a rodent or a squirrel*, she reasoned. The path widened and opened into a circular clearing. Certain that this wasn't on the map, Lucy slipped it out of her pocket once again to examine her position. She froze when she saw two cloaked figures emerge from the shadows ahead.

"Whoa," she muttered, trying to calm the horse as it whinnied and reared. Whatever was up ahead had the horse spooked. Lucy's heart began to race and her throat constricted in fear. She jerked the reins, yanking the horse around to discover three more hooded figures pacing toward her from behind. Her heartbeat was in her throat now.

"What do you want?" she called out, her voice weaker than she'd expected. There was no reply. She couldn't make out their faces, but she was sure they were the same cloaked figures she'd seen in the forest before. Her heart raced in terror—she was surrounded, and they were closing in.

The horse reared again. Lucy clung to the reins, squeezing with her legs to keep her balance, but she was too late. She was thrown to the ground, her head whipping back and smacking the packed dirt. Brilliant flashes of light exploded all around her, obscuring her vision. The air was forced out of her lungs and she was paralyzed by pain, lying on her back staring at the black canopy of leaves high overhead. She couldn't breathe. The hooded figures entered her field of vision as the starry explosions of light faded. The creatures encircled her, leaning in as her senses weakened and the world faded to blackness.

CHAPTER 28

⁎

Lucy heard voices all around her. They were high-pitched and they seemed to be in the midst of a number of different conversations. Someone was laughing up ahead. Was she moving? She wanted to open her eyes, but her eyelids were so heavy. She was so weak... so exhausted. She couldn't focus on the conversations floating through the air around her. Every part of her body ached with throbbing pain. Her limbs felt weighted like lead poles. Someone was laughing again, a loud impish snicker.

Determined, she summoned all of her energy and lifted her eyelids a sliver. Through blurred vision, she made out a train of hooded figures. But they were not the same hooded figures who loomed over her in her last memory after being thrown from the horse. These creatures were much smaller, wearing colorful ragged cloaks and carrying staffs lit by glowing orbs. She was lying on her back, being carried on a litter. She struggled to turn her head to see who was carrying her, but the effort drained her and she succumbed to the darkness, her eyes closing as she let go. The voices faded into an indiscernible hum. She felt herself slipping back into blackness, where she wouldn't feel the pain...

CHAPTER 29

⁂

When she faded into consciousness the first thing she became aware of was the sound of voices. She was lying down somewhere, and two people were having a conversation in the room. She felt better. Stronger. Her limbs were still heavy, but the pain was more dull than before. She still ached from head to toe, and the back of her head throbbed.

"I think she's waking up," said a familiar voice somewhere nearby.

"Oh, good! Lucy, can you hear us?" another familiar voice asked.

She opened her eyes with effort. Two blurry outlines leaned over her in a chamber aglow with dim candlelight.

"Ahh..." she moaned, lifting her hand to rub her forehead. Her arm was heavy, as though it were made of stone.

"Lucy, it's us. You're safe now," the first voice assured her.

It took a few seconds for her vision to sharpen. She blinked twice and squinted, bringing the room into focus. She almost wept with relief to see Cadmus and Luke leaning over her. Cadmus put a hand on her shoulder.

"You've had a rough day," he joked, but concern deepened worry lines across his forehead. "You took a hard fall off your horse. You must be in a lot of pain. Here, drink some water when you can."

She tried to sit up, but pain shot through her back and down her right leg.

"Ah!" she winced and lay back down.

"Just take it easy," Luke said. "Try not to move too much."

"Where am I?" she asked, her mental fogginess fading. She peered around the room. It was all rock, a small cave with all the amenities of a bedroom. She was lying under a brown wool blanket on a cot against one wall. Luke and Cadmus sat on wooden chairs by her side. There was a wooden table on the other side of the room, and a small chest of drawers with a wash basin adjacent to her cot. The cave was dim and windowless, lit by four sets of wall-mounted candleholders. A plain woven rug covered a large portion of the stone floor.

"We're in Abodox," Cadmus replied. "Lucy, so much has happened since you've been gone. We have a lot to catch you up on."

She was so elated to see them, her heart felt as though it might burst. Tears sprang to her eyes. "I'm so happy to see you," she replied, grinning at Cadmus and Luke. "When I came back to Praxis, the village was deserted and the queen said you were all dead and—"

Cadmus placed a reassuring hand on her shoulder. "It's okay," he interrupted her. "It's okay. We'll talk later. For now, just rest. You need to get your strength back before we talk it all out. We're just so glad you're okay," he added, his eyes reflecting his sincerity. He took her hand and squeezed it.

She squeezed back, holding his gaze. "All right, but where is Mack? And how did I escape the Wardens and make it here in one piece?"

"Mack is with the others in another room," Luke answered. "They're planning. We'll tell you all about it tonight at dinner. And by the way—the kobolds saved you." Luke smiled and rubbed her shoulder as he stood. "For now, try to drink some water and sleep a little longer. You're not in the greatest shape right now, sis."

"What are kobolds?" she mumbled, her eyelids growing heavy and beginning to droop.

"They're little forest sprites who are known to be mischievous, but they are good-hearted and will help a creature in need. They have limited magical powers that deceive the mind. The queen of the kobolds, Cleo, informed Zadok that she cast a quick enchantment that tricked the Wardens into thinking that a forest buck was Lucy. While the Wardens chased the imaginary buck, the kobolds whisked you away and brought you here. They are the keepers of Doldrums Forest. At all times they know who is present in the woods, and can sense when creatures have foul intentions."

Fascinated but exhausted, Lucy allowed Cadmus to lift a bronze cup of water to her lips. She took a long swallow and then laid her head back down on the feather pillow.

"Cleo and the kobolds..." she smiled, closing her eyes. Sleep overcame her.

※

Six hours later she awoke feeling alert and well-rested. She was starving. She got up, stretched, and wiped her face and neck with a damp cloth that someone had left next to the wash basin.

Over a hearty meal of roast pheasant, boiled beet weed, and baked cinnamon-encrusted arrowroot, she was made aware of everything that had transpired during her time in Algid. She sat at one of twelve massive wooden dining tables in the Abodox dining hall, a huge natural cave opposite the entrance to the cavern. She felt like a child at the centaurs' oversized table. The centaurs sat on their plush elongated cushions, legs folded beneath them. They had comfortable cushioned chairs available for their guests. Lucy sat between Zadok and Cadmus at the table of clan leaders. Also present were Adalia, Odessa, Auriel, Enzo, Glump, Mack, and Luke.

Lucy wolfed her food, washing it down with generous gulps

of honeyed mead from a simple copper stein. The pheasant was hot, tender, and juicy.

"I could eat centaur cooking for the rest of my life!" she proclaimed. Zadok flashed an appreciative grin, scooping a modest forkful of arrowroot into his mouth. He was a genteel diner compared to his fellow centaurs at the next table, who ripped fistfuls of greasy pheasant off the bone with their bare hands. The other clan leaders at the table poked at their dinners with sullen disinterest. No one had much to say. Lucy could sense the intense melancholy of the group, though she didn't yet know the extent of the damages the Wardens had caused.

The townspeople sat at a third table, filing out as they finished their meals to make room for others. The elves occupied one of the other tables, utilizing a similar system to ensure everyone had a chance to eat. The gnomes crammed around the table furthest from everyone else, isolated in a corner of the cavern. The goblins chose the table in the opposite corner of the room from the gnomes. They growled and snapped at one another as they gobbled their food. A few Bellaux picked at their meals at a table beside the elves.

When the clan leaders had eaten their fill, the dishes were cleared and the honeyed mead replenished. Lucy was satisfied, though she dreaded hearing the story she knew was coming. She caught Cadmus' eye. He gave her a halfhearted smile and put his hand on her knee under the table. Her heart lurched at his touch. She covered his hand with one of her own, grateful for the comfort of his touch.

"Ms. Barnes, we will begin by filling you in on what has happened," Zadok announced, taking charge of the discussion. "Cadmus, I believe you were the last to have contact with the Mapkeeper before she was transported."

"Right," Cadmus confirmed. "Lucy, one minute we were standing together on the edge of the cliff overlooking the valley, and the next, you were glowing and then you disappeared into thin air! I had no idea what had just happened or where you went. Needless to say, I was worried sick." His eyes exposed the pain she'd caused him. She longed to explain that she didn't leave on purpose… that she still had no idea why it had happened. "I rushed back to the castle, but no one there had seen you. Before we could send out a search party, the castle sentries blew their horns. They'd spotted an army of Wardens emerging from Doldrums Forest in the valley."

"Unbeknownst to them at that time," Adalia interrupted, her eyes dull pools of bereavement, "the Warden army had already launched a surprise attack on the elves at our hidden tree lair deep in Doldrums Forest. This marks the first time in history that anyone, enemy or friend, has managed to penetrate the spells cast on our lair which make it impossible to find. They managed to kill nine elves before moving on," she finished, her face paler than usual. Like many others, Lucy noticed Adalia hadn't eaten much at dinner.

"On their way out of the forest, they came across a group of five centaurs on patrol. They too were killed," Zadok added, his hands balling into fists in his grief. Cadmus put a hand on his friend's shoulder, sharing in his anguish.

There was a moment of silence among the leaders, each absorbed in his or her own thoughts. Cadmus resumed the narration of the painful story.

"They emerged from the forest in vast numbers. We had no idea they had the potential to form an army this large. They filled the valley, a great black hooded throng. They made their way to the Tree of Virtue—" he paused, glancing at the Bellaux. They were pale, their expressions detached. Odessa had the vacant look of someone who had cried all the tears she had within her. Her face was drawn, her eyes dull and lifeless. She glanced up at Lucy, aware that her turn to speak had come.

"They burned our home. They surrounded us and torched our tree. We lost everything. Six of us managed to escape by jumping into Glacial Lake and swimming out as far as we could. The Wardens didn't follow us into the water. The rest of our sisters..." she stopped, choking on her words. "I'm sorry, please excuse me." She pushed back from the table, covering her beautiful face with both hands and running out of the dining hall. Auriel's chair scraped the stone floor as she scooted her chair back and ran after her sister. They disappeared, rounding the bend onto the main cavern footpath.

Lucy's heart broke for the Bellaux. At the table, no one spoke or even looked at one another. It was a moment of shared anguish. Even Glump had the decency to twiddle his thumbs rather than make a smart comment.

Sighing, Cadmus continued. "What the Wardens did was beyond awful. It was an attack unlike anything we have ever seen. After burning the Tree of Virtue, they stormed the village, where they began to gather up the townspeople. Men, women, children, it didn't matter. They did not discriminate." He met Lucy's gaze, his blue eyes strained with pain. Hot, silent tears slipped down her cheeks.

"By that time, the castle guards, your brothers, and I were riding to the village at top speed, ready to fight. But suddenly, the Wardens stopped the attack. The lead Warden, who is no different from the others by outward appearance, waved them off and they retreated back across the valley into the forest. We still don't know why they stopped. They were receiving very little resistance from the villagers." He pounded the table with a fist in anger. "If we'd gotten there sooner, we would have saved lives." His eyes watered. "They took a number of people away with them. The taken ones haven't been seen since."

Once again the leaders were silent. Lucy wiped tears from her cheeks. She found that she was as devastated as the rest of them. As the Mapkeeper, she was supposed to protect them, but she hadn't been there when they needed her most. *I failed them,* she thought with frustration.

"I saw them, you know," Lucy spoke up. "The Wardens had me surrounded in the forest. It was the strangest thing—I was tracking myself using the map, but I didn't seem to be making any progress along the trail. I knew you were all here because the map showed me."

Cadmus and Zadok appeared surprised.

"That's a useful tool," Zadok remarked.

"Yes, it showed me everyone's locations after I left the castle," Lucy agreed. "That's how I knew the queen's story wasn't the whole truth. She told me some of what you just told me, but she believes you are all dead. I think she's under some sort of spell. She refuses to leave the king's side, and she seems almost... weighed down by the chamber. She's not herself in there."

"I noticed the same thing before we left the castle," Mack agreed from the other end of the table.

"And the guards. I don't trust them," Lucy added. "In fact, I'm not sure who I can trust anymore, except this group."

Zadok met her gaze. She'd only spoken a partial truth. She never doubted Zadok's credibility, but there were others at the table that she did not trust. She eyed Glump. He was glaring at his hands, which were clasped in his lap.

Looking around the circle, she noticed several leaders were missing. "Where's Bade? And Rhys?"

"Bade left several hours ago, claiming to be going to the Dour Mountains to secure the allegiance of the trolls." Adalia muttered. "That was when we all met and decided that Abodox was the safest place for us. It's large enough to provide more than enough shelter for all the clans. The network of caves is so vast, it seems endless. We are very grateful to you and your clan, Zadok."

"It was the least we could do," Zadok replied, nodding.

"As for Rhys," Cadmus added, "we haven't seen him since the attack, though he has been the subject of several discussions. Some of the villagers claim they saw him whisper something to the lead Warden before the attack was called off. That is a grave accusation. I prefer to give him the benefit of the doubt, but if the accusation is true, it can be inferred that Rhys may be collaborating with the Wardens. We have been discussing and debating various theories as to exactly what role Rhys played in all this over the past few hours."

"It's obvious he's involved in some sort of foul play," Glump snarled. "He is seen whispering something to the head Warden and then without warning, the attack is called off. It doesn't take a genius to figure out why those creatures didn't chop his head off like they were doing to the rest of Praxis," he remarked, his tone dripping with sarcasm.

"On the map, I saw him working in his lab when I rode from the castle to the forest," Lucy added.

"He's probably helping them—making potions for them to use against us!" Glump shouted as he jumped to his feet. His standing height wasn't much taller than his sitting height. In his anger, his oversized, pointed green ears were tinged red at the tips. "I know some of you are thinking I shouldn't have a say since the goblins weren't attacked, but I signed on to this alliance, and I'm sticking to it. Just because our mountain caves weren't in the path of destruction doesn't mean the Wardens wouldn't have attacked us too, given the opportunity." He slid back into his seat with a dramatic swallow of honeyed mead.

Odessa and Auriel rejoined the table, their faces red and tear-streaked.

"You're as much a member of the alliance as any of us, Glump," Zadok assured the goblin leader. "But we can't jump to conclusions about Rhys. We need to speak to him ourselves. As a group."

"Agreed," Cadmus chimed in. "We must summon him to the centaur cavern to explain what happened for himself."

"I believe I can help with that," Lucy replied, pulling the map out of her pocket. She had a sudden idea, and she hoped it would work. The eyes of most of the clan leaders settled on her as she spread the map on the table before her. Some appeared skeptical, others hopeful, while some hung their heads in dejection.

She examined the map. "He's active on the map right now. If I can manipulate the map, I should be able to manipulate him, too."

"Like the water from the moat!" Mack exclaimed, grinning.

"Exactly," Lucy's eyes twinkled.

CHAPTER 30

⁘

She exhaled and focused on the crude sketch of the little satyr slurping soup in his kitchen. Drumming her fingers against his little hut, she willed the structure to tremble. As she focused on a specific portion of the map, like Rhys' hut, it became more detailed and animated before her eyes. She was pleased when pots and pans dangling from wall-mounted hooks in the hut began to sway and clang against one another. The animated satyr leapt up in alarm as the whole structure began to shake, his soup splashing out of the bowl onto the table. Lucy watched as Rhys struggled to keep his balance, bracing himself against the counter top as objects came crashing down around him. Drawing focus from her grief, she maintained her concentration. She drummed harder and harder, until he shuffled across the hut and burst through the front door, stumbling out onto the grass.

Lucy stopped drumming and pressed a firm finger against the front door of the hut, causing it to slam shut. The animation of

Rhys scratched between his horns and looked around, confused. His world had stopped shaking. He tested the doorknob, and finding it sealed shut, began to stomp and kick the door in a fit of anger. Unflustered, Lucy held the door shut.

The clan leaders leaned closer, fascinated to watch the scene unfold. Stamping in a circle and shaking his fists, Rhys shouted his rage at being locked out of his own hut. This elicited a snicker of delight from Glump. As Rhys stomped around to the back side of the hut, no doubt intending to test some alternate method of entry, Lucy released the front door and began to draw large, sweeping waves in the grass outside the hut with her finger. The land under Rhys' hooves began to undulate like waves on the Dark Sea. Losing his balance, Rhys slammed sideways into one of the shingled sidings of his hut.

"Whoa..." Luke murmured.

Lucy continued the steady undulating movements, but moved her finger away from Rhys so that the land was unsteady just south of him, while the land to the north remained stable. She slowly pushed the waves toward him. The satyr threw his little arms up in disbelief, spotting the force moving toward him in the form of waves through the earth. He stepped back toward the path that led into the valley, away from the waves. Lucy continued to move the unstable land waves toward him, herding him onto the path and down into the valley.

She stole a glance at her companions. In her concentration she hadn't noticed them gather so near. The clan leaders stood in a tight circle around the map watching her work, mixtures of amusement and utter wonder on their faces. Even Enzo, who had remained silent throughout the meeting thus far, couldn't hide the fact that he was impressed.

Lucy refocused on using the map to make waves in the earth, corralling the unwilling satyr into the valley and toward Doldrums Forest. She suspected that at this point, he might have figured out who was causing this to happen. After all, he'd witnessed her make the whole castle shake at the first clan leader meeting, and later, her incredible feat with the moat. Seeming to give up, Rhys cooperated at last, trudging down the path leading across the valley, past Glacial Lake, and into the forest.

She stopped making the land waves when he proved he would continue to walk without prodding. Even on the map, his detailed facial expression divulged his resentment, much to Glump's delight.

"Hee hee hee!" the goblin leader cackled, clutching his green pot belly with his claw-like hands.

When Rhys entered Doldrums Forest, the map lost all life and color. It reverted to its most basic form, with no creatures, labels, or animations. Lucy was at a loss, unsure of what caused the sudden and inconvenient change. She slammed a fist on the map in frustration, but it remained dull and unresponsive.

"I lost it," she said, her eyes darting across the map. "The map just fizzled out on me."

"Well, we know he entered the forest," Zadok replied in his calm, matter-of-fact manner. "I can send a search party to find him."

"No. It's not safe out there," Adalia insisted.

"We can't leave him on his own," Zadok countered. "I will send a group of armed centaurs. They will proceed along the main path to the spot where we saw Rhys enter the forest. If he is not found, they will return to the cavern straight away."

Lucy nodded, seeing no other choice. Zadok trotted off to pass his orders to Axel and Lance. Lucy was glad to see those two weren't among the centaurs killed in the Wardens' attack. They were gruff around the edges, but she liked Axel and Lance.

The clan leaders left the dining hall and went to their separate chambers to rest during this lull in the planning process. Zadok promised to send for them the moment his search party returned.

Back in the chamber where she'd slept, Lucy sighed, collapsing into one of the ceiling-suspended hammock chairs she remembered from their first visit to the centaur cavern. *That felt like ages ago*, she reflected. Mack, Luke, and Cadmus sunk into hammock chairs on either side of her. Zadok joined them, reclining on a cushion opposite Lucy.

"I'm glad it's just us for a moment," she admitted, "because I discovered something about the map that I want to share with you." She picked up a pitcher from the low table beside her and filled a tin cup with water. Pulling out the map, she sprinkled a few drops onto the lower right corner, smearing them with her thumb. She stood, holding the map up against the backdrop of one of the candelabras.

Luke gasped. "It's the Commune seal!" he announced.

"I know," Lucy replied. "I found it by accident when I... when my..." she hesitated, looking away. "...when a few tears spilled on the map back in Algid." She was ashamed, though she knew her brothers and her friends would not judge her. *I'm supposed to be strong*, she chided herself.

Mack put a hand on her back. "It's okay, Lucy," he reassured her. "This is all so much to take in, and you have been doing a great job. Better than I would be doing," he added, meeting her gaze with sincerity. She didn't think that was true, but her love for her brother welled up like a fountain in her chest, bringing tears to her eyes. She could only nod her thanks, looking down and dabbing the corners of her eyes.

"What does it mean?" Cadmus asked.

"Where we come from, everyone is governed by the Commune," Mack explained. "They regulate every aspect of our lives. But we were raised to be mistrustful of the Commune. Many people, including our father, have been treated badly by the Commune, but are unable to speak about it for fear of the Commune retaliating." Mack glanced at his sister, pain behind his eyes. She knew they were both thinking of their mother. It hurt just to think about her, let alone *talk* about her.

Lucy couldn't bring herself to tell her brothers what had happened to their father back in Algid. It was far too painful to bear, so she forced the memory from her mind in a concentrated effort to control her emotion.

"The Representative of the People, as he calls himself, was the one who had custody of the map before I took it," she spoke up, her voice wavering. "He is the leader of the Commune. And with the way the watermark Commune seal is blinking..." She held the map up to the light again so they could see the faint, blinking imprint.

"It looks just like the tracking devices they use in their ankle straps!" Luke finished her sentence.

"That's what I thought too," she agreed, "which is why I think the Commune has been tracking me since I took possession of the map." The thought sent a harsh shiver down her spine.

Mack's eyes were wide with fear.

"It has always been a power struggle for the map," Zadok sighed, scratching his chin in thought. "The position of Mapkeeper comes with much power and responsibility. But throughout history, there have always been those who envy the Mapkeeper... who want that power for themselves. This seems to me another example of someone trying to take control of the map."

"Yeah, but this time, that someone is pretty dangerous," Luke added. "The Commune is ruthless! They punish people for crimes they can't even prove were committed. Not only are they brutal, but their authority can't be questioned. As citizens, we are at the utter mercy of the Commune."

"If the Representative of the People can track you, I wonder if he's taken any other steps toward controlling the map." Cadmus asked. "Based on my research, the Mapkeepers of the past have been the only ones able to control the map. Lucy, you and I agreed that it's your ability to harness and focus your emotion that allows you to control the map. Can you think of a time when you tried to use the map but it didn't work?"

"Yes. When the map transported me back to Algid. That was unexpected and not at all what I wanted at the time. Do you think it's possible that Mr. Quincy has some sort of control over the map?" Her stomach tightened with dread.

"Anything is possible," Zadok replied. "But know that you are never alone, Lucy. We will fight by your side for what is right."

Cadmus nodded his agreement. "You are the Mapkeeper, and because of the original spell cast on the map, you are the only one with the ability to control it," he added. "You are Praxis' defender, chosen for your courage and purity of heart. I will fight to the death if need be to preserve you." He held her gaze as he spoke. Lucy's heart swelled with affection for him.

"I know you mean it, Cadmus," she held his gaze in the flickering light of the torches. "You are the truest allies I could hope for," she told her four companions, her courage renewed by their support.

The search party returned with Rhys in tow a half hour later. Zadok gathered the clan leaders back in the dining hall, which was now empty of guests. Everyone had gone back to their respective chambers to wait. An air of restlessness hung over the shadowy cavern as the clan leaders waited for Rhys to be brought in.

"Where's Luke?" Lucy whispered to Mack, who was seated beside her.

"I don't know. He was right behind me when we were coming into the dining hall. Then I sat down, and he was gone. Maybe he had to use the restroom."

Five minutes later, Axel came into the dining hall and addressed Zadok: "The satyr was brought inside the cavern and the main gate has been confirmed locked and bolted shut. But the little beast has run off. We can't find him. I have ten centaurs hunting him down now, sir."

The clan leaders erupted in tense chatter. Lucy could see that it hurt Axel's pride to have to report Rhys missing to his boss.

"All right, Axel, keep up the search. There's only one way in and out, so he's here somewhere." Zadok remained calm.

"Yes, sir." Axel trotted out of the dining hall, barking orders to the other centaurs.

"Would he run off if he were innocent?" Glump shouted

over the others. "This proves he's guilty of conspiring with the Wardens!"

Lucy was incredulous. Even gruff little Rhys wasn't evil enough to collaborate with those creatures... right? Her nerves were on edge. *Where is Luke?*

Pairs of centaurs trotted the cavern pathways, calling out to one another as they cleared caves and chambers on the hunt for Rhys. Their shouts and the heavy clopping of hooves echoed off the cavern walls, fading in and out of audible range as they traversed the network of interconnected caves.

In the midst of a tense silence among the clan leaders, Rhys and Luke walked calmly into the dining chamber.

"Luke!" Lucy jumped to her feet in shock.

"There he is!" Adalia shouted, pointing at Rhys.

Zadok stood from his position at the head of the table and addressed Rhys in his typical calm, collected tone. "Rhys. We've been awaiting the pleasure of your company. Please, take a seat." He gestured to the end of the table opposite himself.

The agitated satyr tugged on the high-backed wooden chair at the head of the table opposite Zadok and hopped up into the seat. Luke slid into an empty seat beside Lucy. She gave him an exaggerated look of consternation. He shrugged and mouthed the words, "I'll tell you later."

The flames of the tabletop candelabras flickered, casting

light across the solemn faces seated around the table. The clan leaders stared at the satyr in shock. Axel peered into the dining hall as he trotted by. Seeing the back of Rhys' head, he stopped and entered.

"He's in here!" Axel called to a companion. "Spread the word and call off the search. The little bugger is here. We won't let him out of our sight again sir," he promised Zadok.

"If you wanted to talk to me, you could have just sent a messenger," Rhys barked at Lucy, his hairy arms crossed over his chest. "You know, the old fashioned way."

"Not all of us are on such good terms with the Wardens that we can just venture out without fear of being attacked!" Glump shouted, jumping out of his chair.

Rhys was on his feet in an instant. "That's a weighty accusation you're making, Glump!" he snarled, pointing at the goblin across the length of the table. Lucy was glad they weren't seated side by side. She was sure a fight would break out if they were within reach of one another.

Cadmus stood, seated halfway between the two. He held an arm out to each of them. "Take it easy, both of you. Glump, we aren't here to fire off accusations. Rhys, we just have some questions for you based on things that were seen during the Wardens' attack, that's all."

The fuming satyr sat back down, cheeks bright red beneath his furrowed brow. "Fine. Ask whatever you want. But hurry up about it. I don't appreciate being interrupted during my supper, locked out of my own home, and herded like an animal!"

"Right. This won't take long," Cadmus replied. "Rhys, several villagers reported seeing you whisper something to the lead Warden in Central Square just before they called off the attack. What did you say to him?" The clan leaders leaned forward in anticipation of his reply.

"I was, uh, I was..." Rhys fumbled. "It's not what you think!" he shouted. "I'm not conspiring with the Wardens, okay? It was just business, that's all. The king's official business. I can't tell you." He sealed his lips and crossed his arms.

Lucy and Cadmus exchanged a glance.

"Rhys," Cadmus began, "you saw the extent of the damage caused by the Wardens. It was *horrific*. Even *you* must have lost friends among those killed or taken by the Wardens. Please. Help us. We need to know why the Wardens retreated before storming the castle, and it seems like it may have had something to do with whatever you told them."

Rhys shifted in his chair, uncomfortable. His eyes bounced from one clan leader to the next.

"Friends?" he burst out. "You say even I must have lost friends? Hah! I haven't had a true friend in a long, long time." Rhys' eyes flashed. "It's like you always say, Cadmus, I'm a dying breed! The last of my kind. The only satyr in Praxis. Who do I have to call a friend?

271

"As the king's alchemist, I do what is required of me. But who among you would call me friend? Who among you has ever reached out to me except when you needed something from me?" he looked around the table, challenging them to meet his gaze. Lucy stared at her hands in her lap, guilt washing over her. Rhys had a point.

"That's what I thought!" He jabbed the air in triumph when his question went unanswered. "And you should all be thanking me, because I *stopped* the bloodshed that day. I told the lead Warden that the one they were after—the Mapkeeper—wasn't at the castle. So they turned back." He sat back with a smug sneer. "You're welcome."

Lucy glanced up in alarm. "How did you know I wasn't at the castle?" she asked. "I'd just been transported back to Algid without having a chance to tell anyone what was going on. Even Cadmus, who was with me at the time, had no idea where I went."

Rhys glared at her, grinding his teeth. He had set himself up. He had to explain himself further now.

"All right!" he exclaimed, slamming his hands on the table. "I'm in too deep, I'll admit it! But I never wanted anyone to get hurt!" His voice broke. "I had no idea it would come to this. No idea. I swear!"

"Tell us what happened, Rhys. It's all right," Zadok assured him from the opposite end of the table.

"It's like I already told you—I'm alone here. Praxis isn't a home to me. It hasn't been for many years..." His expression was pained. "I needed something *more*. I needed a way to escape. And I found it, so I took it. It started out innocently enough! The previous Mapkeeper was ill, so I was tasked to create a concoction capable of generating a clone. With much tweaking and countless hours in the lab, I was able to get it right. The clone was almost perfect, except he didn't have the memory of the original Mapkeeper. He would have to relearn everything from scratch." He scratched his goatee. "A minor setback, if you think about the complexity of the operation."

Lucy's jaw dropped. "I met him in the castle dungeon! *You* created the cloning potion?" she asked, incredulous.

"That's right. And like I said, it was with good intentions. With a clone in place, the map could be controlled using the clone as a puppet. My benefactor would get what he wants—map control, and I would get a second chance at life. I was promised a new beginning in another world: my benefactor's world."

"Who were you working for, Rhys?" Cadmus ventured, his eyes narrowed in suspicion.

"A man who goes by the name of Mr. Quincy," the satyr replied.

CHAPTER 31

Lucy's jaw dropped again. She glanced at her brothers, who were also at a loss for words. "But... but how..." she stuttered, dumbfounded.

"Like I was saying," Rhys continued, "the first clone was supposed to be my ticket to a new life. But the map ruined everything." He sneered at Lucy. "Your name appeared at the bottom of the map when the previous Mapkeeper died, and just like that, our plan was in shambles. The map wouldn't work for Aodhan's clone. It had to be you."

Her cheeks flushed with anger. She felt a sense of possessiveness over the map—it was *hers*. She clenched her teeth and touched the map through her pocket.

"So Mr. Quincy gave you the map," Rhys continued. "We were brainstorming a work-around, but by that time, the dark magic of the Wardens was already showing strong signs of returning. That changed the direction of Mr. Quincy's plan. He figured if the Wardens were going to rise again, he could use that to his benefit. So we began to work with the Wardens, assisting them in the creation of clones of Praxian people and creatures. They were creating an army of clones to replace the real creatures and people of Praxis."

Lucy's head spun. She glanced at her brothers, whose mouths hung agape. She felt like the world she was just beginning to understand was being flipped inside out. Confusion and frustration welled up in her throat as she balled her hands into tight fists.

"The Wardens wanted map control," Rhys continued with a sigh. "Their ultimate goal was to get to the castle, which was already infiltrated entirely by clones with the exception of the queen and king. Of course, you were their main target," he added, gesturing toward Lucy.

Cadmus sat back in his chair, eyes agog. The rest of the clan leaders were in shock as well, mouths hanging open like slack-jawed marionettes.

"Cloning the Mapkeeper didn't work before," Rhys reiterated. "As always, the map named a new keeper when the previous keeper perished. So this time, they planned to keep you alive—to find other means of coercion to enable them to control you and the map." A chill ran down Lucy's spine as she considered what "other means of coercion" might mean. She shook her head in disbelief, shocked and disgusted with Rhys.

"Meanwhile," he continued, "Mr. Quincy's plan was to clone and kill the lead Warden. Once the Wardens achieved their goal of replacing all of the creatures of Praxis with clones, Mr. Quincy would clone the lead Warden—and through it, control the map." Rhys sighed again, pausing to glance around the circle. He swallowed hard. "But the Wardens did evil things. At the onset of it all, I had no idea it would come to this... no idea they would destroy and kill like that. I'm in over my head, and I am so sorry, so sorry to you all. This was never what I envisioned..." he took his head in his hands and wept. "I just wanted a fresh start, that's all. But now I don't deserve to live."

Lucy was shocked to see the satyr reduced to tears.

"Rhys, how many creatures have been cloned?" Zadok asked calmly.

"I've lost count," Rhys sniffed. "Dozens. Maybe hundreds."

"Where are they keeping the real people and creatures that were cloned?" Cadmus asked through clenched teeth, the knuckles of his fists white. He leaned forward as though he wanted to pummel the satyr.

"The Wardens hold them prisoner somewhere in Doldrums Forest, I'm not sure where." Rhys whispered. After spilling his secrets, he seemed to deflate as he shrank back from the table, gazing from face to face with sunken eyes.

"So you're saying that hundreds of people and creatures in Praxis right now have been cloned? And that some of the clones could be living among us right now?" Auriel shook her head in disbelief, her cropped, light blonde hair swishing back and forth.

"That's right."

"So how do we know for sure who is real and who is a clone?" Mack asked.

"Well, there are certain distinguishing characteristics of a clone," Rhys replied, wiping his face. "They lack emotion and possess no memories of anything prior to their creation. They have been put under a spell and they don't know any better than to play along."

Sudden realization hit Lucy like a freight train. *I should have seen it sooner!* she thought.

"That explains why Pip and Quinn didn't recognize me," she mused aloud. "And Prince Puck," she added, looking at Cadmus. "I always assumed he was just a strange boy, but he fits that description too."

Cadmus nodded gravely. "You're right! In fact, the king and queen both voiced concerns about their son's change in behavior on separate occasions. Rhys, did you *really* clone the prince?"

The satyr nodded, resting his head on his arms on the tabletop. "I'm not proud of what I helped them do," he muttered, massaging his forehead with a thumb and two hairy fingers.

"The castle guards..." Cadmus wondered aloud.

"All of them," Rhys confirmed, misery evident in his voice.

Lucy sat back, still stunned. They'd worried about a traitor within the castle, when all along they were completely infiltrated, surrounded by an army of clones controlled by the Wardens!

"How do we know that one of us here at this table wasn't cloned?" Glump barked from across the table.

"I can't prove it to you, but I've been honest thus far. I give you my word that you are all who you claim to be," Rhys replied. "My word is about all I have left," he added, more to himself than anyone else.

"What else have the Wardens done?" Adalia asked.

"They have also been cloning themselves. That is how they've been increasing their numbers."

Lucy's head was spinning. "How do I know you're not here to trap me?" she blurted out. "I'm the one they're after most of all." Her heart raced and her palms began to sweat. *What have I gotten myself into?* she wondered.

"Now that I've come clean, I'm of no use to the Wardens. I'm with you, or I die." He looked her in the eye. "They'll kill me if I go back to them now. I am not here to trap you. I am ashamed of what I did, and I want nothing more than to turn my back on the past. I'm here to help you in any way possible, although you have every right to hate me."

"You lied to me!" Luke burst out suddenly. Everyone

turned to stare. "You said we were working on a serum that would clone healthy genes to replace unhealthy genes in sick creatures!" His voice cracked with emotion. "You said I could help you! That we'd be partners in making Praxis a better place!" He pointed a trembling finger at Rhys.

"Luke..." Lucy touched his arm, confused but wanting to comfort her brother.

"No! It's over, Lucy. I... I helped him do this! He let me work with him in his lab. That's why I was always sneaking off—to help him with what I thought was a project for the greater good. He said to keep it a secret because he wasn't supposed to be working on side projects in addition to his assignments from the king." Lucy had never seen her youngest brother so hurt, his chest heaving as he sucked in uneven breaths. It wrenched her heart. "I am an accomplice to murder," Luke whispered.

CHAPTER 32

"The Wardens are coming! The Wardens are coming!"
Axel, Lance, and four other centaurs burst into the dining hall.
Clang, clang, clang. Someone in the main entrance to the cavern
tolled a warning bell. Abodox exploded into chaos, with creatures
shouting and scrambling over one another in a frenzy to prepare.

"Sir," Axel reported to Zadok, "we just received word from
one of our patrols. A whole army of Wardens is headed this way
from the forest to the east. We are mobilizing the centaurs and will
prepare to defend the cavern."

"Very well, thank you Axel. Lock up the satyr before things
get too chaotic." Zadok dismissed his right hand man. Lance and
another centaur lifted Rhys by the arms and carried him away as if
he were a small child. He was a limp, miserable sight.

Zadok stood and pressing his hands against the table,
leaned forward to address the clan leaders. "You heard Axel, the

Wardens are coming! Assemble your clans by the main gate of the cavern and rally them to fight. Tonight we are not the centaurs, the gnomes, the humans, the elves, the Bellaux, and the goblins. Tonight we are Praxian and we fight as *one* army against the Wardens to defend our homeland!"

Goosebumps sprouted on Lucy's arms as the clan leaders leapt to their feet and scattered to gather their clans. The thought of an army of Wardens approaching terrified her. She looked at Luke and saw that his eyes were rimmed with redness. Battling back against her own mounting fear, she stood and folded him in a hug.

"Luke, it's not your fault. You thought you were doing something for good," she assured him. "It's okay. Please don't beat yourself up over this...we *need* you now." He was stiff, not returning her embrace. "*I* need you now." She looked him in the eye and held him at arm's length. He flinched and looked away. She let him go, turning to Mack. "Well, we said we were all in, didn't we?" She knew she was trying to convince herself more than either of her brothers. Athletic, honorable Mack wouldn't hesitate to fight for Praxis, and now that Luke felt as though he had to make amends for what he'd done, he would want to fight, too. "Let's go. We'll need swords, armor, and our bows and arrows." She swallowed hard, putting on a brave face.

Lucy and Mack joined the chaos, running to their chamber to gather the armor and weapons the boys had brought from the castle armory. As she'd hoped, Luke fell into step behind them. Lucy's heart raced and the map glowed in her front pocket. She could sense the enormity of an impending battle. Soon, the opportunity to prove herself would be upon her. *Nothing will stop me this time*, she decided.

As they exited the dining hall, Odessa ran past them, her elbow brushing Lucy's shoulder. Lucy glanced up as the tall, slender Bellaux rushed past.

"...Nothing left for me now, I have nothing to lose anyway," Odessa murmured. "I've got to save him!"

"Hold on a second, guys." Lucy reached out and stopped her brothers, watching as Odessa sprinted toward the locked and bolted gate sealing the centaur cavern. There were four centaurs guarding the entrance.

"Odessa! Stop! What are you doing?" Auriel ran after her sister. Mack took an instinctive step toward the Bellaux.

As if from thin air, Enzo appeared beside Lucy. "Don't do it, Odessa! It's not worth it!" the little gnome shouted, cupping a hand beside his mouth.

The armed centaur guards squared off facing Odessa as she approached the gate. If she heard Auriel and Enzo's cries, she didn't show it. Instead, she continued to run toward the centaurs.

"You can't leave," one of the guards announced.

"The gate is locked, and it's staying that way," shouted another.

Odessa, a head taller than the tallest centaur, tucked her

chin as if to brace herself as she ran toward the gate, ignoring them.

"Stop!" yelled the first guard. She was almost upon them.

Odessa threw her hands out in front of her, and in a blast of white light, the four centaurs were tossed aside like rag dolls. The blast blew a gaping hole in the iron bars of the main gate and she charged into the tunnel leading to the forest. She did not pause or glance back, but charged ahead, fading from view into the darkness of the tunnel. Auriel hopped through the hole and followed her sister, calling to Odessa as she ran.

Lucy stared in shock.

"Bellaux magic," Zadok said from behind her. "It hasn't been seen in decades. They are only allowed to use in the gravest of circumstances—although more and more it seems as though what were steadfast rules are now mere guidelines in Praxis." His smile was grim. "We will have to fix the gate quickly." He started to move to assign a team to repair the gate.

"Wait!" Lucy grabbed his arm. "I can fix it." He paused, eyebrows arched.

She pulled out the map and located Abodox. Closing her senses to her surroundings and focusing her mind, she rubbed a finger over the main gate, which separated the tunnel from the cavern. Behind closed eyes, she willed the iron to repair itself. With a resounding groan, the warped iron bars untwisted and the strewn pieces rose from the dirt, straightened, and fused with the broken bars. Lucy opened her eyes to see the last iron bar smoothing into solid form. She smiled and let out her breath. The map glowed and was hot to the touch.

A small crowd of creatures preparing for battle had stopped, captivated, to watch the Mapkeeper do her work. Zadok clapped her shoulder with a broad smile.

"You are a wonder," Zadok uttered. The creatures began to disperse, chattering in awe.

"Come on, we have to get ready." Lucy turned to her brothers, whose mouths hung open. They shook their heads and followed their sister to their chamber to strap on armor.

"What was that all about with the Bellaux?" Mack wondered aloud as they fastened the buckles of their sword belts. "Don't they know it's not safe out there? We have to go after them!"

"I have no idea," Lucy replied. "I heard Odessa say something about having nothing left to lose, and that she had to save him. Who 'he' is, I don't know." She shivered with a terrible sense of foreboding.

They helped each other buckle the straps of their leather and steel armor, slung bows and arrows over their shoulders, and pulled on reinforced leather gloves. Lucy had selected one of Prince Puck's forged steel swords. It was lightweight but its sharpness was lethal. She sheathed it in its scabbard and buckled the thigh strap to prevent it from swinging when she ran. She looked her brothers over, tugging on one of Luke's chest plate straps to tighten it. They were ready.

"Let's do this." Mack's voice was firm and steady. Lucy wished she felt the same level of confidence that her older brother exuded.

They hurried back to the main gate, where groups of creatures had begun to gather. The centaurs wore simple helmets and chain mail armor, but their haunches and legs went unprotected. They carried bows and arrows, shields, and spears. The four Bellaux stood in a tight circle in one corner, their height making them easy to pick out of the crowd. They were grim and silent, clutching bows and arrows at their sides. Their two leaders had left them, and based on their disturbed expressions, it seemed even the Bellaux didn't know why.

Despite their squat stature, Enzo and his pack of gnomes were nothing short of menacing. All manner of pointed metallic objects protruded from their throng—spike-dappled chest plates, maces, swords, and iron helmets with long, forehead-mounted barbs. The gnomes were strong, gripping heavy shields that were longer than they were tall.

"They're big on spikes," Lucy commented to her brothers, pointing to the gnomes. Mack and Luke nodded with nervous smiles.

The goblins looked fierce with heavy helmets, maces, long spears, and steel swords. Their armor was fortified with large, dense sheets of steel mined from the Dour Mountains. They growled and paced, eager for a fight. Glump stood at the head of the group beside Gnurt, his chief adviser. They shifted their weight back and forth, impatient for the gate to swing open and release them. Their pointed green ears poked out from beneath polished steel helmets. Compared to the rest of the clans, the goblins seemed to crave a fight.

Adalia gathered her clan in a tight circle and offered the elves words of encouragement. The fervor of the thin, lovely creatures was palpable. They were eager to avenge their fallen brothers and sisters. They raised their weapons in a rally cry that filled the cavern, echoing throughout the vast network of stone walls.

A shiver slithered down Lucy's spine. She didn't know what to expect from the Wardens. She searched for Cadmus, spotting him through the crowd of creatures talking to a group of villagers. That the villagers were not warriors was apparent. They were clothed in the simple attire of a farmer, a baker, or a housewife. Lucy recognized Rolf and Bernie Shuman among the group, their arms around one other, expressions grim. Tall, curly-haired Fritz Brawne, the butcher's son, appeared focused and ready to fight. Lucy searched for his father Arnold, but couldn't find him among the crowd of villagers.

Zadok appeared by her side. "You're ready," he stated, placing a gentle hand on her shoulder. She smiled, confident that he was right. A surge of tenderness for the leader of the centaur clan welled up in her chest. She was sure they could not lose with Zadok on their side. He stepped toward the main gate to address the crowd.

"Creatures of Praxis, the time has come to defend our homeland against the atrocities of the Wardens. They threaten our very existence and our way of life. They hope to wipe us out, establishing a new order using clones controlled by dark magic."

Several gasps of astonishment escaped from the crowd. *The majority of the creatures still didn't know about the clones,* Lucy realized. *Could there be clones among us in this room?* She envisioned Aodhan Orman, Quinn, and Pip, all emotionless in their interactions. They were like mindless machines. Pawns of the head Warden. Distracted, she shook the image from her head and refocused on Zadok.

"The Wardens have invaded our homes and killed our brothers and sisters. Together, we will unite and stand against their dark brand of magic. We will exit the tunnel and form a line in the clearing beyond to wait for the enemy." He drew a line in the air with one arm, illustrating his plan. "These are historic times. Your children's children will tell tales of your bravery! Now, stand together, and hold fast for Praxis!" He pumped the air with a fist.

The cavern erupted with whoops, screams, and shouts, the clanging of sword butts on shields, and the thumping of hooves and feet. Only the Bellaux remained somber and silent. Lucy's heart raced as the centaur guards unlocked and unlatched the gate she had mended. With a gentle push, it swung open and the roaring creatures spilled out through the tunnel and into the forest.

CHAPTER 33

※

They formed a wide semicircle in the clearing around the entrance to the cavern, locking the young and the elderly inside. For once, Doldrums Forest was quiet. The low hoots and scrapes of squirrel claws against dry leaves were replaced by a profound silence that clung to the dense layers of mist shrouding the tree trunks. They waited.

Lucy gripped the shaft of her bow, her knuckles white with rigidity. Positioned between her brothers and Cadmus, she shifted her weight, realizing she had been standing stock-still for several minutes. They scanned the forest, straining their eyes for signs of movement. With a shiver, she noted the striking coolness of the forest air in comparison with the air inside the cavern.

She pulled out and unfolded the map, but to her disappointment, it was lifeless and held no clue as to the position of the Wardens. She was anxious and couldn't focus, so she folded it and slipped it back inside her pocket.

Cadmus grabbed her hand and flashed a handsome, reassuring smile. "We've got this," he said, squeezing her hand. Lucy smiled, knowing he would protect her at all costs.

"They're here!" came a cry from someone at the apex of their protective semicircle. There was no sudden charge or explosion of chaos. Instead, a quiet as deep as a starless night saturated the air. Lucy strained to see through the low-hanging mist, peering between bodies in the direction from which the voice had come. At last, the shadowy profiles of a long row of hooded figures materialized from within the shroud of mist. Lucy's blood went cold.

The Wardens marched toward them in silence, row after row, an endless army of identical black cloaked creatures. Lucy tried to push the image of the beheaded castle guards and horses from her mind as her heartbeat quickened. Praxis' defenders loaded and aimed their bows. The Wardens halted fifty yards from their position, armed with large swords and shields.

Though her hands shook, Lucy strung an arrow and prepared to fire. She slowed her breathing and aimed at a Warden in the second row. There was a moment of stillness in which it seemed as though the world stopped moving—it was almost peaceful. She took the opportunity to focus on her breathing, maintaining a relaxed, steady rhythm.

Then, from somewhere amidst the Warden army came a hair-raising, inhuman cry that made Lucy cringe. The front row of Wardens charged, with the exception of three Wardens who stood still and raised their bony gray hands, casting a spell. The army of Praxis released hundreds of arrows and with a collective roar, surged toward the enemy.

Wardens screamed as they dropped to the ground, pierced by arrows. The armies met with a cacophonous clash of swords, spears, and maces. Lucy and Luke shifted to one side, hopping up and perching atop a large boulder with their backs against the high stone wall of the cavern. It was an ideal vantage point for precision shooting. They unleashed arrow after arrow at the tall, dark-hooded creatures, which stood out as obvious targets among the motley army of Praxis.

Lucy's heart thundered as she aimed and let fly another arrow. Three goblins had been turned to stone where they stood, victims of black magic. The Wardens that had cast the spell moved among the groups of fighting creatures, turning others to stone. Lucy took aim and pierced one of the spell-casters in the shoulder. It fell to its knees with a scream but whipped its faceless head in her direction, raising its gray, claw-like hands in her direction. Lucy's blood went cold. She was quick to load another arrow and released it with lethal accuracy, slaying the creature before its spell was cast. *That was too close*, she thought, taking a moment to wipe her sweaty palms on her pant legs.

Lucy tried not to focus on the gore, but she could not block out the screams. From the corner of her eye, she saw a centaur go down to her left. She pierced a Warden squarely in the face, though she was unable to see the arrow's entry point in the darkness beneath the oversized hood. Without a sound, it collapsed in a heap. Rather than allowing herself to dwell on the atrocities around her, she moved on to her next target.

Smooth. Steady. Precise.

To her right, two gnomes hacked at a Warden with their heavy swords, its blood spattering them like an abstract painting. The stocky creatures lunged at the Warden from both sides and skewered it. A moment later, another Warden cut one of the gnomes down. Bellowing in anger, the second gnome sliced the back of the Warden's legs and with a war cry, pierced its heart when it fell to its knees. With a strong gulp, Lucy forced herself to look away. She let another arrow fly, saving one of the townspeople from being attacked from behind.

Shielded from behind by the main cavern wall, she and Luke were able to pan left and right without watching their backs. It seemed as though most Wardens were armed with swords, but that some were designated spell-casters, responsible for disabling Praxians using dark magic.

To the left, she caught sight of Mack engaged in a sword fight with a tall Warden. It was backing her brother up against the cavern's outer wall! Heart racing, Lucy steadied her bow and loosed an arrow aimed at the Warden. She missed.

"Luke!" she cried as she reached for another arrow, terrified that she wouldn't reload, aim, and release in time to help Mack.

Luke whipped around to see their brother pinned against

the natural stone wall, hacking with his sword in wild arcs aimed at the Warden. With an arrow already strung, Luke took steady aim and released, piercing the Warden in the neck just as it raised its sword high in the air to kill their brother. It collapsed, dead on the spot. Mack mouthed "thank you" to his siblings. Lucy shook her head, a cold trickle of sweat slipping down her neck. That was too close. Her heart was still racing, but she was shocked to find that she remained calm and collected, the adrenaline of the moment carrying her on.

Lucy and Luke continued their methodical sweep of the battlefield, felling Wardens as the dark creatures poured into the clearing. It was too soon to tell which army had the upper hand, but Wardens continued to spill onto the battlefield, emerging from the mist of the surrounding woods. Lucy hoped there weren't many more of them, or she worried the army of Praxis would be overwhelmed. She killed two Wardens back-to-back as they charged a muscular centaur. The centaur reared up and kicked a Warden with its front feet, crushing its chest. The hooded figure flew through the air and crumpled in a lifeless heap. When the centaur faced her, Lucy recognized him as Axel. She cleared the area around him of Wardens. Nodding to her in thanks, he raised his sword and trotted off to find another fight.

She saw one of Luke's arrows strike a Warden a moment before it was about to club one of the Bellaux with the blunt end of its sword. Lucy repositioned herself to help defend them. The Bellaux stood in a group, slashing at charging Wardens with their swords. Though the Bellaux were untrained fighters, their height and long limbs afforded them a natural advantage. They towered over the Wardens, letting the weight of their swords guide their heavy blows. So far, not a single Bellaux had been touched by an attacker. Lucy picked off three Wardens trying to sneak up on the Bellaux from a side angle. Odessa and Auriel were not among them, she noticed with a pang of unease. *Where did they go?*

A loud cry pierced the air to her right, and she glanced over in time to witness Zadok stab a Warden with his long iron sword. She noticed he hadn't strayed far from her position, and had the feeling that he was protecting her. Cadmus, too, remained near at hand. Lucy didn't dare shoot at the Warden he was fighting for fear of hitting Cadmus. He was just out of range of a clean shot. An experienced swordsman, Cadmus fought very well. He made it seem easy, annihilating whole groups of Wardens and coming to the assistance of his less experienced clansmen. He glanced up at her, nodded, and ran to help Fritz Brawne fight off two Wardens.

A large blast of white light suddenly blinded Lucy. When her vision returned, she saw the bodies of nearly ten Wardens scattered at the feet of the Bellaux. At first, they looked as stunned as the rest of the witnesses, but then they grinned at one another in delight. Bellaux magic was back! The battlefield in the vicinity was temporarily muted as creatures regained their vision and balance. The fighting continued. Lucy scored a direct hit on one of the spell-casting Wardens who was making its way toward the Bellaux. It had just turned two elves to stone. Their expressions fierce, the elves had been turned to stone just as they'd brandished their swords high above their heads. Lucy recognized one of them as Tryste, an attractive, grim-faced elf, who was one of Adalia's most trusted advisers. She'd seen the two engaged in solemn conversation in the cavern earlier that day. She couldn't allow her focus to linger.

A teenaged boy came running out of the tunnel, two full arrow quivers tucked under each arm. His long blonde hair whipped in strings behind him as he made haste to Lucy and Luke's boulder.

"I'm here with resupply," he gasped, heaving the quivers up to Luke, who caught them one after the other.

"Thanks!" Lucy called down to the boy. He nodded, wheeled about, and jetted off to hand the other two quivers to a pair of elves who had taken station on the other side of the cavern entrance. They were performing the same duty as Lucy and Luke, picking off Wardens from a high nook in the cavern wall. When they wedged themselves into the rocky recess, Lucy could only see the tips of their bows peeking out. It was brilliant! An even better position than her own. The blonde boy stood on his tip toes and passed the quivers up to one of the elves, then sprinted back into the cavern tunnel.

One of the Wardens caught sight of the boy and broke into a run, tailing him. With nimble fingers, Lucy threaded an arrow and took the Warden down. Her arrow pierced the Warden at the same moment as did an arrow from one of the crevice-bound elves. Deep within the tunnel, she heard the distant hollow rattle and clang of the cavern gate slamming shut behind the boy. She grinned, relief washing over her in the form of goosebumps.

"Good timing, I'm out." Luke dropped his empty quiver and shouldered one of the full ones. Lucy peered over her shoulder to assess her stock. She had about five arrows left.

"I'd better catch up!"

She emptied her quiver with four hits and a miss, and then shouldered the full quiver. Wardens still spilled into the clearing from all directions, converging on the battlefield. The Praxians who had never fought before grew weary, their muscles unaccustomed to holding heavy swords and shields. Lucy stopped a Warden in its tracks as it raised a sword to slash at little Bernie Schuman. Bernie's arms quivered under the weight of her sword as she struggled to hold it in a blocking position. She sighed with relief and let her sword fall to her side when her adversary crumpled before her. Rolf nudged his wife back toward the cavern, urging her to rest. Bernie resisted for a moment, but thought better of it and agreed. She linked arms with another exhausted housewife and together they hiked up their dresses and scurried toward the cavern. Lucy covered them, ensuring they made it inside the tunnel without incident. The distant clang of the iron gate admitting them to Abodox was a welcome sound.

An instant later, a man who Lucy recognized as the husband of the woman with Bernie was impaled. He sunk to his knees, clutching his stomach at the feet of his killer. Lucy's heart wrenched. She directed a shot at the Warden, but her sweaty hand slipped and she missed. As she reloaded her bow, the Warden looked up at her. It turned and marched directly toward her, purposeful. A chill ran down her spine. She wiped her palm against her jeans and took aim again, but missed for a second time. The Warden touched companions as he marched and they abandoned their skirmishes to join him, all staring at the Mapkeeper in horrible, faceless unison. Luke shifted to help.

The group of marching Wardens was now six strong. The Barnes siblings had managed to kill two, when suddenly the pack of Wardens changed direction and dashed out of sight behind the cavern wall near the elves in the crevice. Lucy and Luke exchanged a glance of unease. Once again she eyed the cavern wall behind them. It towered at least four times the height of an average person. There was no foreseeable way anyone could sneak up on them from behind.

Brushing off the feeling that those Wardens were coming for her, Lucy continued to rain arrows down on the enemy. The Praxians as a whole seemed to be losing ground. Zadok and Cadmus still fought valiantly, close at hand on her right side, and Mack was working well with Fritz Brawne to her left. Mack and Fritz stood back to back, each battling a Warden. Lucy was proud of her older brother's natural athleticism. He took to swordsmanship as though he'd trained in hand-to-hand combat all his life.

Almost imperceptibly, the earth began to shudder. At first, it was gentle and rhythmic, and Lucy wondered if she were imagining it. But the tremors increased in magnitude with each beat, and after several seconds she knew it wasn't just a figment of her imagination. She glanced sideways at Luke. Their eyes met, confirming that he felt it, too.

To her left, Enzo paused, head cocked to one side. Soon, many creatures and Wardens paused mid-scuffle and looked around, mystified by the pulsating, ever-intensifying tremors. Soon, the trees began to shake, and then the rhythmic shaking grew so strong that Lucy and Luke had to crouch to maintain their balance on the boulder. Many on the battlefield did the same.

Suddenly, Lucy saw Enzo break into a wide grin. He chuckled, leaning back and holding his armor-clad belly in both hands. Confused, she followed his gaze in time to see several enormous shadows—four times the height of a man—materialize from within the layers of mist. As the shadows permeated the mist, they multiplied until Lucy could make out a thick line of bodies. She gasped in awe, clapping a hand over her mouth. The trolls had arrived.

CHAPTER 34

* * *

The trolls demolished clusters of Wardens with ease, crushing the screaming creatures beneath their massive, stumpy feet with great, earth-shuddering stomps. They took the battlefield by storm, dispersing among the trees. Praxians leapt out of the way, allowing the hulking creatures to thunder past. They annihilated Wardens with stone clubs, the girths of which equaled those of the thickest trees in the forest. The trolls were shifting the tide of the battle in favor of the Praxians!

Lucy grinned at Luke. For the first time since the battle began, the glowing hope that the end was near and that Praxis would triumph reassured her. She restrung her bow and loosed a well-aimed arrow, piercing a Warden that was attempting to cast a spell on a centaur from behind a tree trunk. Then her eye was caught by two familiar figures emerging from the mist. One was a tall, slim robed man and the other was a short, stout companion. They strode into the clearing side by side. *Bade and Hobart*, Lucy thought, torn between relief and loathing.

Bade stopped at the edge of the clearing. He was tailed by two club-wielding trolls who hovered at his heels. *Personal body guards*, Lucy thought with annoyance. Bade crossed his arms and surveyed the battlefield, which was now dotted with unoccupied Praxians searching for enemies to engage. The remaining Wardens were retreating, Lucy realized with a flicker of hope. She observed as Bade's sweeping gaze locked on Cadmus and he motioned for his colossal pair of body guards to follow as he approached the leader of the human clan.

Cadmus was wiping the blade of his sword after coming to the aid of Rolf Schuman, who'd almost been driven to exhaustion before he'd stepped in. The sweat-soaked shoemaker mopped his brow and patted Cadmus on the arm in thanks. Cadmus pointed to the cavern, insisting that the aging man take a break from fighting. Glancing about, Rolf acknowledged that the battle was winding down and jogged across the clearing into the haven. Several other Praxians were doing the same. They were exhausted, unaccustomed to the physical rigor of hand-to-hand combat.

Several creatures guided injured comrades to safety. Lucy's chest tightened at the sight of an elf closing the eyelids of a fallen female elf. Gathering his clan-mate in his arms, the slim elf carried her toward the cavern. His gaze met Lucy's for an instant and she saw the sheen of a tear streak on his cheek. He averted his eyes and disappeared into the tunnel leading to the cavern gate.

By now, the Wardens that weren't killed had retreated.

Nonetheless, Zadok, Axel, and five other centaurs patrolled the battleground, unwilling to retreat into their sanctuary until they were certain the enemy was eliminated. Adalia and a group of elves did the same. Lucy noticed that a large, blood-soaked bandage sheathed Adalia's left forearm. She pressed on the wound, applying pressure to stymie the bleed.

"Let's stay up here for a bit longer to be sure they don't come back," Luke suggested.

"Good idea," Lucy replied, stringing an arrow and scanning the forest for any sign of a returning Warden. She only now realized that her shirt was sweat-soaked and the strands of hair framing her face were matted against her forehead.

She allowed her gaze to linger on Bade, who had just reached Cadmus. They were discussing something. Bade shook his head, spreading his arms in disgust and gesturing to the trolls, who at this point had reached the outskirts of the battleground, chasing the last Wardens away from the centaur cavern. Cadmus shrugged and said something in reply. Lucy wished she could hear what they were saying.

Suddenly, Cadmus glanced across the clearing at Lucy. His eyes went wide and he dropped his heavy shield. The hair on the back of Lucy's neck rose in apprehension as he broke into a full sprint toward her. Something wasn't right. She turned to follow his gaze just in time to see four Wardens sliding down the steep, angled cavern wall behind her. Cadmus reached the boulder and scrambled up to join Luke and Lucy just as the first Warden regained its balance atop the boulder and charged, sword brandished. Lucy jumped back, grabbing Luke's wrist and pulling him with her. Cadmus sprinted between them and blocked the Warden's blow in a deafening clang of steel on steel.

Lucy's senses were heightened with the instinct for survival. The next three Wardens slid down the rock and jumped to their feet, charging Cadmus as Lucy and Luke regained their footing and each released an arrow, piercing two of the creatures at the same time. The Wardens clutched at their wounds and screamed, but continued to shuffle toward Lucy. Cadmus was occupied, barely able to fend off the other two uninjured Wardens. Lucy's heart pounded in her ears. Her hands fumbled when she attempted to string another arrow.

Her subconscious took note of a frenzy of shouts and the thundering of hooves galloping toward her from behind, but her vision was tunneled. Her focused mind did not allow her to acknowledge anything but the imminent threat closing in atop the boulder. With a cry, she unleashed a second arrow into the Warden she had already injured, bringing it to its knees. The hooded creature screamed and dropped its sword. Lucy scrambled forward and snatched up the weapon, bringing it down upon the Warden with all her might. It stuck in the creature's shoulder, delivering a swift death.

Lucy shuffled back to the edge of the boulder in time to see six more Wardens slide down the rock, pushing the others forward into Cadmus. Another cluster of the dark creatures hovered above them atop the cavern wall. Lucy's body went cold. She strung another arrow, her hands shaking. Luke did the same, holding his position beside her bravely. Cadmus was a skilled swordsman and had already killed two of the attackers, but Lucy doubted whether *anyone* could hold out against a whole mob of Wardens. Petrified, she glanced around for help. With her peripheral vision, she saw a group of centaurs thundering toward them. Mack and Fritz were running to help, too.

"It's me they want!" Lucy cried aloud, to no one in particular. She knew she had to fight with every ounce of focus and energy she possessed, so she unleashed an arrow with lethal accuracy. *I have to help Cadmus*, she thought.

Cadmus still blocked the throng of Wardens from approaching Lucy and Luke, but they were beating him back, step by step. Lucy's heart wrenched as the seconds ticked away. He blocked blow after blow with his sword, but without his shield, he was losing energy too fast. More Wardens slid down the rock face and joined the advancing group. Cadmus was the only thing standing between the Wardens and their prize. He fell to his knees from the force of blocking a fierce double-blow from the heavy swords of two Wardens at the same time.

Time seemed to slow down as frantic thoughts raced across Lucy's mind. *Can I do something with the map to help? We need backup, now! Cadmus can't hold them off much longer...*

Zadok's wide, glossy brown body punched through the space between Lucy and Luke, nearly pushing Lucy off the side of the boulder. Mack and Fritz scrambled up the side of the rock to her right, and the other centaurs gathered around the boulder, raining arrows into the mob of Wardens.

But they were too late. With a cry that pierced her heart, Cadmus was struck in the side. He palmed the flat side of his sword above his head to shield himself from another forceful blow from above, his breath sharp and audible through his gritted teeth.

"Cadmus!" Lucy shrieked, gaining the strength to wrench free the sword she'd lodged in the shoulder of the dead Warden. Wielding the blade overhead, she ricocheted off Zadok's haunch as she scrambled forward, sneakers slipping on the granite beneath her feet. With mindless abandon, she charged the horde of Wardens, chest heaving, blinded by her savage need to protect Cadmus. His blood was spattered across the boulder before her. She screamed, raising the sword high, deaf to the noises and blind to the action surrounding her. She was unable to feel the burn of the map that glowed with ferocity in her front pocket.

Lucy was two steps away from Cadmus' side when the sensation that time was passing more slowly than usual stopped. The abrupt, perceived fast-forwarding of time was brought on by the flash of sharp steel slicing through the air to Cadmus' left side. One of the Wardens delivered a powerful thrust of its sword, impaling the man she loved before her eyes.

CHAPTER 35

Lucy heard herself scream as she clenched her fists and her legs collapsed beneath her. She watched Cadmus slump, his bloodied body collapsing against the granite in a motionless heap. A pair of strong, hairy arms encircled Lucy from behind as the sword fell from her grasp, clattering against the boulder. She was dragged back, away from the Wardens as Mack, Fritz, and Axel leapt between her and the throng, weapons carving the air with lethal dexterity. Yet she could hear nothing but her own prolonged scream—a soul-splitting cry of anguish.

"Cadmus! Cadmus! You have to let me go to him!" Tears flowed down her cheeks as she heard herself sobbing and begging her captor, writhing to escape his strong grip. She twisted, recognizing the pair of arms suspending her in the air as belonging to Zadok. He was preventing her from approaching Cadmus.

"Zadok, let me go! He's bleeding! Zadok! You have to let me help him!" she screamed, desperate to make him understand.

Though she struggled against his grip with all her might, she could feel nothing but the searing pain of her heart breaking at the sight of Cadmus splayed out on the rock between her defenders and the Wardens. His light brown hair was matted in thick locks, but his back faced her so that she could not see his face. Her heart fluttered out of control in a state of utter panic. *Is he alive?* Each ragged breath was painful, as if she were forcing a massive volume of air through compressed wind pipes.

In an instant, Mack, Axel, and Fritz were transformed to stone statues. Their bodies froze in the midst of swinging and blocking with their swords. Lucy's world blurred as the Wardens moved around the three statues and advanced on her, unobstructed. The thud of her heartbeat in her ears drowned out all other sound. She glanced to her left. Luke, too, had become nothing but a stone effigy. Her heart broke anew and she became aware that her mouth was parched. Her fat tongue took up too much space in her mouth, and she could barely breathe. To her right, Lance, Adalia, and her troop of elves were also frozen, turned to statues in their final act of rushing to her assistance.

She was torn between fierce rage and hopeless apathy. Glancing down, she realized that the arms suspending her were still fleshy and warm. Zadok was still with her. Some part of her subconscious registered that the map was as hot as fire in her pocket.

More Wardens continued to slide down the face of the cavern wall. An imposing group of them now faced her atop the boulder. She and Zadok didn't stand a chance against what was now a whole mob standing several paces away.

The creature closest to her began to speak in a tongue Lucy did not understand. Zadok's grip tightened as the Wardens formed a semicircle around them. Desperate, she tried to peer between the robed creatures toward Cadmus, but he was blocked from sight. Her heart raced, fueled by a blinding fury at these creatures for cursing and killing the people she loved.

"It's me you want! Take me, leave the centaur behind!" she screamed, writhing to free herself from Zadok's grip, but his grip only tightened.

"Shh, Lucy," Zadok whispered in her ear, catching her off guard. "It's not too late. I can still fight, but I need to toss you to safety first. I'm going to throw you off the rock. When you land, get up and run as fast as you can. Find Bade and the trolls. Find anyone that's not a Warden. And hide!"

But the Warden was speaking again, a succession of murmurs and croaks indiscernible to Lucy.

"No!" She spoke aloud. "Zadok, it's me they want. I won't let you fight this battle for me. I won't run. I have to face them." She wouldn't leave Cadmus lying broken and bloodied upon this rock. She couldn't. Fierce loyalty surged through her veins like a shot of pure adrenaline. She narrowed her eyes at the muttering Warden standing before her.

"What do you want from me?" she cried in angst.

The Warden paused, and then addressed her in her

language. "Mapkeeper," it began, in a low, growling voice. "You are right. It is you and you alone whom we need. You will come with us and fulfill the plans we have for you. The centaur is irrelevant. He will be turned to stone like the others."

An icy chill ran down Lucy's spine at the unnatural tone of the creature's voice as it spoke in her language. A loathing stronger than any she had ever felt overcame her.

"Centaur, release the Mapkeeper," the Warden commanded. Zadok ignored the creature, his grip remaining firm. "Do it now, or we will take her by force," the creature snarled.

"Lucy, you have to try. We have no choice!" came Zadok's urgent whisper in her ear.

Dry nausea clenched her throat as she realized Zadok was right. There was truly nothing else she could do but go along with his plan, as much as she wanted to fight for herself.

"Okay, I'll do it," she replied in a whisper. Zadok's grip relaxed the slightest bit.

"You leave us no choice," the Warden began.

In a single swift motion, Zadok flung Lucy off the side of the boulder, drew his sword, and charged. Lucy did not look back. She collapsed in a heap, then sprang to her feet and began to sprint. The map pulsed with heat against her leg.

She hadn't taken three steps when she realized her movements were sluggish, her leg inching forward even as she willed it to slice through the air with her usual athletic speed. In fact, her entire body was almost immobilized, as though she were trapped inside a dense bowl of gelatin! A sickening horror came over her as the air around her became icy. *What is happening?*

Then the Wardens appeared in a slow-moving procession, encircling her from both sides. She turned her head in slow motion and peered down at her arm, which slowly lifted in sync with her stride. Unable to move her body at a normal rate, she could only watch in terror as the Wardens completed their circle and she was surrounded by the enemy.

"We warned you, Mapkeeper," the one facing her began. "Now you will come with us." It raised its cloaked arms, revealing bony gray fingers attached to skeletal wrists. Her vision blurred as she felt her consciousness fading. The last conscious thought she had was that it felt as though she were sinking through the massive bowl of gelatin, descending ever-so-slowly into a pit of blackness.

⁙

This time, she did not awaken in Abodox surrounded by friends and family. The kobolds did not rescue her from the dark magic of the Wardens. Instead, when her eyes blinked open, she found herself in a large, dim-lighted stone chamber. The large, flat stone slab she lay upon was cold, and her arms and legs were shackled and chained to its corners. She was shivering in the dark, frigid air. The flickering of occasional torches located far-off against dank, moist walls caught her eye next. Lifting her head to peer around, she sensed that she was not alone.

As if to confirm her fear, three cloaked Wardens emerged from the shadows, pacing toward her in a rhythmic cadence. They muttered in unison, droning in their throaty foreign tongue. Lucy's mind reeled as she struggled to control her shivering. The memory of the events of the battlefield came back to her with sickening clarity. *How much time has passed? Where am I? Is Zadok...? Mack and Luke...* A dozen thoughts clamored for her attention at once.

Cadmus. The image of his limp body splayed out on the rock sent a searing pain through her body, originating in her heart and coursing to the tips of her arms and legs. She squeezed her eyes shut, unable to bear the thought of Cadmus as she last saw him. She wouldn't allow herself to acknowledge that he might be dead. She couldn't. Combined with the thought of her brothers, Zadok, and all the others, it threatened to put her out of her mind with grief.

The Wardens approached, chanting. Lucy opened her eyes and tugged the chains, testing the shackles. Icy steel pressed into her wrists. She swallowed, willing herself to focus and remain calm as a lump formed in her throat. Even if she were the last one alive in Praxis, she refused to go down without a fight. *Do I still have the map?* She couldn't lift her head high enough to peer down at her pocket, but she felt no sign of its warmth... no familiar pulse to bring her comfort. She yearned for it now more than ever. Without the map, she knew she was powerless against the Wardens' dark magic.

The three Wardens continued to chant as they reached the stone slab. Two flanked her on her right and left sides, and the third took position beside her head. Heart pounding, she looked up into the faceless black hole of its hood. In place of the fear she had expected to feel, she was surprised to find only a fierce sense of loyalty—a potent resolve to fight these creatures with all her might to avenge her brothers, Cadmus, and all the creatures of Praxis.

"Are you going to clone me now?" she taunted the one looming over her head. "Because I don't think that would be a very good idea. I'm allergic to needles, so I'll die if you try to inject me," she fibbed, imagining with a stab of pain how her brothers would have laughed at her ridiculous lie.

The Wardens ignored her, continuing to chant in unison. Through the shadows, more of them emerged, once again forming a large circle around her.

"Mapkeeper," came a hiss from within the circle. A tall Warden stepped forward, striding toward her. "I am Doelech, the leader of the Wardens, the true heirs of Praxis. With your blood, I will gain control over the map and wipe out all other creatures. It is the dawn of a new era! An era in which Wardens will reign supreme. We will not be stopped. All that remains is to create your clone."

At this, Lucy's body froze in fear, but she steeled herself against the creature's words.

"You will never control my map!" she cried out. She *had* to be strong despite the helplessness she felt. She refused to lie down and die without putting up a fight.

Doelech approached the stone table carrying a glass flask. She caught a glimpse beneath the creature's hood as it approached, at last beholding the face of a Warden. Its eyes were yellow slits and its nose was small and pointy. It had a pinhole of a mouth with dry, cracked skin where lips should have been. Its face was flat and gray.

"You will drink this draught, and afterward your hair will be ready for harvest to grow your clone. And of course at that point, we will no longer have need for you, Mapkeeper." The goosebumps on her arms intensified. She forced her fear back once again, steeling herself against the creatures surrounding her. *If I could get to the map...* she thought.

Doelech growled something to the Warden standing over Lucy's head. It drew a long key out of its robe and unlatched the shackles binding her wrists. Its cold, clammy gray flesh brushed her wrist, making her skin crawl. She was hesitant, knowing that if she did something brash the two flanking her would curse her.

"Sit up," Doelech commanded.

Lucy obeyed, casting a discreet glance down at her pocket. The familiar outline of the folded map was not there.

"Did you really think we would leave you with the map?" Doelech sneered in his deep, hollow voice. "You are a fool." It pulled her map out of its robe, unfolding and examining the parchment. "Soon, this irreplaceable prize will be under my control, along with the rest of Praxis."

Lucy scanned the cavern, desperate to formulate a plan. Her ankles were still shackled to the stone table.

"Now, you will drink this serum and fulfill the destiny of Praxis!" Doelech tucked the map back inside its sleeve fold and approached her, uncorking the glass vial. A bright blue liquid sloshed inside. Lucy's stomach churned and the nausea began to rise in her throat once again. She swallowed hard. Doelech's bony gray hand thrust the neck of the bottle against her lips.

She sealed her lips, rejecting the vial. Closing her eyes, she envisioned Cadmus, bloody and lifeless atop the boulder. She envisioned Mack and Luke, turned to stone in the act of protecting her. She fueled a ferocious fury within her heart. For Cadmus, for her brothers, and for all the creatures of Praxis who had fought valiantly to save their home, she refused to cede to the Wardens. The true love she felt for her brothers and Cadmus coupled with her agony over their loss saturated her with the most intense passion she could summon.

"*Drink*, girl!" Doelech hissed, prying at her upper lip with the edge of the glass vial.

She willed the map to come to her. She focused her passion, channeling her emotion into her desire for the map. *It's my map*, she thought. *It belongs to me.*

"What is this?" Doelech jerked the vial away from her lips.

Lucy opened her eyes in time to see the map float out of his sleeve and into her outstretched hands. She reacted instantly, gripping the map with all her might and willing it to shield her. A bright white ball of light emanated from the map, encasing her in a protective bubble. She threw her head back and with one flat palm, smacked the image of the Warden lair on the map.

The cavern ruptured in a deafening, violent explosion of rock on all sides. The last thing Lucy heard was Doelech screeching in anger as he lunged for the map.

CHAPTER 36

Minutes passed. Lucy opened her eyes to find a mountain of rock debris and dust settled around the shield created by the map. The map still glowed and pulsated in her hands. Her heart soared and she felt a stronger connection to the map than ever before. She clung to the strength of the passion she felt, willing the map to sustain her protective cocoon. Looking up, she realized that rubble pressed against her cocoon of light on all sides. The entire cavern had collapsed!

On the map, the image of the hidden Warden cavern deep in Doldrums Forest was reduced to a great pile of rocks. Until she was inside, it has been invisible on the map. *They must have cursed it so it wouldn't show up on the map*, she thought.

She had to free herself from the wreckage. With the swipe of a fingernail across the parchment, she slashed the shackles that bound her ankles. She closed her eyes and touched the image of herself, lifting up with her finger. As if lifted by an invisible elevator, she rose through the deep pile of rocks as smoothly as a ship plying the sea. Emerging from the mountain of rubble, she left the flat stone table far below and took to the sky. A strange calm came over her despite the trauma of what she'd been through.

Tracing a path with her finger, she glided above and between the tops of the trees of Doldrums Forest toward Abodox. The stunning serenity of the view of the vast forest from above contradicted the violence that had taken place beneath its canopy. She soared between the tips of the great evergreens, the evening sun an exquisite golden ball dipping through a pink sky toward the horizon over the Dark Sea in the distance. But she could not relish the splendor of the view. Her heart was broken, laden with more competing sorrows and horrors than most people experience in an entire lifetime. A constant stream of silent tears flowed down her cheeks as she neared Abodox.

She descended through the trees and touched down a short distance from the cavern on the outskirts of the clearing where the battle had taken place. Landing on both feet, Lucy released her finger from the map. Using her sleeve to wipe her wet cheeks, she drew in a shuddering breath, suddenly aware of her utter exhaustion. Though she was terrified to approach the rock where she'd left Cadmus and her brothers, she knew she had to. However irrational, she clung to the hope that somehow he had survived his horrific wounds. Bracing herself for the worst, she began to trudge toward the entrance to Abodox.

Voices ahead made Lucy catch her breath. She darted

behind the nearest tree and crouched, straining to hear the indistinct voices. A man shouted something and a female answered as distant hooves pounded the ground. Lucy held her breath and leaned out, peering around the tree trunk in the direction of the noises. Her heart pounded with anticipation as the sound of hooves drew nearer.

She let out her breath in a gush of relief when she recognized Axel and Lance rounding a bend in the path, cantering toward her. Lucy's heart soared—the spells must have been lifted when the Wardens were crushed beneath the stone! She stepped into the open and cried out to her friends, tears of joy spilling down her cheeks.

"Axel! Lance! You're all right!" She fell to her knees, weak with relief.

The centaurs' stoic faces lit up when they saw the Mapkeeper on her knees before them.

"Ms. Barnes, you're all right!" They reached her and bent, lifting her up by her arms. "We thought... We didn't know what happened to you," Axel said in his calm, baritone voice. "But come, you must see the others. They'll be elated you're all right!" Before she could object, Axel scooped her up in his arms as though she were a small child and galloped toward Abodox.

They passed Adalia, Tryste, and several of her other trusted advisers along the path.

"They are patrolling the area, as were we before we found

you," Axel explained. The elves were overjoyed to see Lucy waving at them from the centaur's strong arms.

"Ms. Barnes!" Adalia exclaimed. "What a relief! We are so glad to see you!" But Axel did not slow his pace.

"The others are keeping watch at Abodox," he explained.

They were back in the clearing in several minutes. Lucy's heart seized up with joy when she saw her brothers, Zadok, and Fritz standing at the entrance to the cavern. Axel set her on her feet beside them and she was smothered with simultaneous hugs from Mack, Luke, and Fritz. Zadok stood to the side, grinning with joy.

She laughed, wiping tears from her cheeks.

"Lucy, you're okay! We were so worried!" Mack exclaimed.

"I was worried about you, too! They turned you to stone, and I didn't know if you'd ever be back to normal again!"

"All the spells were lifted! But where did they take you?" Luke asked.

Lucy's expression darkened. "They took me to their lair," she said, still hardly able to believe what had happened herself. She would need time to process it. "They tried to make me drink the cloning potion so they could use my clone to control the map. Then they were going to kill me. I was surrounded by Wardens, and they had taken the map from me." Their eyes bulged as they listened to her story. "But I focused on my anger at what they'd done to you and…" she couldn't bear to utter his name. Her eyes filled with tears once more, so she averted them from her brothers and stared at the ground instead.

Luke looked away as Mack stepped toward his sister and touched her arm. "Lucy, I am so sorry," he said with sincerity.

She broke down in tears, unable to bear the intensity of her emotion. Mack pulled her into a hug and let her cry while the others stood by in respectful silence. The pain of her broken heart pierced her anew.

"Where…" she began between sobs, but couldn't finish the question. *Saying it aloud will make it true*, some irrational part of her subconscious chided.

Mack placed a gentle hand on her back and guided her toward the boulder where the final fight had taken place. Each step was agonizing, the pain of her broken heart weighing her down like an iron anchor. When at last she lifted her eyes to look upon him, she found Cadmus had been laid on his back on a patch of grass beside the boulder, arms crossed over his chest. His light brown hair formed a perfect frame around his face, even in death. Lucy fell to her knees beside him and sobbed, the reality of his death at last hitting her with the force of a freight train. The pain that coursed through her was physical, and so intense that she lost awareness of everything but the body lying before her.

Tears poured down her cheeks as she wept without reservation, clinging to Cadmus' lifeless arm as she leaned over his body. Her hair fell around her face and her tears began to drench the strands. After several minutes she opened her eyes and taking a deep, shuddering breath, summoned the courage to look at his face. She couldn't believe how handsome he was in spite of the dirt and dried blood marring his face and clothing. His profound love and courage had cost him his life, but his sacrifice ensured that she would live to save Praxis. She rocked back and forth as she knelt, somehow needing the motion to distract her from the pain of losing him.

"You were the true hero," she choked out between sobs, grasping his cold hand between her shaking ones and kissing it. "I love you, Cadmus." She squeezed her eyes shut, hot tears gliding down her cheeks and dripping off her chin onto his chest plate. The pain of speaking her love aloud and not hearing him say it in return penetrated her to her bones. She'd never known such emptiness. She stroked the stubble along his jawbone with the back of her hand, committing his face to memory.

She knelt beside him for so long that when at last she stood, darkness had cloaked the forest for the night. Everyone except her brothers and Zadok had retreated back inside Abodox. She slowly stood and turned to face them, wiping her sticky cheeks once again. Fatigued and filthy, Mack and Luke plodded into the cavern tunnel beside their sister. No one felt the need for conversation. When Lucy reached her cot, she lay down without bothering to change her clothes and succumbed to the deep slumber of utter exhaustion.

She awoke many hours later, disoriented and unaware of how much time had passed. The events of the previous evening flooded back into her mind in succession, and her heart grew heavy once again, overburdened with grief.

But she was still the Mapkeeper, and there were many questions left unanswered. Swinging her legs over the side of her cot, Lucy forced herself to stand and stretch her sore muscles. She shuffled to the wash basin and took her time lathering and scrubbing her face, neck, arms, and beneath her fingernails. The centaurs had provided simple, scentless lye soap and a rough cloth, but Lucy didn't mind. The roughness of the wash cloth was a welcome distraction from the torment of the incessant replay of her memories in her mind's eye. She dried herself with another rough cloth, then, in a single gulp, drained the contents of the tin cup of water left on the table beside her cot. She left her chamber to find the others.

"Good morning, Ms. Barnes," a centaur greeted her as they passed in the cavern corridor.

"Good morning."

She proceeded straight to the Abodox dining hall, where the clan leaders had made a habit of meeting. Mack, Luke, Zadok, Adalia, Gump, and Enzo were seated at their usual table. Auriel stood at the head of the table, her arms stretched wide, explaining something in exasperation. The other four Bellaux—all that remained of her clan besides her sister Odessa—stood behind her, solemn as ever. Their collective height and beauty made the

Bellaux an imposing group.

"Ah, there she is," Auriel said as she caught sight of Lucy entering the dining hall.

"Good morning, Lucy," Zadok greeted her. "I hope you slept well?"

"Like a baby. What's going on?"

"It's Odessa. She's still missing." Auriel's reply was tense. She wasted no time catching the Mapkeeper up. "We must go find her. We would have gone already, but the others convinced me to wait for you to wake up before we go out into the forest. We need to know the status of the Wardens."

Lucy sank into a chair beside Adalia and explained to the whole group what had taken place inside the Wardens' hidden lair. The clan leaders were rapt. She opened the map and showed them the location of the hidden cavern that had served as the Warden lair. It was now exposed, the dark magic that concealed it having been lifted when the Wardens were buried alive. Even Enzo failed to stifle a gasp when she showed them the pile of rubble on the map deep in Doldrums Forest. Her explanation of how the map had created a protective bubble around her and how she managed to raise herself out of the debris and soar over the treetops back to Abodox astounded them. Even level-headed Adalia, who was two-hundred years old and had lived through the reign of three previous Mapkeepers, was wide-eyed. Their reactions bolstered Lucy's confidence.

Zadok filled Lucy in, explaining that the leaders were operating under the presumption that Bade and Hobart had returned to the mountains with the trolls, as they were nowhere to be found when the dark spells were lifted. There would be a memorial for the deceased Praxians, regardless of clan, the following day at noon.

"Ms. Barnes, your deeds were nothing short of heroic," Auriel praised. "You saved Praxis by your quick thinking and focus under pressure. We are forever indebted to you, and you will always have the support of the Bellaux." Auriel's voice was melodic. Mack ogled her as she spoke, spellbound. "But we are eager to begin the search for my sister. Armed with the certainty that all the Wardens were killed in their lair, will you join us in the search?"

"Of course I will, Auriel. I am eager for Odessa's safe return," Lucy replied with sincerity.

"But where do we start? She's still not showing up on the map," Mack pointed out, eager to help. He leaned forward, clutching a forgotten copper stein of cider between his hands.

"If my hunch is right, I know where she is," Enzo interjected. The group was silent. In unison, they all turned to stare at the fierce-faced gnome.

CHAPTER 37

"We had a pact," Enzo explained with a sigh. Auriel's jaw dropped, her gaze darting around the room to gauge the astonishment of the others. Enzo narrowed his eyes at her. "Auriel, I can assure you with near-certainty of your sister's location. I know you're afraid of the repercussions, but you must remember that we are among allies here. Odessa's secret is not so terrible that it cannot be forgiven."

"I knew that my sister had a secret, but she refused to divulge it to me. How—how did you discover what it was?" Auriel asked, her face pale.

Enzo sighed again, folding his hands in front of him. "I stumbled upon Odessa in the forest. She was tending to an injured creature. Rare as it is to see a Bellaux alone and out of the Tree of Virtue, I snuck closer to find out what drew her so deep into Doldrums Forest all by herself.

"She had the injured creature hidden beneath a rock outcropping against the side of a sheer cliff. It was a large creature, though it never made a sound as she cleaned its wounds. I was able to creep within paces of her position, hidden by the tall ground ferns until the creature sensed my presence. I still hadn't had a good look at it yet when it snorted and lifted its head in my direction. Odessa whipped about and discovered me squatting among the plants." Enzo paused before finishing. "At that point I saw the thing clearly through the plants. She was caring for an injured unicorn." The leaders gasped in unison.

"No!" one of the Bellaux cried in disbelief. "It's not possible!"

"Unicorns have never been seen by anyone alive today except for the most ancient of the elves!" Adalia scoffed. "How can you be sure of what you saw?"

"It was a unicorn all right! It had a pure, silken white coat and a long silver-white horn. It was magnificent!" Lucy noticed the other clan leaders lean in, engrossed by his tale. "Odessa made me swear to keep her secret, and in return she gave me leaves from the Tree of Virtue to help heal my ailing son." The Bellaux gasped again.

"My son had been very ill for a long time, and no amount of medicinal or magical healing helped before we tried the leaves. His condition deteriorated, until he grew so weak he was unable to walk! I had no choice but to do whatever it took to help heal him." Enzo peered up at the Bellaux, defensive, and eager to justify his position.

"She would *never* do such a thing!" Auriel exclaimed, her pale blue eyes flashing. "To give away fruits or leaves of the tree is a grave sin among our clan. Your accusations are bold, Enzo." Auriel crossed her arms. "But if you claim to know where Odessa is harboring this injured unicorn, you must take us to her."

"Forgive my ignorance, but why is a unicorn such a big deal?" Mack voiced the same question Lucy had been pondering.

"Like Adalia mentioned before, there have been no known unicorn sightings except by the oldest of the elves, who are now hundreds of years old," Zadok replied. "Not only are unicorns among the rarest creatures of Praxis, they also possess exceptional, quite powerful magic. It is said that looking into the eyes of a unicorn will heal whatever ails you. It is also known that the powder of unicorn horn can heal a wide variety of illnesses, though it is illegal to hunt and dehorn them. It is recognized among all clans that they are a protected creature. Anyone who takes the life or horn of a unicorn will be put to death, by order of the king."

Enzo pushed back from the table and stood, gulping the last of his cider. "Auriel, I'm ready to go whenever you are."

"I'll arrange for armed escorts," Zadok added, trotting to the entrance of the dining hall, where Axel was stationed and awaiting instruction. Enzo, Auriel, and the rest of the Bellaux hurried out of the dining hall.

Adalia followed. "If there really *is* a unicorn, this isn't something I'm going to miss," she muttered.

Lucy was left alone with her brothers. "I've been thinking about something," she began, her voice just above a whisper. Unease coursed through her veins. "When I... when I brought down the Warden lair around me," she paused, struggling to find the words to describe what she saw. Mack and Luke looked at one another, unsure what their sister was trying to tell them. She swallowed, knowing she had to tell the truth. She looked from Mack to Luke, hoping they would stand by her side when she revealed what she'd done. She gathered her courage and continued: "I saw one other thing on the map inside the lair—besides just the Wardens." She looked from Mack to Luke, hoping one of them would finish her sentence so she didn't have to.

She looked down, her eyes welling with tears. She wasn't sure she could stand any more turmoil and loss of life. "It was the people and creatures the Wardens had kidnapped," she choked out, tears slipping down her cheeks.

Mack and Luke's eyes widened.

"Ohh," Luke breathed, covering his mouth with one hand. "I was beginning to wonder..." he shook his head side to side, overcome with the weight of it.

Mack put a hand on Lucy's shoulder. "Lucy, it's not your fault." His voice was firm. "You did what you had to do. You saved the map... and the Mapkeeper. Both are essential to the survival of everyone else left in Praxis. You have to believe that. What you did was *right*," he emphasized. She drew in a shuddering breath. "The Wardens are responsible for the deaths of those people and creatures, not you."

"But I brought the cavern down around them! They could have lived!" she insisted, her voice rising with emotion.

Mack jumped up from his seat and rounded the table to sit beside her. He grabbed her by both shoulders, making her face him. "They were gone the moment they were kidnapped and cloned," Mack told her, looking into her eyes. "Yes, of course it's tragic, but Lucy, I swear to you, it's not your fault." He held her gaze, his expression fierce and loyal. "You have to believe me."

She nodded, wanting to believe her brother, though she felt a dozen different emotions at once. Luke gazed at her with hurt behind his eyes, seeming to share in her pain.

"We need to focus on rebuilding now," Mack stated. "The map shows no more Wardens, but we can't be sure that we're out of danger." The three Barnes siblings looked down at the map together. It still glowed, pulsing with faint light and warmth. They saw themselves in Abodox, each with a miniature inscription beside them labeling the individual in meticulous script. Lucy noted that Enzo, Auriel, Adalia, Axel, and Lance stood in a circle somewhere deep in Doldrums Forest. If a unicorn was indeed at her feet, it didn't show it on the map. Odessa was nowhere to be seen on the map.

"When it stops glowing, it goes blank," Lucy explained. "I'll lose the ability to track people. I'm getting better at keeping it activated, though. I just have to keep my focus."

The siblings watched as the five creatures shifted around a bit and then began to move back toward Abodox.

"I have a bad feeling about this injured unicorn," Lucy muttered.

Zadok reentered the dining hall. "How are you holding up?" he asked, taking a seat at the head of the table beside Mack.

"I've had better days." Lucy's smile was weak.

"You fought well, and your bravery saved us all," he replied in his kind, wise way. He sat straight-backed and showed no signs of discomfort despite a blood-soaked bandage covering his left shoulder and a large part of his upper arm. Lucy stared at the wound. "It will be fine. It's a superficial wound," he assured her. She grimaced. Seeing Zadok, the strongest creature she knew, in less than perfect health made her uneasy. She brushed the discomfort away, determined to focus on the responsibilities she had to fulfill.

"Zadok, it looks like Axel and Lance are on their way back with Auriel, Adalia, and Enzo," she began. "In the meantime, do you have another set of trusted advisers you can send to the castle to check on Queen Oleksandra? We still don't know what has become of the clones. Everyone at the castle except the queen and king were clones."

"Great idea," he replied, standing in a smooth motion. He beckoned to two centaurs standing guard at the entrance to the dining hall. They came at a gallop. "Tobias, Zandar, take along two others and make haste to the castle." Zadok placed a hand on the shoulder of the centaur nearest himself. "Check on the queen and king, and report back the status of the castle guards and groundskeepers, all of whom are clones. We need to know whether they lived, and if so, what state they are in. We don't know how the killing of the Wardens may have affected them." Both centaurs nodded, stoic and resolute. "I will await your report here at Abodox. Be fast and effective, but be careful, my friends." They nodded and galloped out of the dining hall. Two more silent centaurs took their places outside the dining hall without being summoned. Lucy marveled at the discipline of the centaur clan.

"Lucy, you and your brothers are welcome to stay here at Abodox as long as you please. My home is your home," Zadok offered.

"Thank you, Zadok. I appreciate your kindness," she replied. "I think we will stay here until we receive word that it's safe to return to the castle. The king and queen are going to need help sorting everything out in the aftermath of all this," she predicted. Her heart ached as Cadmus sprang into her mind once again. Hot tears welled in her eyes.

Suddenly, the entire cavern shook with a vengeance. Lucy's chair danced beneath her, thudding against the stone floor with violence. Lucy, Mack, and Luke dove under the table as opaque mineral stalagmites broke from the ceiling and plummeted to the stone floor, shattering in explosions of crystals. The quake was the most ferocious they'd experienced yet. Lucy closed her eyes and covered the back of her neck with her hands, fragments of rock and mineral crystals pummeling her. Over the low rumble of the quake, the rattle of chairs jumping up and down on the unsteady ground accompanied frenzied shouts. The tremor ceased with the same abruptness it began with.

Lucy removed her hands from her neck and opened her eyes to a thick cloud of dust. Coughing, she scooted backwards out from beneath the great wooden table. "Mack? Luke? Are you guys all right?" she asked as her brothers emerged beside her, coughing and brushing dirt off their sleeves. Luke shook his head, his long locks flapping back and forth around his head and forming a dust cloud of their own.

"Yeah," Mack replied, wiping his face with the back of his sleeve and looking around the dining hall. "Zadok!" he shouted, running to a corner of the room. Lucy froze. The leader of the centaurs was sprawled, motionless beneath a massive chunk of fallen stone.

CHAPTER 38

⁙

Mack threw his weight against the boulder, straining to push it off his friend's body. Lucy and Luke sprinted to his side, weaving among heaps of broken rock to heave against the boulder beside their brother. Lucy gritted her teeth, summoning all her strength.

"Ahh!" Mack cried out, exerting with all his might. Though it was slow to move, the boulder gave way, inching off Zadok's pinned body. At last, the great rock rolled and thudded onto the stone floor, crushing one of his legs and hooves on the way. Zadok did not move.

"Zadok!" Lucy bent down to his face, patting him on one cheek. "Zadok, wake up!" she was frantic.

Mack began to pat down his abdomen, sides, and haunches. "He's got a lot of internal bleeding from the blunt trauma," he reported.

Lucy rubbed Zadok's shoulder, willing him to wake up.

"I'm going to check the area for anyone else who might be injured," Luke stated, moving away.

"Zadok, please..." Lucy pled with her unconscious friend, who was always so strong and unwavering. She realized what a source of confidence and comfort Zadok was for her. The thought of losing him in addition to Cadmus was almost unbearable.

Her heart skipped a beat when his eyes fluttered open. He moaned, moving an arm up to his head and brushing his flowing brown hair out of his eyes.

"You're alive!" Lucy exclaimed as her body flooded with relief. "Zadok, you were hit with a large rock, but we're here and we're going to help you," she comforted her friend, stroking his shoulder. "Don't try to move yet."

"What happened?" Zadok blinked his eyes. "Ahh!" he cried out in pain as he attempted to move his legs.

"Take it easy, Zadok," Mack ordered, his hands resting on either side of the impact area. "We need to get him to the castle maesters," Mack told Lucy. "He needs medical attention, fast."

"We centaurs have our own healers," Zadok huffed through clenched teeth.

"The castle maesters are the best doctors in Praxis and you know it," Lucy countered. "Zadok, we have to get you the best. Your life may depend on it..."

"Ahh!" he winced again. Her heart wrenched, his pain agonizing her.

"Everyone else seems okay in here!" Luke called across the cavern. Most of the dust had settled. Lucy scanned the room. Several creatures from a variety of clans were picking themselves up and dusting each other off. The two centaurs who replaced Tobias and Zandar trotted into the dining hall to assist their leader.

"Good," Lucy replied. "We need to get him to the castle," she addressed the centaurs. They nodded.

"I'll get a litter and some more centaurs to accompany us," one replied, galloping out of the hall.

"We'll go with you," Lucy assured Zadok.

"No, no, you don't have to do that—" he began to protest between strained breaths.

"We're coming."

In the distance, the entrance gate clanged shut. Lucy's hand jerked to the map in her pocket to see who had arrived. The map! She rushed back to where she'd left it open on the dining table.

"The map! It's gone!" Her stomach dropped. Mack rushed to his sister's side.

"No!" Mack cried. "Who could have…?" He scanned the room, but there was no one anywhere near the table.

Enzo, Auriel, Adalia, Axel, and Lance entered the dining hall.

"Is everyone all right?" Adalia led the group. "We were almost back to Abodox when the quake struck. We took cover and everyone is all right in our group. We didn't find Odess—" her eyes fell on Zadok, splayed against the cavern wall and struggling to breathe. "Oh, Zadok!"

Axel and Lance rushed to his side, kneeling beside their leader.

"As far as we know, everyone was okay in here except Zadok," Luke replied, grimacing.

"The map is gone!" Lucy exclaimed, distraught. She ran from creature to creature, stuffing her hands in the pockets of their garments, in total disregard of their personal space in her desperation.

Auriel and Adalia's eyes went wide.

"What do you mean it's gone?" Enzo growled as his eyes narrowed.

"When the quake happened we took cover under the table," Lucy explained, frantic. "Then we stood back up and saw Zadok was hurt. We went to help him, and by the time I came back for it, it was gone!" Her heart raced as she shook a young male elf by the shoulders, barely aware of what she was doing.

"I don't have it, Ms. Barnes!" he insisted, both hands in the air.

She regained enough composure to release the young elf. Stepping back, she paused, her heart still thundering out of control. She whipped around.

"Scour Abodox," she ordered the group at large. She took off running toward the main gate. "Did anyone leave when Auriel's group arrived?" she demanded of one of the centaur guards.

"Yes. There were two humans and the satyr," he replied.

Lucy's blood went cold. *Rhys.* She sprinted back to the dining hall.

"Let's go!" She motioned to her brothers. "Axel, make sure Zadok is transported to the castle and seen right away by the maesters. Whether they are clones or not, they have the knowledge and skill Zadok will need in order to survive." Axel nodded, overseeing Zadok's careful transfer onto the litter. "My brothers and I must go. Three creatures left when your group arrived: two humans and Rhys," she told the remaining clan leaders. "You stay here and scour Abodox. Let no creature, no room, and no corner go unsearched. My brothers and I will track down the three who left. We have to find the map!" she emphasized, wheeling on her heels and racing to her chamber to strap on a quiver and grab her bow.

"Did you find the unicorn?" Mack asked Auriel as he backed out of the dining hall after his sister.

"We found a carcass with the horn sawed off," the Bellaux

murmured, her face ashen. The hair rose on Lucy's neck as she heard this, jogging out of the dining hall. She sprinted to her chamber, forcing the image of a dead unicorn from her mind.

"Got everything?" she asked her brothers as she cinched the belt of her scabbard, looking them over. "Let's go." She ran down the torch-lit passageway to the main gate, Mack and Luke beside her. A centaur had saddled three horses for them. Lucy grabbed the saddle horn of the nearest mount and stepped into the stirrup, swinging her leg over the animal. "Which way did they go?" she addressed the guards, turning the horse to face the gate.

"We saw them head down the main path away from Abodox. They disappeared into the trees soon after that," one of the centaurs answered with an apologetic shrug.

She dug her heels into the horse the moment the gate creaked open, and the three horses thundered out of Abodox into the forest, leaving behind a cloud of dust.

Mist clung to the trees like an enormous burial shroud. Mack and Luke flanked her, urging their mounts to maintain a fast pace. The only noise was the collective clop of hooves, yet the forest possessed an ominous ambience, as if it were crawling with mysterious, well-hidden life. Though Lucy estimated it was about midday, only a few rays of sunlight managed to poke through the infrequent breaks in the dense canopy far overhead.

The ambush was swift and overwhelming. Three trolls stepped out from behind the trees bordering the path, using their massive clubs to bludgeon the horses with brutal accuracy. Lucy was thrown, her momentum carrying her onward after her horse was brought to a vicious stop beneath her. She smacked sideways against the trunk of a tree, the massive blow forcing the air out of her lungs. She crumpled against the base of the tree, paralyzed by shock for an instant before intense pain ripped through her body. Her chest was tight and devoid of air. Willing herself to breathe, she relaxed her back muscles and heaved a shallow gulp of air into her compressed lungs. Her vision cleared in time to see a troll's boulder of a fist swing down and connect with a ruthless blow to her head.

CHAPTER 39

"Sit her up," a familiar voice ordered.

Lucy felt her body bend at the waist, forced into a sitting position by two large, scratchy hands. Her head throbbed with immense pain, and her entire back and neck ached. She felt like she'd been hit by a train. She blinked her eyes open. Opening and closing her mouth, she peeled her dry, sticky tongue off the roof of her parched mouth. She was leaned up against the cold stone wall of a dark cave. To her left and right stood two enormous trolls. Through sheer willpower, she managed to stifle a moan of pain. Tight ropes bit into her wrists, which were bound behind her back. In front of her, Bade and Hobart stood in the center of the cave, arms crossed, peering down at her with hideous grins.

"Excellent." Bade's grin widened. "You're awake. Welcome to my home away from home, Mapkeeper! I hope you're ready for some fun, because I want to play a little game." Hobart giggled, his short, round frame bobbing up and down with glee.

Total-body stiffness made even the slightest movement painful. Lucy's hands were numb from the tightness of the rope binding her wrists. Despite the pain that wouldn't even allow her to take air into her lungs in comfort, she somehow sensed that the map was nearby.

Ignoring the throbbing in her head, she croaked, "Where are we? Where are my brothers?" Her parched mouth made forming words a challenge.

"Ahh, but if I told you all that, then there'd be nothing left to surprise you with!" Bade spread his thin hands. "You see, things are changing here in Praxis. And we are fortunate enough to be at the forefront of it all! Together, we can establish a new world order, Lucy." He flashed a maniacal grin. "The monarchy is archaic, and the royal family doesn't hold any real power anymore. What Praxis needs is a real leader from within. For centuries, the map has chosen an outsider to come to our world and attempt to lead us. This has to end. Praxis needs a leader of its own, and I am ready to step forward and become that leader."

"Why would anyone follow you?" Lucy spat, shifting her position but finding no relief from the pain afflicting her entire body.

"He has the map." A huge, pot-bellied troll stepped out of the shadows behind Bade. His deep, loud voice echoed off the damp walls of the cave. "He has a plan. And he's right. We don't need outsiders coming to Praxis to lead." Like the other two trolls in the cave, he wore nothing but a large brown loincloth.

"Ms. Barnes, have you met Digby?" Bade asked with false politeness. The beast bared a cringe-worthy collection of gaps and square brown teeth that Lucy interpreted as a smile. "As you can see, the trolls are already with me. With the Wardens out of the way, the goblins won't be difficult to convince. They don't play well with others, so the happy little team effort that your late love interest had organized is over."

Lucy seethed, hatred burning within her. "You're not even worthy to mention Cadmus by name," she growled. She longed to plunge a sword into his skinny belly. She looked down, but her weapons were gone.

Bade threw back his head and cackled. "Very good, Ms. Barnes. I like that anger. Stoke that fire, that's good."

"Where are my brothers?" she repeated. The numbness in her hands began to spread up to her elbows. She shifted, trying to stimulate blood flow. Her back and neck screamed in protest and her head throbbed harder.

"That's all part of the fun!" Bade took several steps toward his prisoner. Digby grinned, crossing his trunk-like arms across his barrel chest. "You see, Ms. Barnes, I've got your brothers in a very special place." Lucy's stomach dropped. She looked away, sickened by the sight of Bade's face. He knelt down in front of her. "And I have big plans for them."

Fear bubbled up in her throat and a sudden loneliness unlike anything she'd ever experienced overcame her. She looked once more at the trolls to her left and right, then back at the pale, gaunt face of the man kneeling before her.

"That's right, Ms. Barnes. You're all alone now." He lowered his voice. "The gig is up. Playtime is over. But don't worry, because I still need you," he added, standing and walking back to where Hobart and Digby stood. "Because unfortunate though it is, the map still takes orders from you." He reached into the pocket of his robe and pulled it out. It was inactive. A plain piece of parchment. Lucy's heart pounded. She ached to jump up and snatch it out of his hands.

"Lucy Barnes." Bade unfolded the map and read the script in its bottom corner, his upper lip curling on one side. "It makes me sick. And one day, I will find a way to fix the only flaw this otherwise beautiful artifact retains. But until then, your assistance will be a necessary hindrance."

Lucy willed herself to remain calm. She focused on drawing in long, slow breaths.

"Now. The first order of business in which your help will be necessary is in regards to your brothers." Bade began to pace, clasping his hands behind his back, the map still in his grip. Lucy's heart began to pound once again. She stared down at the dirt. "I have a problem. There is only enough space in my new headquarters in the Dour Mountains for one... guest. And with both your brothers there, it would seem that I have two, would it not?" he stopped pacing and faced her.

Lucy's mouth was so dry she was sure she wouldn't have enough saliva to speak. Her mind raced. She couldn't bear for anything to happen to Mack or Luke. Her heart ached at the thought of it. Closing her eyes, she took a long, deep breath and swallowed, willing herself to remain calm.

"What do you think about my predicament, Ms. Barnes? Wouldn't you agree that something must be done to rectify the issue?"

She ignored him. Her mind whirred as she tried to come up with a plan. She'd done it in the Warden lair. Why not now? But self-doubt assailed her—Bade had the map! She felt useless, tied up and beaten on the floor of a cave surrounded by her enemies.

I can't give up, she urged herself. *I am the rightful Mapkeeper and I was chosen for a reason. Zadok believed in me*, she recalled with sudden clarity. Cadmus had believed in her. Her heart soared at the thought of the centaur and the man she admired so much placing their faith in her. There were others, too: her brothers, Adalia, Odessa and Auriel, the king and queen, the villagers, and even Enzo and Glump had placed their trust in her. *I can't give up on them!*

"Since you seem to be at a loss for words, I'll fill you in on my plan. Because I make the plans around here from now on, Ms. Barnes." She looked up at Bade and his brow furrowed in sudden anger. "You will choose. One will live, and one will die." His sneer broke into a sudden maniacal grin. "It'll be fun, like a game. Don't you think so, Ms. Barnes?"

Lucy's heart constricted and her pulse skyrocketed. "No!" She croaked, unable to formulate words to express her anguish.

Bade chuckled. "I thought you might react that way." He looked down at the map, which began to pulsate with faint light. His expression sobered. "So here's the deal: either you decide, or my hospitality runs out and I kill them both."

She sucked in shallow, rapid breaths. Somewhere deep in the cave, the steady drip of water permeated the silence. Bade took a step toward her.

"Well, who will it be, Ms. Barnes? I don't have all day," he snapped.

Thunk.

"Gah!" One of the trolls guarding the cave entrance fell to his knees with a roar. An arrow was sticking out of his chest.

Thunk. Thunk. Two more arrows sunk deep into the neck of his companion.

"Arrrrrgh!" the second troll gurgled as he grabbed at the arrows sticking out of his neck, breaking them off at the shafts. Blood gushed from his neck. He ran out of the cave toward his assailant, club raised high overhead.

"What is going on?" Bade demanded. "Digby, get more trolls!"

Digby roared, waving an arm toward the recesses of the cave. Four trolls emerged from the darkness, dazed as if they'd been torn from a deep slumber. They advanced into a spray of arrows as Lucy looked on in disbelief. These arrows were thicker than the ones she and Luke used in the battle against the Wardens. Dozens of them pierced the thick flesh of the trolls with ease, taking the unarmored creatures down in seconds.

"We're under attack!" Bade screeched, retreating into the depths of the cave, Hobart hot on his heels. "I thought you said this cave was charmed and unfindable!" He smacked Digby on the shoulder as he passed the leader of the trolls.

"It is," Digby growled in his deep bass voice. "Hold your ground," he directed, holding one of his massive hands out toward the two trolls flanking Lucy and looking toward the cave entrance. The arrow-riddled bodies of six trolls now lay heaped in the dim light penetrating the cave.

"Who's there?" Digby thundered, squaring his shoulders to face the threat.

With a flourish of his bow and a deep bow, Rhys hopped over the bodies of the trolls and bowed low before Digby.

"Why it's just the satyr," Rhys replied, looking up from his bow and wiggling his thick eyebrows at the creature towering over him. "Oh, and I've got a few friends with me." He turned and waved an arm. A swarm of waist-high hooded creatures flocked into the cave and surrounded Rhys.

Digby backed up, uncertain of the capabilities of the small army standing before him. Many shouldered bow slings and quivers. They buzzed with energy—a dozen high-pitched conversations at once muddled into a continuous hum. Lucy was hit with the distinct memory of the same mélange of conversation noise somewhere before, but she couldn't quite place it.

One of the short, hooded creatures stepped forward. It wore a deep crimson robe and carried a walking stick longer than it was tall with a luminous, opaque orb encased in wooden prongs at the tip. The throng of creatures hushed themselves.

"We come for the Mapkeeper," the creature announced in a high-pitched, feminine voice. "And the map," it added with a giggle. The odd gathering dissolved into tittering laughter, but the giggles ceased as soon as they'd started.

Bade and Hobart crept out from the depths of the cave.

"And what makes you think we will give it to you?" Bade sneered.

"You will give it to us," the little creature squeaked, "or we will be forced to take it from you."

Bade looked up at Digby. "Well? Go ahead! Squash them!"

Digby frowned and backed away. "Not today, Bade. They have some kind of magic. There are only three trolls left here. And too many of them." The cave shook with each step the great creature took away from Rhys and his companions.

Bade's face fell. "What do you mean not today?" he roared, stomping his foot. He crinkled the map in one hand. Lucy winced, longing to rip her treasure from his undeserving hands. Keeping quiet, Hobart backed away from his leader.

"We will take the map," the leader of the mysterious creatures repeated herself. She extended a tiny, thin hand toward Bade as if expecting him to hand it over.

Bade looked around, frantic. Unnoticed, Hobart had retreated back into the shadows with Digby. Bade was left standing alone. Screaming in rage, he threw the map down at the feet of the crimson-robed creature.

"I'm not through with you!" he spat hatefully, pointing at Lucy before he sprinted into the depths of the cave. Hobart, Digby, and the two remaining trolls who had been guarding Lucy lumbered after him. Rhys leapt forward to chase them down, but the crimson-robed creature stopped him by placing a tiny, gentle hand on his arm.

"Don't bother, they'll be gone," she squeaked. "It's a tunnel with many forks and turns. As with the rest of the forest, we know it well. But it's no use chasing after them now. We have what we came for."

At last she faced Lucy and her army of companions followed suit. Lucy ogled the little creature, unsure of what to expect. Her dark face bore the deep creases of age, but her eyes sparkled with youthful mirth.

"Rhys, how did you—" she began, her voice cracking. She shifted her weight. Her arms were numb from her hands all the way up past her elbows.

The satyr hurried to her side. "Lucy, are you all right?" He

347

knelt and pushed her away from the stone wall, picking at the rope that restrained her.

"Here, let me." The mysterious creature appeared at his side and touched the milky orb that topped her walking stick against the rope. It fell to the ground in loose folds.

"I told you I was on your side." Rhys winked, helping Lucy to her feet. She swayed, a rush of lightheadedness sweeping over her. Her back screamed in pain.

"Whoa, you better sit back down," Rhys huffed as he supported most of her weight, easing her back to a seated position. "You don't look so good." He squatted beside her on his stubby, coarse-haired legs. Her blurred vision sharpened as blood made its way back to her head.

"I've had better days," she murmured, exhausted and aching all over. "Rhys..." She mustered the energy to look him in the eye. "My brothers. Bade kidnapped them. He's holding them somewhere in the Dour Mountains. I've got to go..." She leaned her pounding head against the wall of the cave.

"Lucy," Rhys objected, "I'm all for saving your brothers, but you're in no condition to—"

"I believe this belongs to you, Mapkeeper." The orb-wielding creature handed the map to Lucy with a smile. Lucy took it, a surge of relief flooding her. The parchment felt smooth and perfect in her hands. "Mapkeeper, my name is Cleo and I am queen of the kobolds. We owe you our sincerest thanks for leading

Praxis to victory over the Wardens, who possessed an ancient magic but were gone astray.

"We kobolds are the keepers of the forest. We know the secrets of the land and all the creatures that inhabit it. And we try to do good by those whose intentions are pure." She smiled, her eyes sparkling. "Mapkeeper, we will help you find your brothers." The rest of the kobolds erupted in raucous cheering, their whoops and squeals echoing off unseen walls deep in the blackness of the cave. The steady dripping of water was, for a moment, drowned out.

Exhausted, Lucy looked up into Cleo's eyes. She clutched the map against her chest, ignoring the uncomfortable tingling of blood prickling its way back into her arms and hands. The map commenced its familiar pulsing glow, the warmth penetrating to her core. Drinking in a deep, shuddering breath, the Mapkeeper nodded to the queen of the kobolds.

ABOUT THE AUTHOR

Katie Cash is an active duty military officer who lives in San Diego with her husband and their cat. She enjoys running, surfing, world travel, competing in triathlons, and, of course, writing. She also hosts an annual badminton tournament, rides a 150cc Vespa scooter, and plays the cello. She can most often be found exploring new running trails, at the beach, hunkered down writing in a coffee shop, or sampling a new local craft beer at one of San Diego's many craft breweries.

www.ingramcontent.com/pod-product-compliance
Lightning Source LLC
Chambersburg PA
CBHW071041250626
47159CB00002B/327